Blue Violet

Blue Violet

Scarlet Clearwater

GSH

ISBN: 978-1-956074-99-4 (Paperback Edition)
ISBN: 978-1-956515-03-9 (Hardcover Edition)
ISBN: 978-1-956074-98-7 (E-book Edition)

Some characters and events in this book are fictitious. Any similarity to the real persons, living or dead, is coincidental and not intended by the author.

Book Ordering Information

Phone Number: 315 288-7939 ext. 1000 or 347-901-4920
Email: info@globalsummithouse.com
Global Summit House
www.globalsummithouse.com

Printed in the United State of America

Table of Contents

Chapter 1

Jenny burst through Lila's door and slammed it shut behind her. Theatrically, she held her arms out wide. "Honey, I'm home," she rang, beaming.

She was clothed in shredded blue jeans and a black tank. Her tank was complimented by a faded black hoodie, adorned with patches which read things like, "What the Fuck Are You Looking At?" and "Vampires Rule." Jenny wasn't completely goth, but she was hardened with a sharp edge. Mostly, she was all about shock value. Lila thought of her as a live wire. Any unknowing person could cross her and get the electrocution of their life. She starkly contrasted Lila's introverted ways.

Lila was lying back in her bed, in her night clothes. The cute ones with the different-colored polka dots, and they were flannel, since the cold weather was unbearable to her. It was almost December, and her mother, Pearl, kept the heat low to save money. Pearl believed in layers and bundling and hot chocolate to stay warm.

Lila often found she wanted to flee to Florida, but North Carolina would have to suffice for now. She was twenty-two and had finally decided to go to North Carolina State for college, come spring. She wasn't fleeing anywhere. No time too soon, anyway.

"So, tell me again," Jenny said, her blue eyes piercing holes through Lila's green ones.

She slipped into the bed next to Lila and shivered slightly. She had heard stories about Lilith a hundred times, but never seemed to get bored with them.

"Do I really have to?" Lila whined. "I'm tired."

"Yes. I have a hot date tonight, and the stories empower me. I haven't heard one in months," Jenny laughed. "Tell me, pleeease." She cuddled up to Lila and rested her head on her shoulder.

"Fine, I'll tell you one. Again," Lila sighed.

"Okay, but tell one of the sexy stories," Jenny said.

Lila ignored her. She wasn't in the mood to tell a steamy sex story.

"No. I've never told you about Lilith's beginning. Aren't you the least bit interested?"

"Sure. Go ahead." Jenny waved her arm in a the-floor-is-yours gesture.

"Well, Lilith was made for Adam, God's first human. For a while, things were blissful, until Adam realized his sexuality. Once procreation was imperative to human existence, he propositioned Lilith. She was glad to oblige, but when Adam told her to come up from her side and lie underneath him, she had a fit. She didn't want to feel dominated by a man who was meant to be her equal.

"So, she left the Garden, and once Adam and Eve populated the lands, Lilith set out to satisfy her sexual needs. She succumbed to her dark side and used her beauty and clout to bed and kill numerous men out of her hatred for God and Adam. Meanwhile, angels fell from the heavens to mate with the female humans they found so beautiful."

Jenny tapped Lila on the shoulder, but Lila batted her away and continued.

"Lilith became consumed by sex and continued on with her ways until she met Samael, a fallen angel with whom she fell madly in love. Once Lilith was content, God cursed her as a demon, hoping no man or fallen angel would ever bed her again. He made her body like a snake's and her head like a cat's. Her eyes were emerald, and she had the wings of a bat and the talons of a large bird. But Samael did not leave her. Instead, the two had scores of children.

"These children, the Lilin, were said to be captivating and miraculous creatures. Because they had the blood of angels, their ejaculations produced supernatural lubricants that caused humans to orgasm within seconds. They were incredibly strong, hypnotic to the opposite human sex and highly charismatic. The Lilin spread their sinful ways across the lands."

Jenny tapped Lila on the shoulder again. "You're leaving out all the juicy sex parts," she whispered.

"Shut up, Jenny. This is *before* the juicy sex parts. The *reason* for the juicy sex parts."

"Okay. Go ahead. Geez."

"With the world immersed in filth, God brought about a great flood to cleanse it. He charged Noah with taking two of each species of life with him onto an ark, including the hybrid spawns of the angels, which He cursed. But God put the abominations to good use. They would serve Him by temping humans so He could distinguish the good from the evil and…Ummm, yeah...to be continued." Lila rolled over in the bed.

"I wish I was like her," Jenny said with her hand under her chin. She was gazing out Lila's window, into the darkness, speaking in a dreamy voice. "Lilith was the perfect feminist. There are a few guys I'd love to kill by fucking them. Ha!" She rose on her elbow and hopped out of the bed.

"Well, I haven't met one man who is worthy of my attentions," Lila said objectively.

"'I haven't met one man worthy of my attentions,'" Jenny mocked in a robotic voice. She did a little robot dance to match.

"Fuck you," Lila said, throwing a pillow at her.

"Whatever, Li. Doug seems really into you. You should give him a chance. And your virgin ass doesn't know what it's missing," Jenny coaxed, twirling a lock of golden hair around her finger.

"Yeah, I like him, but not too terribly much. I don't know. It's not like he's even made a move on me." Lila shrugged and then pulled her pink floral comforter up to her shoulders.

"And if he does?" Jenny's eyebrows raised.

"I don't know. Maybe I'm like Lilith. Maybe I'll kill him." Lila hardly smiled, but Jenny broke out in a giggle.

"Well then, it's settled. When Doug makes his move, ravage him. If he dies, that means you're a badass," Jenny joked. "I'll be back before you know it. Ginger's been up my ass to move out.

We need to look at some places. 'Kay?" Jenny winked at Lila, who gave her a thumbs-up.

Jenny crept out of Lila's room so she wouldn't wake Pearl or Perry. She would slip out the front door to go to Greg's house and then come back to Lila's around four in the morning. Lila had given Jenny a key a while back because this was a pattern of hers.

After Jenny left, Lila thought about what she had said about Doug. The truth was, she deeply wished she had a boyfriend, a normal life, but Pearl had finally admitted to her, a few years back, that she was a Succubus. That Lilith was a Succubus. Lila's demonic side would take hold of her at some time or another, and after that, nothing could be done to halt her lethal desires.

Her mother had terrified her into keeping her virginity intact. Pearl said that once she allowed a man to enter her, the curse would fully activate. That she would make men ill, or perhaps even kill them, during sex. Even worse, she would suffer immensely without sex. With every sexual encounter, her body would start to burn internally, and the burn would greatly intensify until the man she was with ejaculated inside her. There were still holes about her demon side that needed to be filled in. She only knew the basics and didn't feel like she had enough information to make a wise decision about her virginity or her future as a Succubus.

Her mother had made the plunge into the turbulent lifestyle when she was young—way younger than she was now, so it couldn't be all bad. Now her parents lived like everyone else who was human. Why couldn't she do the same? There had to be a trick to it, something her mother hadn't told her yet. She would talk to her mother tomorrow.

She felt herself becoming more restless with each passing hour, thinking about how the dreams were more frequent now. Dreams where she woke to find herself humping her pillow and screaming out with pleasure. She had bought vibrators, dildos, and porn magazines to keep her yearning at bay, but they no longer did the job. She had to get off at least five times a day to be somewhat satisfied, and still wished she had a man to do the job for her. She was lonely and slowly becoming depressed.

Lila's phone rang. She looked at the clock. It was ten thirty. Doug called her often around that time just to make plans with her and say good night.

"Hello?" she asked in a sweet voice. The guy had been chasing her for years without letting her know head-on, but she hadn't been interested until recently.

"Hey, Lila. I was wondering...," Doug stammered. "Do you want to go out tomorrow night? Movie or something?"

The anticipation in his voice was enough to make her laugh. She heard him take a deep breath. They had always hung out, but for some reason he sounded really nervous.

"I mean... as a date."

Oh. "Yes. That sounds like a good idea, Doug." She smiled to herself. *Ironically perfect timing.*

"Okay. I'll pick you up around six, then?"

"Get me at Jenny's."

"Sounds good."

"'Kay," Lila giggled.

"Okay, Lila. Uh, bye."

Lila hung the phone up and wondered what she had just gotten herself into. But the unknown possibilities made her giddy. She was flooded with excitement and plopped herself onto her bed, smiling widely. She texted Jenny that she had a date with Doug.

Her stomach fluttered as she thought about what Doug might look like naked. As she lay back in her bed, she moved her hand under her pajama pants and between her legs. She was warm there and grew warmer as she skimmed her hood with one finger.

She closed her eyes and imagined that Doug's hands were touching her most private parts. After she massaged herself to climax, she put her earbuds in and fell asleep listening to her bedtime playlist.

By the time Lila woke, Jenny was fast asleep in the bed next to her. She watched her friend for a while and then started pulling her hairs out one at a time. After about five pulls, Jenny woke abruptly, scratching at her scalp.

"What? Hey, there," Jenny said groggily, as her blue eyes focused on her Lila. "You pulling my hair out again, you bitch?"

"So, when did you get in last night?" Lila smirked at her.

"I think it was around four. I kind of lost track of time," Jenny yawned.

"What is it like? Tell me about it." Lila stared at Jenny wide-eyed. She placed her cheek in her hand and waited for all the juicy details. She had never asked Jenny about her sexual escapades before, and Jenny had never offered to tell because Lila seemed to get all huffy when she talked about her boyfriends.

"Really? You want to know?" Jenny asked, in shock.

"Yeah. I think I'm ready to get all of this over with," Lila answered.

They both sat up excitedly and Jenny dove right in.

"Well, the first time it was awkward and kind of painful. It felt like my pussy was tearing. Then it got better, and there was no pain. Now that Greg and I are used to each other, it's actually quite nice. He still needs a little direction, though. Like when he goes down on me, he misses the mark almost every single time," she said as she rolled her eyes.

"Do you do it every time you're together?"

"No. I'm not a sex addict, Lila. We do it when it's convenient, or when we're horny, which isn't all the time. For me, at least. Sometimes we just watch TV and fall asleep with each other. It's comforting."

Lila noticed that Jenny still had that sex afterglow. She had always seen the shimmery golden halo on certain people, even on her parents. She never knew what the glow meant until she realized she saw it after Jenny had sex, after her parents came downstairs in the morning or at night, after she saw drunk kids at parties stumbling out of bedrooms together. She knew it was a way to tell who had recently had sex, but she didn't know why she needed to know that information, and she definitely didn't need to know when her parents did it. That was totally gross. She had asked her mother about the glow when she was younger, and Pearl told her she would explain it as she got older, but the subject never came up again.

"Jenny? If you were like Lilith, would you want to stay a virgin?" Lila asked in a small and unsure voice.

"Hell, no! Sex is great. It wouldn't be so bad relying on it to survive. That's kind of what we do anyways. I think we'd all shrivel up and die if we didn't have sex. I know I would."

"Really?" Lila didn't know it was *that* good.

"Really. It's not just the orgasms, it's the bond you create with a person. It's also a great cure for loneliness, bad moods, good for revenge against past boyfriends, good for all sorts of shit." Jenny looked at her fingernails. "I need a mani." She got up and went to Lila's vanity and started wiping her makeup off. "Any more questions?" she asked as she rubbed under her eyes with cotton balls doused in cleanser. She looked slyly at Lila in the mirror.

"Does it feel wrong? Like it's a sin?"

"If it's a sin, then I'll gladly burn in Hell," Jenny said, tossing the cotton balls onto a silver makeup tray. She stood up from the vanity chair and made her way over to Lila who was still sitting on the bed. Jenny sat down next to her but turned her body into Lila's. She had shed her hoodie and one of the straps of her tank was falling off her shoulder. She wasn't wearing a bra.

Lila found herself aroused at the sight of her. Jenny was beautiful even without makeup, even with her curly locks in a mess. For a moment, she sensed something in her friend. A wave of something that smelled like roses and almonds. She had smelled the fragrance before, but it had been much less potent. Now, she instinctively pegged it as the smell of lust.

Jenny reached for Lila's face and ran a thumb along Lila's pouty bottom lip, which she sucked into her mouth in response. Jenny smiled that beautiful toothy smile of hers and then moved her hand to the back of Lila's head, lightly stroking her brown waves.

Lila's breath caught, and she found she couldn't move. Didn't want to. She was magnetized to her friend.

Jenny leaned into her, and as she did, her breasts pressed into Lila's, making her nipples harden and peak. Lila felt her core tightening, and her panties became moist. She closed her eyes, and then Jenny brought her mouth down on hers. The kiss was soft and angelic, innocent, with a slow exploratory brush of tongues.

Lila moved closer to Jenny on the bed and wrapped her arms around her waist. She massaged her tongue against Jenny's more bravely but still hesitantly.

Jenny moved a hand down to Lila's leg and it slipped in between her thighs. The thin flannel of her pajamas did nothing to hinder the roaring sensation her touch caused.

Lila moaned into Jenny's mouth as Jenny moved her hand inside the flannels. Lila could no longer kiss her, because she had to smother a squeal by pressing her face into her best friend's shoulder. Jenny giggled and slipped two fingers in between Lila's folds, which were warm and moist.

The smell of roses and almonds grew even stronger now.

Lila closed her eyes again and allowed Jenny to take her over. Her body tightened in anticipation.

Jenny circled Lila's bud three times with a wet finger, and Lila stirred beneath her touch, forcing her hips up, pressing her sex into Jenny's palm.

Jenny gently kissed her neck up to her ear. "You're gonna love this," she whispered, and as Lila moaned again, she thrust her fingers deep inside Lila's heated entrance.

Lila cried out, and Jenny hushed her cry with another passionate kiss. She felt Jenny's thumb stroke her knot of nerve endings once more with gentle but firm pressure, and with a blinding light flashing behind her eyelids, she came apart. She shook and trembled, and as Jenny retrieved her hand from the flannels, she fell back onto the bed.

Jenny bent over her quivering body. Her golden hair fell around Lila's face, tickling her. Jenny laughed quietly and watched as Lila took in a big breath of air.

"If I can get you off like that, imagine what some dick could do for you. I'm gonna hop in the shower." Jenny giggled.

Once Jenny left the room, Lila found herself staring into her canopy, breaths coming in strong, steady pulls. She relished the post-orgasm pulse she felt between her thighs.

Wow, that was so much better than touching herself. Better than her toys and movies and fantasies. Her mind was on overdrive, and her sex throbbed, ready for more. Ready for so much more. Her friend had awakened something in her. Something insatiable. Something dangerous.

Lila smiled widely and sighed. Then she remembered her parents would be out all night with the neighbors. The neighbors always threw a big barbecue in the fall, when the weather was soothing, and the autumn smells were extra inviting.

She and Doug would be all alone after the movie. She almost grew nervous. Almost. She told herself that she was going tear that boy apart. She couldn't wait to feel what his hot, engorged member would feel like buried deep inside her.

Suddenly, her desire spun out of control. She was invigorated. All she had needed was the jump-start Jenny had given her. She felt wild and reckless, but she liked the feeling. She had been so used to suppressing her sexual desires that she had had no clue how powerful they could be until now. She felt alive for the first time.

Jenny entered the room after a while, smiling at Lila, who was still lying on the bed.

"So ... how do you feel?" she asked, towel-drying her hair.

"Really? I feel ... I feel ... fucking great! Like my real self, I guess, which is weird. I feel like you knocked a ton of shit loose in me and the pieces are falling together in the right places now." Lila laughed, and her eyes glistened.

"Well, what are best friends for?" Jenny dropped the towel from around her body, exposing a smooth expanse of caramel skin, compliments of the tanning salon down the road. She had a thin frame, with firm, perky breasts. She was beautiful and not the least bit inhibited. She pulled on a fresh set of clothes: a short skirt and a partially see-through shirt—all black, of course—then she grabbed her backpack off the ground and kissed Lila on the cheek.

"See you, sister."

"See ya. And … thanks," Lila said back.

Jenny shook her head and put a finger to her lips, intimating that the incident had never happened. But it so had.

Lila hopped off her bed, fully revitalized, and looked at the alarm clock on her side table. It was only eleven. She had hours to kill before she saw Doug.

She undressed and got into the shower. Each bead of water that ran between her legs reminded her of Jenny's touch. She had never been so consumed by sex before, probably because she had never allowed anyone to touch her in that way. Now she felt like she was defenseless against her desire.

Jenny had said she wasn't a sex addict, but Lila sure felt like one. She needed more. She soaped up her shower pouf, creating a creamy lather and she spread the lather across her breasts and hardened nipples, sending a tremor straight to her clit. She turned toward the cascading water so that it could beat against her swollen nub as she washed over her breasts again, increasing the pleasure building inside her.

She moved her soapy pouf to her curls and lathered in between her thighs. She dropped a hand to her lips, separating her folds so she could rub her most sensitive spot. In under thirty seconds, she found herself against the cold shower wall, shivering and unsatisfied. A need swam inside her. Jenny had created a void that begged to be filled.

She finished washing the remainder of her body and reached for her towel. *Dammit, Jenny.* It wasn't on the bar. Jenny always used her towel every time she came over.

"Lila!"

Shit, her mother. She grabbed a fresh towel off the shelf and wrapped her body in it, then stepped into her room to see her mother putting away some of her clothes.

"Hi, sweetheart. How was your slumber party last night? I didn't see Jenny this morning," Pearl said as she shook her grey bangs out of her face. She continued to open drawers and place clothes inside them. Thank God Lila had hidden all her illicit items in the closet.

"Mom, you know I can put my own clothes away. You really don't have to do that."

"I'm of no use if I'm not taking care of you and your father. You know that. It's not like I have a job to go to. It's not my fault your father wants me at home, under his thumb," Pearl said resentfully.

"It's not that. Dad just makes enough money so that you don't have to work. I think he just wants you to be able to relax and enjoy life. I know I wouldn't work if my husband asked me not to."

"He's a typical Incubus. Arrogant and controlling. He wants me home to wait on him hand and foot, and it's miserable. Things will be even more insipid after you go to college. I can't wait," Pearl sneered, turning with the laundry basket.

"Mom, you'll be fine after I leave," Lila said, pulling a corner of her towel to dry her face.

"Lila, I have no social life, no friends to speak of, and no purpose other than playing house. You'll realize what life with an Incubus is like when you find one. Unless you find the *right* one."

"Mom, just chillax. I'll come eat breakfast with you. Your life is great. Quit downing it, and smile more, Sergeant Buzzkill. Things could be a lot worse."

Lila dug through her drawers for something cute to wear on the date she would never tell her parents about.

"Worse." Pearl was staring at nothing in the middle of the room. Then she shook her head and left without another word.

Damn, Lila thought. Her mother and father often argued behind closed doors. But she hadn't known her mother was so unhappy. She'd always had mood swings, but never spoke ill of her husband in front of Lila. Maybe she was just PMSing. Maybe she was menopausal. Lila wasn't sure which. She really wanted to ask her a few more things about her demon side, but she would ask later. Today didn't seem like one of her mother's better days.

Lila felt sexy after her and Jenny's steamy encounter. Once her mom was out of view, she slipped on a black, lacy thong, one she was sure Doug could appreciate. Then she stuffed her large breasts into a matching black bra. She pulled a short-sleeved hot-pink sweater on, which hugged her chest and exposed some of her flat belly. Then she yanked up her knee-high black-and-white striped tights. Finishing the ensemble, she donned a pleated black skirt and some black chunky high heels adorned with hot pink buttons along the straps.

She sat down at her vanity mirror. Never had she thought she was especially beautiful, but today, for the first time, she saw herself as others might see her. She took time to appreciate the way her dark hair fell in waves around her shoulders. She had a complexion models would pay for, too. Her skin was a flawless ivory that defied the sun. Her eyes were emeralds shielded by thick lashes that never needed mascara. And behind her pouty pink lips were shiny white teeth that her dentist said he greatly appreciated.

She smiled at herself and went downstairs to eat with her mother.

"Where's Dad?" Lila asked as she bent to get orange juice out of the refrigerator. Her OJ was the best part of her morning.

"He went to buy something for the computer. I don't know. Another one of his gadgets," Pearl said, while she whisked eggs in a large bowl.

"What a nerd," Lila said under her breath. Her dad had worked with computers as far back as she could remember.

"But he's my nerd," Pearl said back, pointing a spatula at Lila. "Forever and ever and *ever.*" She accentuated each syllable sourly and went back to whisking the eggs.

"*Okay...*," Lila started. "So, Jenny and I are going to a concert tonight. We're leaving at around six." She began texting the details of the lie to Jenny the minute the words came out of her mouth.

"What concert?" Pearl asked, with her back turned.

"Um, The Deep Underground is playing at Coyote's."

"Another one of those gothic bands, huh?" Pearl said, slightly disapproving. She had taken to wearing pastels and khakis, Keds sneakers, and granny sweaters.

"Yes, Mom, another one of those gothic bands." What should she care? They were demons, for Satan's sake.

Lila quickly finished texting the information to Jenny, who wrote back: *You so better get laid tonight.*

"Just be home at a respectable hour. That Jenny needs to get you home well before dawn. I worry about you."

Pearl's tone was quite motherly this morning.

Lila texted Jenny once more. *Oh yeah ... pick me up here at five thirty. Luv ya!*

All she got back was a smiley poking its tongue out.

With all that out of the way, she ate with her mother.

"Honey, I have to run some errands. You want to come with me?" Pearl asked, between mouthfuls of egg.

"What kind of errands?" Lila crossed her fingers hoping something fun.

"Well, I was thinking about getting some new shoes and perhaps a new bag. Mrs. Anderson just got a new Gucci. I want a Chanel."

"Sure, Mom. We'll hit the mall. Sounds like just what I need."

Lila knew a trip to the mall would take plenty of time, knowing her mother, and she always got something really cute and expensive out of it.

Today though, Lila didn't get anything cute or expensive. They spent hours perusing through the stores, shopping without buying anything other than her mother's purse. They had eaten at the food court and gotten ice cream.

Lila told her mother that she would like to talk to her more about what would happen when she succumbed to her curse, and Pearl promised they would talk about it tomorrow when they had time. But tomorrow would be too late. Lila had a date. Her parents had the barbecue that night, and she didn't know if she could hold out any longer.

She could have just told her mother about the date, but that would result in more sheltering and a possible lock down. Who knows? They might even make her kiss college goodbye.

Their last stop was a jewelry store, where Lila's mother had apparently special-ordered something. As the lady behind the desk turned to retrieve the item from the back, Lila saw her shadow display against the wall. It was a lot like her mother's shadow. It had wings, and a long tail. Talons.

The short, round woman came back to the desk and placed a small box into a little green bag and handed it to Pearl. Pearl stuffed it into her larger Chanel bag, then appreciatively shook the vendor's hand.

Lila knew something was up but refused to ask. She had always posed questions to her parents about things she found bizarre, but when she got sick of them never giving her a straight response, she quit asking. They always told her she would learn more with time. *Blah, blah, blah.*

Pearl and Lila walked back to their white Escalade and, once inside, Lila took note of the time on the dash. It was 4:44. She had to get back to do her hair and makeup before Jenny got there.

Pearl pulled into the garage, and before she could even stop the SUV, Lila was scampering out and pulling the interior door open.

Pearl sighed and grabbed her bag. Deep inside, she knew the time had come. She felt Lila's anticipation. She had to have one final talk with her daughter, the talk that would change everything for her. Finally, Pearl would be unburdened. After all, she and Perry had done all they could to keep Lila safe this long. She was beyond legal age and going to college. She was leaving their protective wings. It was time she knew the truth, no matter how hard it was. Pearl just dreaded Lila's reaction to the full reality of being a Succubus. She and Perry had to be ready for the worst.

Pearl walked into the kitchen and set her bag down. "Lila!"

"Upstairs, Mom! I gotta get ready!" Lila yelled back.

Panic lodged itself in the back of Pearl's throat, but she forced it down and went upstairs to her own room to get ready for the barbecue that Perry insisted they go to. Assimilation was one of his greater concerns.

Pearl hoped that Lila was really going to a concert tonight. She had sensed deceit in her daughter when she had told her about her plans, but Lila was not always honest with her. Lies or not, she always came home intact. She hadn't done anything rash yet and had held out far longer than most who were afflicted with their curse. They would speak tomorrow as planned.

Chapter 2

Lila darkly shadowed her eyelids and applied pink lipstick to her mouth. She powdered her nose and blew a kiss to herself in the mirror.

She was bursting inside, needing to get outside herself. Her excitement had built up so intensely that she thought for sure her head was going to pop off. Then she heard Jenny's horn.

She jumped out of her vanity chair and grabbed her leather jacket on the way out of her room. She sped down the stairs and out the door before her mother could say a word. When she got outside, she crashed into her brick of a father.

"Whoa there, little lady. Where are you off to?" Perry asked, laughing.

"Off to a concert. A goth concert, Dad. Spare me the lecture." Lila pulled her purse back onto her shoulder and headed for Jenny's car.

"Well, stay out of trouble, and tell Jenny to get you home in one piece. That girl'll be the death of you someday!" he called as Lila disappeared into Jenny's black Accord.

The girls drove to Jenny's house blasting Korn, Jenny's favorite band. When they got to the driveway, Lila saw Doug's car parked across the street. When he stepped out of it, time seemed to slow down. She wanted him so badly, but everything her mother said about saving herself suddenly came rushing back to her. She told herself to wait. She would wait until she talked with her mom.

Doug was a little over six feet tall and had a medium build. His hair was dark and seemed to shadow his face, shrouding him in a mysterious cloud of wonder.

Lila got out of the Accord and immediately appreciated his gait and the way his clothes fit him. He had a really nice body and knew just how to accentuate all of his best attributes. His jeans hugged his ass just right, and his jacket made his shoulders look broader.

When he was within arm's reach, he raised his head to Lila, and she took in his gaze. He leaned in and kissed her on the cheek. His warmth lingered there long after he pulled away. She smiled coyly.

"You ready to go?" he asked in a deep voice, which was sexy, whether he meant for it to be or not.

"Yes," Lila said.

Doug took her hand and pulled her to his car.

Lila waved at Jenny, and Jenny winked at her then grabbed her breasts vulgarly and stuck out her tongue.

Lila hoped Doug hadn't seen her and, thankfully, he had been opening the car door for her—something he'd never done before.

During the movie, Doug held Lila's hand, another thing he had never done before. He moved his thumb over the top of her hand, creating small circles in a soothing, sensual motion.

While his eyes locked on the movie screen, Lila spied him from the corner of her eye and watched as light danced against his silhouette. His lips were supple lines, and his nose, a perfect, straight slope. His eyes were alive and curious, and his smell was fresh, like aftershave.

She scarcely watched the movie and found herself hoping he would take her somewhere after it was over. The throbbing between her legs was beginning to usurp her need to stay a virgin.

Once the credits rolled, the couple sat in the darkness, waiting for the theater to clear.

"Are you hungry?" Doug asked.

For you. "Uh, no," Lila answered.

"Well, do you want me to take you home?"

"Of course not. It's only nine. My parents think I'm at a concert."

Doug pulled his hand from Lila's. "Your parents don't know you're on a date?" he asked, eyebrows high on his forehead.

"No. You know how protective they are. I've never been on a date until now," she admitted.

"Why didn't you just tell them the truth? We hang out all the time."

"I never tell them when we're alone. I always tell them we're out with friends."

He put his hand over his mouth in apprehension. "I should get you home then."

"No, please don't." She grabbed Doug's forearm. "I mean, I'm an adult. I don't need my parents' permission to do anything. I want to stay out with you."

"And I want to keep my head attached to my body. That won't happen if your father blows it off with a shotgun." He stood up, seemingly ending the conversation.

She was going to have to work him a bit to convince him to stay with her. "Don't you like me?" she asked with an innocent squeak.

"Yes. Yes, I like you, Lila. But I don't feel right going behind your parents' backs. Maybe if we talk to them, tell them we're dating. I mean, I've known you for six years. They shouldn't mind."

Doug was more of a gentleman than she'd hoped for. "You're right. You can take me home, and we'll have dinner with them or something this week."

She would just have to lure him inside and make him submit. Yep. All she was thinking about was his hands all over her body, and the pleasure she would get out of fucking the hell out of him.

"That sounds like a plan," he said, and took her hand, leading her out of the theater.

The ride to Lila's was somewhat quiet. Doug was looking at her exposed thighs when she caught him staring. He audibly swallowed and refocused his attention to the road.

"You're wondering if I'm a virgin. Aren't you?" she asked bluntly.

"Um ... uh, no. That's none of my business. I mean, I figured, if you've never been on a date..." He bit his lip.

"It *is* your business, if you're going to be the one taking my virginity."

He squirmed in his seat, and the car filled with the same scent Lila had detected when Jenny had seduced her. Almonds and roses. Deadly seduction. Doug was becoming aroused.

Lila felt her heart hammering inside her chest. She moved her hand to his thigh. Under the fabric of his jeans, she felt him swelling beneath her fingertips. His hands tightened on the steering wheel, exposing white knuckles, and his Adam's apple struggled down another hard swallow.

"I ... I can't do this. It's too soon. This is our first date, I mean," he laughed nervously.

"It seems you want to. And we've known each other six years, just like you said," she reasoned.

"Lila, I've wanted you since high school. I don't want to take advantage of you though."

"You can't take advantage if I'm willing, silly." She dragged her fingernails across the bulge in his pants.

His mouth opened partially, and he closed a hand over hers.

She moved her palm against him, and then moved her body closer to his so that she could suckle his neck.

"Oh, that feels good." He struggled to speak, his voice rough.

She smiled at how easy it was to get him to surrender to his hunger for her. She flicked her tongue out across his bottom lip and then slowly kissed down his jawline.

"We're here," he rasped. She stopped kissing him and pulled her hand away from his hidden erection.

"Walk me in," she whispered in his ear.

"No. I shouldn't," he protested.

She clutched his face and forced him to look into her smoldering eyes. "Please."

Entranced, he nodded his head. "Of course."

Lila let herself out of the car, and Doug followed her to the front door. The house was dark, and her parents had probably only been gone an hour or so. The neighborhood barbecues lasted for a few hours, because the yuppies really enjoyed getting plastered.

She tossed her keys into a basket that sat on the foyer table, then took off her jacket and hung it from the newel post at the end of the staircase.

She reached back and grabbed Doug's hand and they ascended the stairs together. With every step, she became more alive, as though she had taken a shit-ton of diet pills or something. High anxiety. She was so enthralled with the thought of giving it up. For good. No more bullshit; she was putting her foot down. She had made up her mind. No way would she let her mother talk her out of it again.

The smell of roses and almonds grew stronger as she opened the door to her bedroom. She activated the dim lamp on her nightstand and sat on her bed.

Doug absorbed his surroundings. He was in a room of soft light that bounced off the pink canopy hanging over the bed. There was a cute little makeup station with a mirror and a cool antique chair sat in front of it. The throw rug was a lush neon-green color and the bed ... The bed looked really comfortable. Lila sank back into the numerous pillows scattered against her ornate headboard. He took one step toward her and then stopped.

"We really shouldn't be doing this," he said.

"Why not? It's natural." She cocked her head to the side and licked her lips.

"I know, but you're a virgin." He slapped himself on the forehead and paced.

She giggled. "I'm hoping to change that. And I have dildos, so technically, I've been deflowered."

"Ha." He almost laughed and shook his head. "With me? Why? And why now? You've known how I feel about you for a while," he said, his expression puzzled.

Because you called right when I decided I didn't want to be a virgin anymore. "Because I trust you won't ever hurt me. I know how long you've wanted me. I've wanted you too, Doug. I just wasn't ready. A girl must be careful about these kinds of decisions. The timing has to be right; the setting has to be comfortable, and the man—well, the man is you. Come here." She patted a spot next to her on the bed.

She actually never wanted Doug like this before, and she would have taken any man tonight, in all honesty.

He inched toward her and sat down on the bed beside her, his hard-on raging. She kissed him before he could say another word. His breath got heavy, and he took her face into his hands. He kissed her back hungrily and deeply. She tasted like cherries, probably from her lip gloss or whatever she had on.

She soon pulled away from his mouth and started working the button on his pants, and then his zipper. Quickly, she slid off the bed and onto her knees, between his, pulled his pants down, took off his sneakers, and finished yanking his pants from around his ankles.

He took off his shirt, and then she stripped him of his boxers too. Satisfied, she stood between his thighs and stared at him.

"I don't ... I don't have a condom," he sputtered.

"It's okay, I'm on birth control. You know, just in case." *Total lie.* "And I'm disease-free, obviously."

"Okay. Okay, then." He nodded his head.

"Take me, Doug. Any way you want me," she purred.

He brought her into him so he could push up her sweater. She pulled it off over her head and threw it to the floor. He traced the lines of her bra and then reached for the back of it, to unclasp it and free her. Her ample breasts spilled out in front of him, and he looked at her in awe. She was so soft, so tight, and so innocent. He couldn't believe it was happening. She was all he had ever wanted.

He took one of her nipples between his lips and she almost wilted in his grasp. She had never before been touched by a man, and it was better than anything she ever imagined. He pinched her other nipple between his thumb and forefinger, twisting the light brown bud back and forth.

She crawled onto him, straddling him, pressing his erection against the thin fabric of the thong she was wearing. She rocked into him, grinding her hips into his. Pressure built within her core quickly, and she came right there against him. A loud whimper escaped her and she collapsed against his chest.

"Already?" Doug breathed, pulling back to look at her. He smiled.

"Sorry," she apologized, embarrassed.

"Honey, you can come as many times as you want and as soon as you want. It's me who has to last," he chuckled and swept back the hair that had fallen into her face. He kissed her neck and pulled her closer. "Are you ready? Or do you want to wait?"

"I want you now. All of you."

Lila's need for Doug inside her was unbearable. She could hardly contain herself. She wanted to roam his body; discover male parts she had never seen in real life. She wanted to lick him all over, but she didn't have time. Her lust seized her, and her mind focused on one thing and one thing only: Doug's warm cock inside of her.

She slightly lifted her hips, pushed her thong aside, and guided Doug's erection into her smooth walls. He groaned loudly, which just made her wilder with lust. Immediately, she felt a current of electricity shoot through her. It was jolting at first, but then settled to a low thrum.

She lowered herself onto him. Her toes curled and her thighs clenched.

Using both his hands, he hiked her skirt up and grabbed hold of her round ass, gripping her hard. He helped her move up and down along his shaft, faster and faster, bringing her close to climaxing again. The prickles inside her body morphed into a burning, and while it stung, she cried out in ecstasy a second time. He slipped out of her and tossed her onto her back.

Needily, he removed her panties and brought her hips to his thighs, then, he propped her legs up over his shoulders. Boy, did he like this view. Her lips were sopping and he played around her weeping entrance with his fingers.

She bit her lip and threw her head back into the mattress.

"Please," she begged. The heat was intensifying inside her and her sex swelled again, creating a sensation that laid somewhere between sweet bliss and painful torture.

"Please, what?" he asked, while he teased her.

He spanked her pussy with his cock and she inhaled sharply, her clit pounding, pushing her toward the edge. He dipped his head down to taste her, and when she felt his hot tongue on her clit, she couldn't speak. One more roll of his tongue, and she gripped his head with her thighs so tightly she was scared she might break him.

When she shakily let him go, he readjusted her legs over his shoulders and asked again,

"Please what?" His eyes sparkled. He liked turning her into putty, and he thought about how amazing she tasted. His tongue tingled a bit.

"Please fuck me until I can't stand up. Fuck me until my legs don't work. Fuck me until I can't see straight. Just do it, now!" she begged him, her pleas saturated in desperation.

Without another tortured request from her, he thrust inside her again. She was soaking wet, and they were making quite a mess of her sheets.

Doug had never had a woman who felt so good. His dick was more responsive than it had ever been, and before he could think about how amazing she made him feel, he came. He should have been sated, but instead, he geared up for more.

Lila barely had time to relish the coolness that overcame her before the electrical storm started up again. The more she screamed Doug's name, the harder he pumped into her. Her muscles contracted around his girth, and she orgasmed a third time.

He was thrilled by the sensation. He loved the way it felt when her walls spasmed against him. And again, he became extremely sensitive inside her tingly juices. *Magical pussy*, he thought.

While her body went limp, he pulled out of her slowly and rolled her onto her stomach. She might have been spent, but he sure wasn't. Not yet.

She tried to sit up, but her muscles were too shaky. *This must take practice*, she thought as he gripped her hips and pulled her up on all fours.

Scared to go again, but too lustful to stop, she stretched a hand underneath her and ran her fingernails gently across his taught sac.

He grasped a handful of her hair in response and tugged, easing inside of her again.

"Oh my God!" she cried.

The flaming current in her body intensified and branched out. She needed him to come again or she thought she might combust from the inside out. He released her hair and grabbed her shoulders instead, pulling back on them unmercifully.

Just as Lila thought flames would explode around them, swallowing them whole, Doug pumped his seed deep inside her.

She felt the heat in her body finally fizzling out, and she breathed deeply at the comfort. The internal galvanic storm had ended.

Doug's sweat dripped onto her lower back as he slowly pulled back. Her billowy entrance caught the head of his cock and he hissed as he withdrew from her. She shivered and collapsed onto the bed.

"I need to get the hell out of here before your parents get home," he said as he searched for his stray clothing.

He kind of stumbled and swayed, then he caught his balance and pulled on his shirt.

"It's okay. I'm not a cuddler," she admitted, although she didn't know it to be true until now. All she had wanted was his release. Once she got it, she was perfectly content to lie there alone.

"It's not like that, Lila," he said as he shrugged on his jeans, then his coat. It sounded like he was out of breath. He coughed a few times, then cleared his throat.

"It's okay, really. I'll see you later."

Lila was still lying on her belly, head resting against a pillow. She barely even looked at Doug, which he found a little strange, especially for a virgin. He thought she'd be a little more attached and hoped she was. He had every intention of getting some of that again. And soon.

"Well, did you at least enjoy that?" he asked, almost offended that she hadn't praised him for his performance.

She lifted her head to him. God, he was pale. She hoped she hadn't made him too sick. She actually really loved what they had just done and couldn't wait to do it again. She wished she had done it sooner. "I'm speechless," she sighed.

He smiled weakly and kissed her good night. "I'll call you first thing tomorrow, okay?" he asked, hoping that he wasn't coming down with anything. He felt really ill suddenly.

"Until tomorrow, then." She kissed him back and felt a sudden urge to go for a jog.

Once her suitor was gone, she settled for doing about two hundred jumping jacks. After the expenditure of energy, she fell asleep naked.

Chapter 3

The next morning, Lila woke up suddenly and thoroughly refreshed. She normally laid in bed for about twenty or thirty minutes before persuading her body to wake up, but not today. She felt like she'd had a shot of B-12 or something. Her clock displayed nine thirty-five. Strange. She had made it a rule to stay in bed until about eleven ever since she graduated high school.

She strode to her vanity in need of a ponytail band. She glanced in the mirror briefly and stopped dead in her tracks. For once, she didn't look like a walking zombie in the morning. She looked energized, new, crisp. She could swear that her wavy hair was a little shinier and thicker.

Her lips were crimson, and her cheeks were splashed with a little color, too. Her body felt silken, tight and strong.

As she contemplated her subtle changes, a horrible thought tore through her brain. Her mother would know she had bedded a man; the sex aura would surely give her away. If she went downstairs now, she would actually be doing a walk of shame, in front of her parents, no less. How mortifying! Was the halo a way for Incubi and Succubi parents to tell when their kids had had sex? Eww! There had to be more to it. She'd ask her mom about it again later.

Deciding against the walk of shame, she got dressed and hid out in her bedroom. She couldn't wait to tell Jenny what had happened, but Jenny woke up late, especially after partying, so she didn't expect to spill the beans anytime soon.

She turned on her TV and went into the bathroom to retrieve her nail polish. When she had procured everything she needed for her pedicure, she flipped through the channels and found the court channel, which she really enjoyed watching. It also doubled as prep work for the paralegal degree she decided she would obtain. Her dream was to work with the district attorney or with the most prestigious defense firm she could find. She was excited to start college. It would finally get her out of the damned house.

Smiling, she pushed Styrofoam dividers between her toes, stripped off her old blue polish and searched for a new color.

"Back to the case of a sixteen-year-old boy who brutally attacked his fifty-five-year-old friend with a pickle jar and a knife, resulting in death from blunt force trauma and multiple stab wounds," the reporter on the TV said.

"Ah, Kovarbasich. Sick bastard," Lila muttered while she shoved aside numerous polish colors. She thought perhaps her new shimmery brown would work. It was a good fall color.

After about twenty minutes, she applied the thirty-second topcoat and watched TV for a bit while her toenails dried. She wondered if her sex halo was gone. She didn't really know how long they lasted, and she especially didn't want her father seeing it. Awkward.

"Lila!" Pearl cried out in despair.

Her tone shocked Lila like resuscitation pads. She put her butt in gear, forgetting all about the sex glow that possibly still hovered over her. She yanked the Styrofoam dividers from her toes and padded down the stairs, anxiety-stricken.

Her mother come into view at the base of the stairwell. Tears streamed from her green eyes, wetting the collar of her lavender shirt. "It's Doug. He's ... *Lila*." Pearl said her name as if it were shameful.

Lila realized then that her afterglow was visible. Blushing red, she looked down at the floor. She wasn't really sure what she was sorry for, but she felt sorry. She continued the descent down the stairs and closed the distance between herself and her mother.

Pearl placed a finger under Lila's chin, forcing her daughter's head up so she could look her in the eyes.

Lila noticed that her mother not only looked sad; she looked devastated, like the world's end was near and only she knew it.

"Mom? What's going on?" Lila asked meekly.

"You killed that boy, didn't you?" Pearl's voice was even, but severe.

"What boy, Mamma? What are you talking about?" Lila swallowed back tears and tried to chokehold the seemingly irrational fear that gripped her in its ruthless hands.

"You killed that boy, and it's all my fault," Pearl cried. Her shoulders started shaking.

Lila put an arm around her mother and led her into the kitchen, where her father sat at the table, the paper and his coffee in front of him. He didn't seem interested in either.

"Dad? What's going on? Why is Mom so upset?" Lila asked.

Perry shoved a hand through his thick, grey hair. He cleared his throat loudly. "It's time we tell you the absolute truth. All that we feared has happened. We should have told you everything a whole hell of a lot sooner. Lila, sit down."

She sat down in a chair at the table and listened to her parents explain that Doug was found dead, in his car, which had been found on the roadside. There was no sign of foul play and no obvious cause of death, and nothing would be known until an autopsy was performed.

Lila panicked, flushed, and her hands began to tremble. It wasn't true. It couldn't be. All semblance of reality flew out the window.

"But I was only with him last night. How could he have died?" she asked in horror.

"How long were you ... with him," Pearl asked.

"It was about half an hour."

"There's your problem. You were with him far too long. Did you have an orgasm?"

"Mom!"

Lila was mortified. How could she discuss her intimate encounters in front of her dad? She noticed her father was gripping his paper so tightly it was tearing.

"I had a few," Lila whispered. She bit her lip.

"Then what happened? Why did it take half an hour? He should have been done in a few minutes." Pearl looked at her as if she were an idiot.

She felt like she was being interrogated by the police. "He had a few also." Lila looked down at her hands. They were still shaking, so she balled them into fists.

Pearl took one of her fists, uncurled it, and squeezed her hand tightly. She lowered her gaze to meet her daughter's.

"Honey, listen. Next time you find a target, make sure your tryst is fast. Don't offer him seconds, and especially not thirds. The longer it takes, the sicker he will become." Pearl moved her chair closer to Lila's.

"You have no clue what you've gotten yourself into, young lady. You should have waited until your mother spoke with you," Perry interjected as he shoved himself away from the table.

"Oh, like that helps, Perry. Go find something useful to do with yourself," Pearl spat at him.

"You watch your tone with me, Pearl. This is your fault." He squinted his eyes at her, almost threateningly. "You should have spoken with her sooner." He pointed a finger at his lifemate before he stalked out of the room.

Lila thought perhaps her mother had plenty of reason to be unhappy with her father if he spoke to her like that often. She had never seen this side of him.

"Lila, when you take an Incubus lifemate, choose very wisely," Pearl said flatly.

"What does Dad mean this was your fault? You told me not to have sex. I didn't listen. I think that pretty much makes it my fault."

"I didn't tell you everything. I was scared you would act out or leave or be angry with us. Your father insisted I tell you every detail of our curse, but I chose to shelter you from that enlightenment in an attempt to prolong your normal life. Once you activate the curse, life is the polar-opposite of normal." Pearl teared up again. "Understand, I couldn't risk losing you, my only daughter.

I should have raised you with the knowledge to prevent disasters like this. Our need for sex becomes irresistible with time. I sensed it on you, and I was foolish." Pearl sighed and rubbed her temples. "When you take a human male, you need to get him in and get him out."

Lila nodded slowly. Tears also welled in her eyes. She couldn't stop thinking about Doug. Six years of memories together with him whizzed through her brain in mere seconds. Vertigo attacked without mercy. She was nauseas.

Pearl continued on about the Lilin curse. "There are other things you need to know. Let's start with the easy stuff first, okay? Ask me anything, and I'll fill you in on the rest."

Her mother looked nervous, which frightened Lila. What was she about to learn about her "condition"?

"Okay. The burning. It started the second Doug, you know, was inside me. It was tickly at first, then it got worse and worse each time before he came. I mean, I know it's part of the curse, but why does the burning get so intense?"

"The burning is a gauge. It alerts you as to how much life force you are extracting from a mate. The longer it takes to secure a life force, the more life you are stealing; therefore, the burning gets worse. When it's unbearable, you know you are about to kill a man. You need to secure roughly one life force a week to survive. So, again, make it quick, for your prey's sake and your own. Without his seed, you have not secured the life force, so make sure he ejaculates."

"What happens if he doesn't?"

"You will burn internally, enduring the most excruciating pain of your life for several days, then you'll die."

"God, Mom. You never told me this? Doug wasn't my prey or my victim. He was my friend. He cared about me." Lila became even more disconsolate than when she first sat down.

"Well, from now on, any man you bed will be your prey," Pearl said curtly.

Lila twisted in her seat uncomfortably. She had to repress a few tears before she spoke again. "Why didn't Doug die while we were having sex? Why did he die later?"

"Apparently you left just enough life in him for him to drive down the road a bit. He must have fell very ill on his way home, which is why they police discovered his vehicle on the shoulder. I can't accurately tell you how long it took for him to succumb," Pearl answered.

"He looked sick when he left me." Lila dropped her head to the table with a thud.

"You must know that there are mishaps. You are a demon. Part of you is evil, whether you want to acknowledge that part or not. Just, please, don't become a man-eater or a baby-killer. I'd like to think most of us are above Lilith's revenge by now," Pearl said derisively.

"What else?" Lila choked on her saliva. She wanted to run away and scream. She wanted everything to stop. Her head spun with the veracity of the situation. It was too surreal.

"Mostly just survival techniques. The smell of lust will help you locate easy and willing targets."

"Roses and almonds, right?" Lila hypothesized, her head still down against the tabletop.

"Right. Also, if you can't find a lustful mate, you can look into any man's eyes and will him to bed you, as you have limited hypnotic powers."

"I know, I know. You told me about hypnosis when I was eight years old. Tell me something I *don't* know." Her mind reeled, and she wished she could prevent her knees from knocking together under the table.

"Okay. The glowing halo you see over certain people is another alert system Lilin are equipped with. The halo marks those who have recently had sex. Men shrouded by the halo aren't the safest bet when you need a life force. I recommend younger males, inexperienced males, virgins," Pearl rattled on lightly, as if she were thinking back to more pleasurable times.

She stood to wash the breakfast dishes as if everything were normal again and Lila hadn't just killed her innocent and dear friend.

"Drunks are just dreadful. They can never go all the way," her mother continued.

"What about sexually transmitted diseases?" Lila asked firmly. She had suspected there was more to whole STD thing besides what her mother had told her when she turned sixteen. They were immune. Being immune was a blessing, not a curse. It didn't make sense.

Pearl hesitated before answering the question. "We're immune." She looked hard at the pan she was scrubbing.

"Yeah. And?"

"We are carriers."

"Mom!" Lila cried.

Pearl dropped the pan into the sink and turned to face her daughter.

"Our diseases are spread to punish unholy fornication. You will never know when you unleash a disease or what its nature is. You will spread whatever is necessary, whenever it is necessary, based on worldly trends and cosmic wisdom.

"Demons are God's children too, but do you think He allowed us life without keeping an ace in His pocket? We tempt for God, punish for God, and we suffer during it all for the sins of our ancestors."

"You're always saying that shit. *Lah-dee-dah*. Mom, c'mon, just face it. We're demonic prostitutes," Lila said acerbically.

Pearl had constantly reminded Lila of God's perfect plan for Lilin since she was little. Now it just sounded like horseshit.

"You are not a prostitute. You are a seductress. It will all end when you find an Incubus to bond with. No more burning, no intense energy surges ..."

"Energy surges? After Doug left, I wanted to run a marathon."

Pearl nodded. "Yes, that will happen after taking a life force, unless you are bonded. Then you and your lifemate will exchange your own life forces back and forth evenly."

"So, what else about this bonding with a lifemate?" Lila asked, rubbing her forehead while making a mental list of imperative shit. Her Armageddon list. Screw the burning, the surges, the mystery STDs and, oh yeah, the murder.

"Well, Lilin can only bond with an Incubus or a Fallen because, as you learned the hard way, other species' life forces are either too weak or too impure to sustain you for more than a week or so. Once you have bonded, you and your lifemate will be linked in nearly every facet of your lives. Your counterpart will not be able to ejaculate with anyone else unless you break your bond with him. Only a Succubus can break a lifemate bond and she can only do this by securing another one."

"So, it doesn't have to be forever? It's just like humans and marriage, then," Lila asked hopefully.

"No. Not nearly as pretty as humans and their dysfunctional marriages. Some Incubi are desperate to stop the burning, and they force themselves on unbound Succubi when they find them."

Lila curled her lip in disgust.

"Most Incubi are elusive, loners, and all testosterone. They are rarely emotional, so they aren't easy to access. Some love what they are. Some won't bond out of arrogance, fearing a bond break. If his bond is broken and he approached another Succubus, she would likely turn him away, thinking he isn't suitable. The upside about bond breaks for Incubi is that they can go back to ejaculating however and with whomever they please. Succubi don't have it so great. I highly discourage breaking a bond. When your lifemate finds you've been secured another bond, he will likely hunt you down and kill you and your new beau for revenge and to save his pride."

"How can I tell who's bonded and who's not?" Lila asked. She finally had more than a modicum of interest in the monotonous Lilin lesson.

"You know the tattoos your father and I share? They were cosmically created at the time I chose him. The tattoos appear in relation to your heart. The farther away from your heart the tattoo is, the weaker the connection you will have to your lifemate."

"You and dad have tattoos on your shoulders." Lila had always thought her parents ran off together and got inked in Vegas or something, back when they were young and free.

"Yes. We are close, but not a perfect match. I've never seen a perfect match, myself. Your father and I are actually quite lucky."

"Great! With my luck, I'll bond with the worst match on the planet." Lila slammed her hand down on the table.

"Honey, it is what it is." Pearl shrugged and wiped her hands on a dish towel.

Lila thought for a minute about how being a Succubus couldn't possibly be the most horrific thing a girl had to deal with. She decided she'd rather be tied down than killing people. She'd just find a lifemate and deal.

"So, I have to find a lifemate. Shouldn't be too hard. I'll get right on that. Problem solved." She shrugged.

"You can't rush into this, or you will likely choose your mate unwisely. Bonding requires patience and the utmost discretion. It may take a while to find a desirable mate who is willing to bond," Pearl cautioned.

"How in the hell did you meet Dad?"

"Your father and I were sort of raised together by a demon-snatching witch. She kidnapped us and harnessed our mystical properties for spells and potions. We spent most of our young lives in cages, eating scraps. Through those hard times, we formed a strong connection and found comfort in one another."

"You had it easy then, even if you were treated like pound puppies. How the hell am I supposed to safely find an Incubus who will actually take me?" Lila huffed. "I am a walking death sentence. I can't maintain a normal relationship with anyone. I'm a bigger freak now than I was in school, and you don't tell me all this shit until I've murdered someone?" she was an octave away from screaming at her mother.

"Lila, you knew you would suffer without sex and that it was dangerous or fatal for your human when you had it," Pearl argued defensively.

"Yeah, but had you told me the burning was a death meter, Doug would be alive right now. I figured since you gave up your virginity at fourteen, I could surely deal with this curse at twenty-two. But no. You failed mentioning any of the epic information to me."

Pearl sighed. "Lila, you'll know an Incubus when you meet him by his smell, his shadow, his presence. His irises will be like your father's, like Samael's. He'll draw you in. You'll find him. Trust me. Everything will work itself out."

"Pff. 'Work itself out.' I'll find an Incubus at some point, sure, but I won't find the right one. By the way I've never even seen a picture of Samael or his stupid irises because you sheltered me from all Lilin literature, insisting that you pass the stories along orally. And I don't know what Dad's eye color is either because he's worn colored contacts for as long as I can remember!" Lila barked. "Is that it? Or is there more? Why did you have me? I mean, why did you get pregnant?"

Pearl was so frustrated with all the questions because none of the answers were pleasant. She took a deep breath, deciding to address Lila's last question.

"Honey, the cosmos control Lilin pregnancies. There's no such thing as birth control for us. I had fifteen children, all males; and in my last cycle, I conceived you. Succubi are rare. That's why I sheltered you. I didn't want anything to happen to you."

"I have fifteen brothers?" Lila squawked. She went cross-eyed. She couldn't begin to wrap her mind around having sixteen kids to save her soul. Where the hell were they all? And how could her mother even have sixteen children so far apart that she had never met any of them? If her mother was only forty-something or fifty

... Then she realized that she had no clue how old her mother was. They hadn't celebrated her birthday a single year.

Recognizing just how far out of the loop she was, Lila began laughing uncontrollably. Part of her brain had snapped. It was all a joke. All falsehoods and guises.

Pearl's expression became one of worry as she watched her daughter's mini mental break-down unfold. She didn't know how to approach her or if she even should.

Lila slid down in her chair as her laughter made a conversion to hiccups. She just sat there; shoulders jolting with each annoying one.

When Pearl decided Lila wasn't going to acknowledge her, she backed out of the kitchen, scampered down the hall and up the stairs to her bedroom. Digging through her new purse, she located the custom pendant she'd had made for Lila. Originally, it was intended to be a present for when she left for college, but now seemed like a good time to try and give it to her. Pearl went back downstairs.

"Li?"

Lila heard her mother's voice and it caused searing pain to shoot through her head. She swore it felt like a thousand rusty nails were piercing her skull and delving into her frontal lobe. Then her mother sat in front of her holding the little green jewelry bag from the mall.

"Lila, I know our lives are not cherries on ice cream by any means. You need to have this," Pearl said, retrieving a small box from the bag. She slid it over to Lila, who just stared at it dolefully.

Pearl pushed her chair back and stood, then walked over to her daughter. She picked up the box and opened it withdrawing a necklace. She stepped behind Lila and latched the chain around her neck.

"What is this?" Lila asked wearily, gazing down at the black jeweled pendant. It was the profile of a female beast perched on her heels, breasts protruding and wings rising from her back. A spade tail curled around her feet. A green emerald was her eye. *Expensive.*

"It's a talisman. That necklace cannot be removed until after you bond. Only your lifemate can unlatch it. Until then, it is a constant reminder of your power and purpose. Understand?"

Lila roused in her seat. "Yeah. I think I get it. Fuck Lilith. What a prideful bitch," she ground out. Suddenly, Lilith wasn't as cool as she used to be. Lila plopped her arms onto the table and rested her head on them, mentally exhausted.

Pearl really didn't want to tell Lila what she had to next, but everything else had already been aired. She knelt beside her daughter, placing a hand on her back. She regretted not having eased her into things when she was younger, but the timing had never been right. She was either too young to grasp the concepts, or she was starting her period, upset about bullies or worried about boys. Pearl always justified reasons to keep Lila off demon radar, but she'd been overprotective for far too long. It had all blown up in her face.

Pearl spoke in a low tone. "Lila, once you activated the curse, you began a new life cycle, one that will last a few hundred years. Toward your end, you won't be able to secure as much life force as you need, and you will die and reside in Hell, until after Armageddon. God will then judge you and decide whether you go to Heaven or stay in Hell."

Lila's head snapped up and her jaw unhinged. She couldn't conceive of living so long when her teen years alone had been enough to make her want to crawl into a hole and die.

"That's how you could have had so many kids? How old are you, Mom?" she asked, her face contorted with fear and thoughts of her mother's treachery.

"I'm just over three hundred and sixty years old. You lose count after a while. About ten human years equate to one year of our life. We don't factor in the years of our chastity."

"Whatever, Mom. There's no way we could live, what, eighteen years in the same neighborhood without anyone noticing something was way off with us." She waved her hand, dismissing the possibility.

"Lila, our closest neighbors have changed at least three times, so we haven't had to leave. And your father has switched jobs four times since we settled here. If we bump into someone we knew from a while back, plastic surgery is a great excuse for looking the same as a few years ago, hypnosis works sometimes ... There are ways around the difficulties."

Lila eyed her mother skeptically, but Pearl's face didn't reveal the slightest smile. It wasn't a mean joke. It was as real as the rest of it.

"That's not gonna happen to me. I'm sorry." Lila shook her head violently. "What if I just don't have sex? What if I want to end it now? I could just hang out in Hell."

"Lila, suicide is an unforgiveable sin, in most cases, and it would be a very painful choice to make. Like I said, the burning could last for days. Listen, there are many things you will experience, good things you'd miss out on if you chose that path."

"No, I don't think I'd be missing out on anything. Burning and killing and burning and living. *For-ev-er*. It just doesn't appeal to me."

"Lila, you know your probable strength. You must also know now that you can only die from the most severe of wounds, and from not taking life forces."

"This is fucked." She couldn't breathe. "Are all demons almost impossible to kill? Do they all live for centuries?"

"No. God inflicted different curses on different demons. Most are pesky little beasts. Some heal from wounds, like us. Some are just as fragile as humans."

Lila fingered her new pendant. It would have been really stunning had it not been a gruesome reminder of all the knowledge she just got blasted with. A tear slid down her cheek as she pondered her fate. She was infuriated with her parents for not telling her all the facts. Doug was dead and it was their fault, and they didn't even have to carry the burden she had to now. While she hadn't a clue how the burning meter worked at the time, she was the one who took his life directly, and she was the one who would live lifetimes to remember it.

She stood from the table silently, turned and walked away from her mother.

Pearl called after her, "There is still so much you need to know!"

Lila didn't turn around. Instead, she went into some state of shock. Through her ears, she only heard muffled noises. Her brain filled with darkness and fog. She didn't feel the legs that moved beneath her, carrying her to wherever. She couldn't discern whether or not she was breathing. Her vision blurred, and her body went numb.

She was never going back to her childhood home and her parents were as dead as Doug to her. She was leaving the false life she knew in search for something true. In a stupor, she walked the five miles to Jenny's house.

Exhausted, Lila knocked on the door to Jenny's place. Her mom, Ginger, answered.

The rough woman's red dye job was fading, and she wore an oversized sweatshirt. Her eyes were bloodshot, and she held a glass of scotch in her hands. She never did anything involving energy exertion and had somehow gotten approved for disability. But she never gave Lila or Jenny a problem, and for that, they were thankful.

"She's upstairs, Lila." Ginger coughed and went back to the couch curling up to watch QVC.

Lila rushed up the stairs and into Jenny's room. She shook her friend until she woke.

"I'm leaving, Jenny. I'm getting far away from here," she said urgently.

"Where are you going, baby?" Jenny asked as she wiped the sleep from her eyes.

"Wake up. I need you awake for this." Lila shook Jenny's small shoulders again.

"Okay. Okay. I'm up. What's going on, Li?" Jenny's eyes opened a little more, and she sat up so she could hold Lila's hand. "Wow. You look amazing. New face cream or something?" she asked.

"I am the monster in my mother's stories. I killed Doug last night. I fucked him, and he died. He died, Jenny!"

"Doug's dead? Holy shit!" Jenny sat up, fully alert now, and grabbed Lila's other hand, too.

"He's dead because of me. I am a demon. A Succubus like Lilith. My parents have royally fucked me!"

"Honey, slow down. You aren't a demon. Your 'rents are screwing with your head. I always thought they were a little weird, but this is just cruel." Jenny shook her head and looked deep into Lila's tearful eyes.

"Jenny, I killed Doug. I swear it was an accident, though. And I see things. Like I can tell when someone has had sex because they glow gold afterward. I see shadows of demons that belong to people, but they aren't people. They are monsters hiding behind human masks. Ever since you ... ever since that morning, I have craved sex. But it hurts so badly like my skin is on fire and my insides are lava." Lila took a breath, realizing how this must sound to her best friend, but Jenny sat there taking it all in. Though her eyes were saucers.

"Mom said I can heal from wounds, hypnotize men…and… and… Remember the stories. Remember Lilith. You know all about what's happening to me. It's all true, Jenny." When her friend didn't respond, Lila dropped her head, sighing deeply. It was no use. She withdrew her hands from Jenny's and proceeded to wring them together anxiously.

After a long minute, Jenny snapped out of her overload trance and said, "Listen. Stay with me for a while. We'll figure this out." She embraced Lila.

When Lila understood that Jenny didn't believe her, she began to sob. She pulled away from her, and Jenny grabbed for her necklace.

"Way cool," she said, moving her thumb over the sparkly black diamond pendant.

"Not cool. It's a reminder that I'm a freak," Lila retorted resentfully.

"Well then take it off. I'll wear it." Jenny made a "gimme" gesture with her hands.

"It won't come off. It's been enchanted or something." Lila had tried to rip the thing off on her five-mile hike to Jenny's.

Jenny moved behind Lila and reached for the clasp, trying to open it, but couldn't to save her soul. She peeked over Lila's shoulder, looking at her questioningly.

"I told you," she sneered.

"This doesn't make sense." Jenny yanked on the necklace as hard as she could, yet it wouldn't break, either. It was only a thin strand of silver. She had broken plenty of necklaces to know that this one should break and break easily. She tried one more time, to no avail.

"Lila? Prove it," Jenny said, her voice shaky, as she peered around Lila's shoulder again.

Lila stood from the bed and looked around the room. In one of Jenny's dresser drawers, she found scrapbooking items and a large pair of scissors. She slid the scissors out slowly, turned to her non-believing friend, then closed her eyes and stabbed the scissors deep into her thigh. She loosed a bloodcurdling scream and crashed to the floor. Instantly, she thought she had made a colossal mistake.

Jenny fell to her side. She hastily yanked the scissors out of Lila's flesh, then rushed into the bathroom for a towel. Blood was spurting everywhere.

"Jenny? Everything okay up there?" Ginger called.

"Uh, yeah, Ginger! We're just messing around!" Jenny placed the towel on Lila's wound in sheer panic and applied pressure. "What the fuck were you thinking, huh?" she screamed in a whisper.

Lila moved her leg, and the pain that seared through her only moments ago began to dissipate. She removed the towel from the wound in time to see her flesh mending itself seamlessly.

Jenny's mouth hung open. She was speechless for a long time before taking a deep breath. "So, you killed Doug, huh? Tell me everything."

Chapter 4

"We got back from the movies, and I hinted that we should go somewhere to get it on, but he wasn't having it. He said it was because it was our first date, then there was my Dad, and I was a virgin. He was dead set against it until I looked into his eyes and said 'please.' I think I hypnotized him a bit. He was still unsure at first, but after a while, he ravaged me.

"My skin burned. It started with what felt like light electricity, then the electrical current turned into an inferno beneath my skin. It was unbearable, and it didn't stop until he came."

"Did that happen with me?" Jenny asked.

"No."

"Weird."

"Yeah, Mom said the fiery sensation begins when a man enters me and intensifies until he ejaculates. It's then that I absorb part of their life force. Or all of it, in Doug's case. I guess I can't take female life forces because females don't have semen. Supposedly, Succubi aren't meant to be lesbos.

"Then Mom told me the burning is a gauge that alerts me as to how much life I'm extracting. I'm supposed to get a dick in me and get it out of me as soon as possible. Quickies." She put her head in her hands.

"Well, do you at least get pleasure from it? I mean, how was it with Doug?" Jenny stroked Lila's hair gently.

"It was like the world melted away. I wanted to fuse my body into his. I had a few amazing orgasms. Each time he pounded into me, I craved more and more. I wanted to be with him for hours. Only I couldn't. The burning was killing me."

"How do we stop this?" Jenny asked.

"I have to find a lifemate. An Incubus or a fallen angel are compatible with my breed on account of the angel blood that runs through our veins, but fallen angels are super rare. Anyway, the burning will stop once I bond, then I can have sex like a normal demon. Have little demon children and a little demon home with a demonic white picket fence. What part of this isn't totally batshit crazy? Why aren't you completely freaked out?"

"Lila, since I met you, I wanted your stories to be true. I wanted there to be something other than everyday bullshit. I'm so jealous!" Jenny helped Lila off the ground, and they both sat back down on her bed.

"Great. The one of us who wants to be a demon isn't. This sucks." Lila rolled her eyes.

"Totally sucks. I agree. Well, it looks like we need to find you an Incubus, then. Shouldn't be that hard. I mean, look at your parents. They both are what you are, right?"

"Easier said than done. My parents were lucky enough to have been raised with each other. They didn't have to hunt each other down."

"What were you saying about the shadows?" Jenny asked, immersed in delight.

"I see shadows of demons. I see a human-looking person, but their shadow reveals them to be otherwise."

"Well, can't you just look for the shadow of an Incubus, and we can hook you up?"

"I've never seen one other than my father's," Lila said. "Mom says they're reclusive and mostly not eager to bond."

"Well, Lilith looks like that." Jenny pointed to Lila's necklace. "What do Incubi look like?" Jenny jumped off her bed and grabbed her laptop. She typed "Incubus demon" in the search engine.

What popped up terrified Lila as it had many times before when she researched her roots. Adorning the demon's head were the curling horns of a ram. Razor-sharp claws jutted from his fingertips. Expansive tattered wings spread out across his back, and a spade tail extended from his tailbone. His erection was quite intimidating, too. The Incubus was awful. He looked like a charred seething devil. His nostrils were flared, his teeth were sharp, and... Lila slammed the computer shut.

"I already know what Incubi look like."

"Damn, girl. That's gonna be some erotic shit," Jenny breathed.

"Whatever, we can't transform into this," Lila pulled on her necklace. "Or that," she finished, pointing to the laptop. "Besides, my mother said most of the Internet info was crap, so I never bothered looking into it any further. This is a friggin' nightmare, Jenny. I have one week to figure this out before I have to steal another life force. I don't know if I'm strong enough to stop myself before I kill someone else. Once I get started, I don't want to stop," she admitted shamefully.

"Do you want to come out with me tonight? Get your mind off things? Be a twenty-two-year-old girl just a little while longer? We can get some drinks and figure out what to do next."

"I don't know, Jen. I think I'll just stay here. I don't know what to do. I'm terrified to be in public."

"Okay, well, we can do a movie night or just sit and stress. Whatever you want to do," Jenny offered sincerely.

"No. I need some time to think. Go to Greg's or something and have fun," Lila said back.

Jenny started again, "We could..."

"Go, Jenny," Lila interrupted and lightly pushed her shoulder.

Jenny slowly crawled off the bed and began sifting through her closet searching for something to wear.

"We'll figure some of this out later. Whenever you're ready, I'm all yours. Promise." Jenny really didn't want to leave Lila by herself. She needed someone to help her cope.

She turned and looked at Lila with her big blue eyes. "Sure you don't want to go out?"

"I need some time alone, Jen," Lila answered again, aggravated.

Jenny shrugged and went back to sifting. "Okay, Okay. By the way, you never answered me. New face cream or what? New shampoo?" she asked, pulling a tight black shirt on that had intentional tears across the center to reveal cleavage. The back was shredded too, along the spine.

"I hope you're gonna wear a sweater or something with that. The wind will tear right through those ... exposed areas." Lila pointed to each of Jenny's breasts.

"Sure thing, *Mom*," Jenny retorted, rolling her eyes.

"So, tell me why you look so good. I mean, not that you don't all the time. You just look... really healthy."

"It's a result of sucking the life out of boys, I guess. It makes me new. Like I shed my old skin or something." Lila rubbed her temples. A headache lingered behind her eyes.

"Well, that's just badass. Maybe your problem isn't all that horrible." Jenny was looking in the mirror hanging over her dresser, smoothing a moisturizer across her face.

"You have no idea what that burn feels like, Jen. It's ...there are no words to describe the pain."

"But you're better after and you look like a goddess."

"Yeah, and I killed a human being. Let's not forget that part."

"Okay. If we're going to get through this, you need to start thinking positively," Jenny said, squinting her eyes at Lila in the mirror. "You screwed up. Wasn't your fault. We'll look for your Incubus, and everything will be fine." She started applying blush and powder to her cheeks and nose.

"You're not acting like this is really happening."

"Girl, things were so boring until today! I'm going to pick your brain apart about this," Jenny squeaked, tapping the end of her eyeliner against the mirror.

"You're fucking crazy." Lila shook her head.

"I know, right?"

"I can't even mourn for Doug because of everything
that's happening. It's just not fair," Lila whispered so quietly Jenny almost didn't hear her. She dropped the cosmetics and sat on the bed next to Lila.

"I'm sorry, Li. I'm not sympathizing. I'm being a total jerk. And I wish I had known Doug better. Maybe then I could say something to make you feel better."

"Nothing anyone could say would make me feel better about any of this."

"What do I tell your parents when they call?" Jenny asked, putting her arm around Lila's shoulder.

"Tell them I got on a plane and didn't tell you where I went. Will your mom go with that?"

"Yeah. It shouldn't be a problem. Ginger's out of it half the time anyway. I'll tell her you're having some issues at home."

"Jenny?"

"Yeah?"

"I've got to get out of here. Go somewhere new," Lila said dejectedly.

"I'll go anywhere you want. We're in this together, okay? We'll do some research and pick a place."

Lila grabbed her best friend and hugged her tightly. "Thank you, Jenny. I love you."

"I love you, too," Jenny reciprocated and kissed Lila on the cheek.

Chapter 5

At around five the next evening, Jenny slipped out the door, promising to return early. Lila still refused to go out and Jenny's boyfriend was hounding her to see him again.

She sat on the bed, worrying herself sick, just as she had the day before.

Jenny's laptop was on the dresser and Lila kept eyeballing it, wondering if maybe the Web could offer something that jived with what she now knew to be true.

She finally decided to research more and began scrolling through various topics. She started on Incubi hideouts and found nothing. Next, she focused on demons in America. Then she searched demons in human forms and numerous other key phrases. She came across role-playing websites for freaks and nerds, loosely informative websites that contained basics she already knew and sites full of total bullshit lore. An overwhelming number of sites were devoted to theories about demons (presidents) in the government. Several pages were dedicated to the band Incubus. Total irrelevant and useless information.

Frustrated, she closed the laptop and sighed. She wanted to get out of the house now. It was ten, and she wasn't the least bit tired. Her sex throbbed. It was bad enough that she had to fuck for a living, but to be horny while she was off the clock, too?

A naughty urge washed over her. She locked Jenny's bedroom door in case Ginger came to check on her. Then she laid back on the bed, to unbutton and unzip her jeans. She slipped a hand up her sweater and fondled her nipples. A pleasurable sensation crept along her stomach down to her pelvis. She found herself lifting her hips once she was too stimulated to wait any longer. Her hand then travelled beneath her panties. Slowly she rubbed her clit with two fingers in a circular motion. Closing her eyes, she moaned while she teased herself, but after about three more seconds she stifled an outcry as her orgasm burst through her body.

It was a release, but nothing like the erotic pleasure of having a man inside of her, massaging her walls with his warm, hard flesh until she orgasmed all over him. Nothing like the overwhelming feeling of when the fire inside her was splashed out by a man's balmy semen.

She scampered off the bed, consumed by lust. She shed the sweater but buttoned and zipped her jeans. Haphazardly, she sifted through Jenny's closet, finding a cute top and a sexy pair of heels, then she pulled on her leather jacket and purse.

Ginger was nowhere to be found, so Lila quietly made her way through the hall and shut the front door silently behind her.

The night was clear, and the wind was hushed, which abated some of the chill in the air. Still, Lila shivered. She didn't know where she was going, and didn't care, either.

She walked the street for nearly an hour and arrived at the local bar. Her mom had told her to avoid drunks, but she felt a little masochistic tonight.

Smoke clouds and stale air flooded the dingy space. She sat at a table alone, ordered a screwdriver, and waited.

Soon enough, a man approached her and offered to buy her a drink.

"No, thanks, I have one right here," she told him.

"Oh, yes. I see that. I apologize," he stammered.

"It's all right," she giggled.

"Well, want some company, or is your boyfriend gonna come around any second?"

"I'm single. Sit down." She gestured to the open space in front of her.

The man sat and signaled the waitress. Once she came to the table, he ordered a rum and coke. He smiled at Lila, and she smiled back.

He was very handsome, probably almost thirty, and she notice he wore a wedding band. Her smile widened. She wouldn't feel so bad stealing a bit of his life force.

"So, why are you alone? Surely you have plenty of guys lined up waiting to take you out," the man presumed, his smile half-cocked. His eyes were a cute kind of squinty when he smiled, giving him a subtly playful look.

"Just trying to get away," she answered, and sipped her drink.

"What are you running from, beautiful?" The man casually raked a hand through his spiky brown hair and tugged the collar of his blazer. Beneath the blazer he wore a light blue dress shirt, unbuttoned enough so that she could see a bit of his chest hair.

Lila licked her bottom lip, tasting sugar from the cherry she seductively plucked off the little plastic toothpick in her drink. "What do you say we skip all the meaningless dialogue and just get out of here, huh?" She locked eyes with the stranger. Aromatic lust exuded from him. Great. He was ready and willing. So was she. Or was she? *Dammit, I'm such a horndog.* She should have just stayed at Jenny's.

"Well, my place is just around the corner. We can have drinks there," he suggested. "My bar is stocked. What's your name?" he asked.

"Lila."

"Well, I'm Peter, Lila."

"And where is your wife tonight, Peter?" she asked, brushing a hand across his ring finger.

He laughed, a bit embarrassed, and the waitress returned just in time to briefly relieve his discomfort. He requested his and Lila's checks then took down a healthy swig from his glass.

"Uh, she's actually visiting her mother." Peter swallowed hard and braced for impact.

"Good," Lila said, meeting his eyes, grinning.

He loosened up when he heard her response. Lila was a ten. Hell, she was way more than that. Tonight was going to be intense. He'd bet big money that she was totally kinky and would beg him do things to her that his wife never would.

The waitress stopped by, setting the checks on the table. Peter placed a few bills down as Lila stood.

He looked up at her in amazement. She was the perfect lay. He threw his drink back and followed her to the door. He held it open for her, then showed her to his Jag.

After a quick drive down the block, he pulled into his garage closing the door behind them.

Lila wondered how many times he had picked up random women to bed as he opened the car door for her. She took his hand and followed him inside his expansive home.

Peter asked her if she wanted another drink, but she declined as she eased off her jacket and purse.

He took her things and said, "Well, have a seat in there, and I'll join you in a second." He pointed to a cozy living room, which his wife had probably invested a lot of work, money and time into decorating. Interior designs that he probably didn't even appreciate or notice.

Lila perched herself on the arm of an oversized, cream-colored chair and waited for Peter, who soon rounded the corner with a drink and a condom in his hand. She thought the move was too soon and a bit tacky.

He sat across from her on a matching plush sofa and just stared at her.

She undressed him with her eyes. Her need was raw. *Now. I need it now.* She stood and sauntered over to him, took the drink from his hand and set it on a small table next to the sofa.

He grinned at her, settling back into the couch. Once he was completely comfortable, she straddled his thighs and unbuttoned his slacks.

"I'll make this really easy on you. Just sit back, and let me work," she heard herself say, yet she couldn't believe the words were hers. She had been a virgin not forty-eight hours ago. Now she sounded and acted like a seasoned seductress.

She unzipped his pants, and he raised his hips so she could pull them down. Lila took the briefs he wore down too, freeing his semi-soft and unimpressive penis. He folded his arms behind his head and beamed. She didn't want to take him in her mouth, because it seemed a little too intimate. She didn't want intimacy with him either; she wanted to fuck. Blow jobs weren't the only way to get a guy hard. She learned had all kinds of tricks from her extensive porn collection.

Standing in front of him, she slowly lifted the racy red shirt she borrowed from Jenny's closet and tossed it to the floor. She wasn't wearing a bra.

Peter nodded in approval and licked his lips. Lila moved closer to him, lifted her leg gracefully and placed a stiletto-clad foot on the arm of the sofa. He slid off her shoe, his eyes hungry.

Mini Peter swelled a bit, but still wasn't nearly firm enough to sate her appetite. She put her bare foot on the floor and raised her other leg, resting her heel on his thigh. He started at her hip, running his hands down the length of her leg, slipping the other shoe off as well.

Turning her back to him, she shimmied down her jeans and panties. Then she intently peered over her shoulder at him and raised her arms in the air, rolling her hips sensually as if she were listening to a Sade song.

He reached out to touch her, but she shook a finger at him and rubbed her perfectly shaped ass across his lap, brushing his erection. Her smooth ivory skin, her captivating eyes and her luscious lips...It was too much. After watching her dance another a minute or so, he lost control and fumbled for the condom he had set on the side table.

She touched his hand. "Don't put that on," she said, staring through him with those eyes.

Without objection, he took her by the waist, forcing her down on him, and plunged his fully swollen manhood inside of her. While he wasn't large, he was skilled and moved inside her with precision.

Lila didn't like Peter, but she appreciated the sex. She craved the interaction more than she craved orange juice, and that was huge. She didn't have any other vice to compare the yearning to, but she was sure if she'd had a heroin problem, sex would be more tantalizing than the drug.

Electric pulses ramped through her, spiking her temperature. She ground out a few heavy thrusts, and the man beneath her groaned.

"Hell, yeah, baby. Just like that."

"You like that?" she enticed.

"I love it."

Peter forced her against him aggressively and brought a hand around to caress her bud.

She closed her eyes just when she thought she would peak, but suddenly she thought of Doug. All desire to orgasm escaped her. She attempted to bury the guilt deep but couldn't. It was seizing her thoughts. She had to concentrate on what she was doing now, had to focus and make this man come.

Quickly, Lila cleared her mind and centered her attention on Peter's shaft caressing her swelling walls. She began circling her hips and while the burning inside increased, so did her pleasure.

Peter released her waist and gripped one of her breasts tightly. That, in combination with him vigorously teasing her engorged clit almost sent her over the cliff. Almost. She'd lost it again, and it aggravated her to the point that she almost punched Peter in the thigh.

Needing to try once more, she hopped off his lap and turned, facing him, sliding her thighs along the outsides of his. She guided his hardness inside her and closed her eyes, basking in the delightful feeling, ignoring the passing time. Her skin flamed, but the ecstasy was still more prominent than the pain. As she rocked into the man her center tensed and he clenched her hips, pulled her to his chest and bit her shoulder.

She cried out, then another surge of blazes coursed through her. More excruciating this time. She needed this man to orgasm. Now.

"You gonna come for me, baby?" she whispered into his ear.

"You haven't yet. And I won't until you do," he promised in a rough voice.

Anxiety attacked her and the burning inside twisted her gut and shot up through her chest. With each breath, she felt her lungs threatening to collapse. She couldn't orgasm now no matter how hard she tried. The pangs were too sharp. She'd just have to fake it.

She rode him hard and fast, bucking her hips into him relentlessly. She begged him to release, begged him to exterminate the uncontrollable flames scorching her from within. Feigning an orgasm as theatrically possible, she met his eyes and then ran her tongue from his ear to his collarbone.

"You ready?" he panted.

"More than you know. Come now!" she shouted in despair.

He dug his fingers deep into her hip bones, thrusting into her one last time. His warm liquid filled her, and she gasped at the relief it provided—better than any orgasm. She shuddered and collapsed against his chest, unable to move even though she was flooding with energy. *Close call.*

Peter rose her with her in his arms and whisked her to his bed, resting her under the sheets. Her blood pumped, swelling her veins, and she felt they may crack open if she didn't go for a run.

"Stay with me," Peter requested. "I'll want you in the morning before I let you go." If he let her go. He contemplated taking her as a mistress. She was the best he'd ever had.

"I really can't stay. My roommate is expecting me home. I have to get back."

"Do you need a ride?"

"No, I'm okay," she replied, watching him wipe his prick off with a towel in the bathroom.

She scurried out of the bed. "I'm just going to get my stuff." She was already heading back to the living room.

"Okay, but are you sure you can't stay? How will you get home?"

"Yep, I'm sure. Gotta get home. I'll walk. It's not far from here," she answered, snatching her things up from the living room floor.

Hastily, she shoved herself back into her clothes and spied her jacket and purse hanging on a rack in the foyer. As she grabbed up Jenny's heels from the side of the couch that she and Peter had christened and called out, "Thanks, Peter. It was nice meeting you!"

She darted for the door and disappeared outside. Not bothering to wear the stilettos, she ran down the driveway and down the main street that led out of the neighborhood. Searching around in her purse, she tried to find her phone, but it wasn't there. If she didn't call Jenny, she would really be in for it. Lila decided she would just tell her best friend that she went out to get a drink and was on her way back.

She checked her jean pockets finding nothing. Flustered, she halted and opened her purse, looking through each compartment thoroughly. She felt through her jacket pockets. *Dammit!*

Turning around, she sprinted back to Peter's. Once at the door, she tested the handle. It was still unlocked. As she re-entered the home, dirty regret shot through her body.

"Peter?" she called, tiptoeing through the foyer. "Peter, it's Lila. I just left my phone."

She heard a muffled buzzing sound, but it stopped just as she entered the living room. After a few seconds, the buzzing sounded again. Frenzied, she followed the buzz, which led her to the couch. She crouched down and saw her phone light up underneath it. Bending further, she outstretched her arm and clutched her phone. It must've fallen out of her pocket when she stripped like a pole dancer for Peter.

Standing, she unlocked the screen. Three missed calls. Then her phone buzzed again.

"Hello? Hello? Jenny?" Lila stammered as she answered the call.

"Where the fuck are you?" Jenny barked.

"Oh God. Just gimme a minute. Okay, just one second." Lila wandered toward the bedroom.

"Where the hell are you?" Jenny yelled.

"I went for a drink," Lila whispered back, as she entered the room. It was dark except for the light spilling out of the bathroom, which illuminated part of the empty bed.

"I said, where are you?" Jenny shouted again.

"Cool out. I'm fine," Lila responded quietly.

"Why are you whispering? I can barely hear you."

Lila ignored her. Something was wrong. Peter wasn't in the bed and the house was eerily silent. She wanted to just sneak back out. But who was she kidding? What she really wanted was to make sure the poor bastard was still alive.

"Where are you, Lila? You had no business leaving my house!" Jenny continued to squawk.

"I'm fine, I'm with ..."

Dread suddenly flooded her body, weighing it down. Her stomach turned as she forced her legs to move toward the bathroom door.

She stopped cold. Peter was lying on his beautifully tiled bathroom floor. She disconnected the call with Jenny and rushed into the room, kneeling beside him. It didn't look like he was breathing. She checked for a pulse. Nothing.

Jesus fucking Christ! Her heart nearly popped. She jumped up and back, looking down at the dead man. It was a sight she never wanted to see: her wrath in physical form. The man named Peter was naked, lying in urine, head to the side, eyes wide open. His hand was on his chest.

How awful! She stepped back over to him, ensuring to avoid his piss, then she squatted and ran her palm down his eyelids. The consequences of her actions hit her in the face like a horror fiction baddie with a tire iron.

She covered her mouth, muffling her words. "Oh shit. Shit!"

After a long moment, she stood, readjusted her purse on her shoulder, snatched her heels back up and fled from the bathroom. As she reached the living room again, she glimpsed a picture on the fireplace mantel that made her come to a screeching halt. It was a picture of Peter and two little girls clinging to his neck, smiles all wide. She had just killed a husband and father. She was a monster.

She flew out of the house and once she reached the street, she called Jenny back trembling.

"Where are you?" Jenny asked, highly irritated.

"Come get me. I'll be at the corner of Magnolia and Sycamore." Lila ended the call and shoved her phone in her purse.

Lila saw Jenny's car pull onto the street where she waited in agony. She found herself wanting to return to her parents' house so she could kill them. If Doug hadn't died, she wouldn't be floundering in this unholy mess again.

Jenny stopped the car abruptly and threw open the passenger door. "Get in here now."

Lila paced to and fro, adrenaline coursing in wild currents through her body. She was scrubbing her face with her hands. She wanted to run as far away from everything as she possibly could.

"Get in the car," Jenny commanded again, patting the seat next to her impatiently.

Lila reluctantly grabbed ahold of the car door and hoisted herself inside.

"We'll go home, and you can tell me what's going on with you. Okay?" Jenny asked, but it was apparent Lila's attention was elsewhere. She looked like she was turning green.

Lila didn't answer her. She just sat there bouncing her up and down rapidly. Then she started to rock back and forth with her arms crossed over her chest. Her mind rebelled, streaming wretched images and thoughts that she couldn't ignore or control. Had she really killed another man? A married father? *Shit!* The coroner would say it was a heart attack or something of the sort.

"What's wrong, Lila? Are you okay?" Jenny asked, placing a hand on Lila's leg, to still her.

"Energy surge. Happens after I take a life force," she answered mechanically.

"Lila!"

She confessed to Jenny what she had done when they were close to their street. Tears streamed down her face and she struggled to breathe evenly.

When Jenny pulled up to her house, she threw open her car door, stomped around to Lila's and yanked her out of the car.

The women scurried inside and up to Jenny's room. As soon as Jenny shut the door, she was all business.

"Girl, we have got to get this under control. We need some ground rules. No married men. No men with children. Regular exercise or you'll never sleep."

Lila went to speak, but Jenny pursed her lips like she'd just sucked on a lemon. She pointed her finger in Lila's face, warning her to keep her mouth shut.

"And we need to set aside some time to find you a lifemate. I can't do this with you forever. This shit is too heavy." She stood there with a hand on her hip, her stare menacing.

Lila looked down at her feet. She had shunned her family and killed two men within a week.

"I won't do it again. I promise," she said quietly, only she didn't know if she could uphold her word.

"We'll see," Jenny responded. "Now put my fucking stilettos back in my closet."

Chapter 6

Lila sifted through the small box of pictures and keepsakes she had accumulated. Each seemingly jubilant reminder left a bad taste in her mouth. Six long years had passed.

Over that time, Lila had filled in the cracks about her demon side for Jenny. Jenny had taken everything in stride, never hung her out to dry and continued to aid her through her hardships.

The man Jenny had been with for four years hadn't yet proposed, and she desperately wanted children. She had become a registered nurse at Mission Hospital in Asheville, so she and Lila never left North Carolina like Lila had wanted to. They just moved a couple of times within the state lines.

Lila had gone through internships and training as a paralegal, and eventually earned her degree. She had landed a great job, too, but after five years, she quit, because it would've soon become apparent that she wasn't aging like her colleagues. She finally decided to abandon her career as a paralegal altogether. Bouncing from firm to firm wouldn't get her anywhere. Her professional dreams were shot, so she took bartending jobs and waitressing jobs, never staying at any one place for too long.

She had met a few demons throughout the years, finding that most of them were quite huge assholes, or just downright creepy. For instance, her contact for fake identification records made her chain him up and whip him repeatedly in the back of his business space until he came from the pain she inflicted. It disgusted her to do what he required of her, but the sessions were infrequent and necessary if she wanted to utilize his services.

With a few years of practice and experience gathered, Lila was better able to control her urges and only took one man per week. She never screwed men she knew. She chose college boys, or shy guys, and men who wanted sex with no strings. It was all still so difficult, as resisting her desires could be torturous. The worst part was that even after six years, the leaden guilt she carried about

Doug and Peter staunched her ability to orgasm. Therefore, her conquests weren't always easy.

She hoped each day would be the day that she overcame her hang-ups about Doug and Peter, but the day had still not come. She couldn't fully enjoy the meaningless sex she had to have. The only time she found her trysts gratifying was at the end, when a man extinguished the unrelenting inferno inside her.

Most times, it was effortless to locate men who lusted for her. Other times, she had to entrance them to bed her. Either way, such was her life. She struggled every morning, watching as Jenny took off to begin her normal, mundane day. Every evening, she loathed seeing Jenny kiss her boyfriend while they were curled up on the couch. Every night, she felt alone, cold, and so disconnected from everyone else. She was Pluto.

Lila could never bring a man home and take her time with him, make love to him. She could only dream of what making love felt like. She had never been meaningfully caressed or held. Never had a man whispered honest sweet promises in her ear. Even if a man fell for her, she couldn't be with him. She would never know love or heartbreak; it just wasn't in her cards. She woke each day just wanting to close her eyes again. She felt herself fading away into nothingness.

Jenny returned from her morning jog to find Lila still in bed, staring off into space.

"When was the last time you had sex?" she asked accusingly.

"Jenny, do we have to do this?" Lila whined.

"Yes, I know that you feel the need to persecute yourself, but when you don't get laid, you get sickly and moody and you're a total burden," Jenny said back.

Lila flipped her off. "Spare me."

Jenny's blonde hair was pulled back into a short ponytail, and she wore a sweatband around her forehead. She was gulping out of a water bottle. At twenty-eight, she had come into her own. She had gained a little weight, which settled in her breasts, thighs and hips. The curves of her body were now prominent and sexier than ever. Her hair was short and flirty. Jenny's appearance was a constant slap in the face to Lila, who looked the same as she had six years before.

"Jesus, Jenny, it's only ten-thirty. Leave me alone," Lila growled and rolled over in her bed.

"You know, you need to get out and do something. There's that new club downtown we can go to again. I can't look for Incubi by myself, you know. I don't see their shadows, remember? It's been months since you've gone anywhere to socialize, and I'm starting to think you don't want to find a lifemate, Lila." Jenny stepped into the bathroom they shared and began peeling off her sweaty clothes.

"I give up! We've been looking for six years, Jenny!" Lila yelled, pulling the covers over her head. "That may not be long for me, but it's a damn long time for you," she finished.

Jenny had been quite the trooper, helping Lila search the Web for others that may be like her, accompanying her to numerous bars, clubs, and parties. Lila had seen several demons, but none who were Incubi and few who were willing to socialize.

"It's Saturday you know, and I promised Silas we would meet up with him next week. I got off work and everything!" Jenny called from the shower. "We're going to The Den. Remember that place I keep telling you about? I think Silas can help us out."

Through some research, Jenny recently met a man named Silas in a gothic chat room, and they actually began conversing about different breeds of demons. Jenny told him she believed demons existed and quite possibly knew one. One that needed sex to survive.

When Silas typed back that he knew many Succubi and Incubi, she went apeshit. Silas gave her the name of a club, dubbed The Den, in Barnesville, Georgia, promising to show her a good time.

Jenny kept assuring Silas that she and her friend would make it to Georgia as soon as they could. She just had to persuade Lila to get off her ass and go.

"You know, I've been so selfish. I am so sorry that I haven't been more of a friend and a... human. I apologize that I can't get around the fact that I'm an insatiable whore!" Lila squawked hurtling her alarm clock across the room.

She flung herself out of bed, grabbed a whiskey bottle out of her nightstand drawer, and sluggishly made her way into the steamy bathroom.

"Leave, Jenny. Leave me now. I want to be alone. You're just hindering yourself taking care of me. I don't need you to get by. I'm fine. No—I'm better off alone." She combed a hand through her tangled hair and swigged her booze. "Better yet, I'll leave. You have your dream job and man. I'm the problem. I'll leave. You stay." She swigged from the bottle again and leaned against the counter.

"That's friggin' it!" Jenny screamed. She yanked the shower curtain aside, snatched the bottle from Lila, and shook her violently by the shoulders.

"Get your shit together! *I* need you. You are my best friend. You have given up, and too easily. Get the fuck out of this funk you are in and snap back into reality. I'm going to finish my shower, get dressed and eat some breakfast. I have a date with Luke later, and when I get home, you better be ready to go out. We're going somewhere tonight. Anywhere. And next week, we're taking a road-trip to The Den to start looking for your lifemate. He's out there, Lila. I know it."

Lila turned away from Jenny and rubbed the steam from the bathroom mirror. "I still look twenty-two, Jenny."

"Honey, that's not a bad thing," Jenny said as she stepped back into the shower.

"Not. A. Bad. Thing." Lila poked her face in the mirror accenting each syllable.

After Jenny left for her date with the Lukester, Lila carried her bottle of whiskey to the living room, proceeding to get wasted. She called for pizza and watched Netflix, until the doorbell rang.

Lurching off the couch, half asleep, she shuffled to the door. When she opened it, an adorable tan guy greeted her. He had dark hair and eyes, and she imagined his body might be quite enticing underneath his baggy shirt.

"Here you are, miss," the young man said, handing a pizza box to her.

"Why, thank you...?" Lila paused for him to offer his name.

"Joey. The name's Joey."

He handed her the ticket and a pen. Lila signed the ticket and then looked at the blank line at the bottom where she would enter his tip. She glanced up at Joey's kind eyes.

"What would you like for your tip, Joey?" she asked, settling against the door frame.

"Um, anything you'd like to leave is fine, miss."

"What about something other than money?" She tossed the pizza box to the floor.

"What do you mean?" Joey's face cutely contorted with confusion.

Lila leaned into his smooth handsome face. "I mean, how about instead of giving you money, I fuck you within an inch of your life?" *Literally.*

He smiled widely, taking a step forward and a wave of lust smacked her in the face. "Okay," he said simply.

Lila hadn't felt up to par for the past three days. And she'd need energy if she was going to some stupid club tonight, so she decided Joey would make for a nice refreshment. Taking his hand, she ushered him into the living room. She flicked off his hat and stared at him for a moment. He was so young and eager, his erection full tilt already bulging beneath his black pants. Maybe she would actually enjoy this one.

Lightly, she shoved Joey in the chest. He smirked, falling into the couch. Immediately, Lila proceeded to undress his lower half. *Impressive,* she thought as his thick manhood plopped against his stomach.

He palmed his throbbing cock, stroking vigorously while licking his lips. She noticed a drip of creamy liquid collecting at the slit of his head. She smoothed her finger over the milky drop, circling it around the rim of his tip. He groaned, pressing his head against the back of the couch.

She shimmied out of her pajama pants and straddled the delivery boy. He stopped her advance. "Protection."

"You won't be needing protection," she assured, gazing into his eyes.

"Okay," he said slowly.

She spread herself for him, and he delved inside her swiftly. The alcohol she'd imbibed numbed her sensitivity a bit. But she didn't care; she couldn't orgasm anyway. Sex was just sex. As he forcefully brought her down on his hips; he hit her core. She braced herself with her hands against his chest.

"What do you like?" she asked sensually.

"Talk to me," he answered in a deep tone.

As he fucked her, Lila moaned dirty phrases that she thought would help speed things along. He spasmed a few times but withheld his release and continued ramming into her ruthlessly. Suddenly, the drunken shroud that cloaked her disintegrated. Now fully sober, she tore her shirt off, hoping that her breasts in his face would rile him. Joey grabbed her mounds hungrily still driving into her steadily.

Soon, she was begging him to release, pleading for him to let go. This Joey guy had deceived her. She'd thought of him as young and inexperienced, the kind of mark her mother had told her to look for, but he proved to have the stamina of a bull.

Sweat broke out across her forehead and she panicked. The fierce burning within her warned that she was about to take his life. She needed his release, needed him to splash out the fire. She needed it more than anything, yet with every ounce of her strength, she pulled herself off him. The smoldering heat inside her contorted her body and she rolled to the floor.

"Go! Get out of here!" she screamed at the stunned pizza guy.

He didn't understand what was happening, but it freaked him the hell out. He reacted immediately and pulled up his pants, grabbed his pizza-carrying case, scooped up his hat, and frantically flew out the door.

Lila crawled along the floor toward her bedroom and collapsed just short of the threshold. She laid there, naked, unable to move, crying, and in the worst pain of her life. *I'm going to die.*

A few hours passed by the time Jenny came through the door with a couple friends who were all cackling loudly and obviously drunk. They migrated to the kitchen to put away their beer and take a few shots.

Jenny searched for Lila, hoping she was in a better mood. She called out for her but got no response. When she rounded the corner, she saw legs sprawled out on the floor. Quickly, she ran to her friend, finding her naked and unresponsive. Jenny flipped Lila onto her back and checked her breathing. She was alive. Although Jenny had had years of RN experience, she settled for slapping Lila across the face and shouted for her to wake up.

"Need sex," was all Lila could muster.

"What's wrong with your friend?" a guy named Kevin asked as he staggered into the hallway with a beer in his hand. Kevin had been a college football player before a knee injury demolished his career. Now he was a worthless drunk and a womanizer.

"Help me get her into bed," Jenny said urgently.

The ex-jock stumbled over to Lila's crippled body and knelt down. "Wow, she's fucking hot," he slurred.

"Yeah, she is. Just help me get her into bed, will ya?"

"Sure. Sure."

Kevin set down his beer and grabbed Lila's torso, making it a point to brush one of her breasts with a thumb. Jenny took her legs. The pair hefted her from the floor and carried her into her room, then dropped her in the bed. Lila curled into the fetal position and unleashed a pathetic cry.

"You know what, Kevin, I bet you can help my friend out. What do you say?" Jenny asked, out of breath.

"What do I do?"

"Just fuck her, and she'll get up." She motioned to Lila's naked body.

"Whatever, man," Kevin laughed, waving Jenny off.

"I'm serious. This happens a lot. She has these... spells, and the only thing that brings her back is sex. She's an addict. Wanna hook a sista up?" Jenny asked. She moved toward Kevin and rubbed the bulge in his jeans. "I mean, you can handle it, right?"

"Shit, yeah, I can handle it," Kevin said excitedly, shifting his weight from leg to leg, as if warming up.

"I'm just saying, you've been drinking ..." She rubbed him a little harder.

"I could come in a coma, Jenny. And with a hot bitch like this, I'll be done in a couple minutes," Kevin assured.

"That's what I like to hear," she said, and encouragingly slapped Kevin's shoulder. He was already taking his jeans down as she shut the bedroom door.

She hoped she hadn't just signed Kevin's death certificate. She was so done trying to pick up all of Lila's pieces.

Lila felt a warm naked body settle flat against her back. *Great. I'm gonna get raped now.* It's not like things could get much worse for her at this point. She was still partially fetal, twitching, ablaze, wondering what fate had in store. A hand lifted her thigh, then she was being penetrated, vigorously. Instinctually, her flaming walls enveloped the foreign intrusion. She couldn't swivel her head yet to see who was behind her, but it really didn't matter. She conceded to the fact that she wanted to die.

The anonymous male humped her faster and faster, then she felt a splash into her void, immediately cooling the magma coursing through her veins. She gasped vociferously as if she hadn't breathed in a century.

The mystery man who restored her moaned and rolled onto his back. Lila quickly hopped out of her bed. She strode to her dresser for clothes and pulled on the first things she retrieved from the drawers. Then she went back to the slumbering man on her bed and picked him up. He didn't stir a bit. He was spent from alcohol, fucking, and the life she sucked from of him. She opened her door and dumped the sex savior onto the hardwood floor. Then she turned, picked up his clothes and tossed them onto his naked body. She shut her door and locked it, hoping Jenny would send her visitors away. The night had been far too overwhelming.

Lila pounded out some indoor exercises to expend her exorbitant energy. Then she cleaned up, selected a book from her bookshelf, and settled in bed to read.

About an hour went by when someone pounded on her door.

"Lila! Open up right now, dammit!" Jenny yelled.

Lila rolled her eyes, slowly got out of her bed, and opened the door. She turned away from Jenny, went back to the bed and slid under her sheets.

"Damn you, Lila!" Jenny shouted. "Kevin wasn't sober! What if he couldn't make it happen?"

Lila dropped her head and closed her eyes. Jenny had provided this Kevin guy to her on a bet that he may save her life.

"It was an impossible situation, Jenny. I made a judgment error, and it was either him or me. I chose not to kill him. What was I supposed to do? I'm so beyond fed up with this existence."

Jenny moved closer to Lila so she could hear her better, and Lila looked up at her miserably. "I want you to kill me, Jenny. You are my friend. You owe me that. I see you aging and moving forward, while I stay trapped in a twenty-two-year-old body, spinning wheels. There is nothing in my life other than suffering and life-draining sex. Kill me, Jenny. Please."

Jenny sat next to Lila and hugged her, although Lila didn't reciprocate. She was flaccid in her arms.

"I'm not gonna kill you, Lila. I love you. I know this is difficult for you, to say the least, but Silas swears Incubi are in Georgia at The Den. I know you'll find what you're looking for there. I know it. We have to keep trying."

Lila withdrew from Jenny's embrace and lay back on her bed.

"Is this Silas an Incubus?" she asked, her arms draped over her eyes.

"I don't know. He didn't say. He's kind of guarded," Jenny answered, patting Lila's leg.

"Whatever you want, Jenny. I'm just tired. Today was a real shit-show." Lila slid down into the mattress and turned on her side, laying her head on her pillow. A tear escaped the corner of her eye and ran down her cheek.

Jenny frowned and gently swiped it away. Her heart hurt for her friend. She couldn't begin to comprehend what Lila was enduring. Hell, the woman almost died tonight. As her best friend and confidant, she'd been selfish and a total bitch to Lila about all of it. Regret and sorrow ran through her. "We'll make this right, Li. I promise."

Chapter 7

Jenny made breakfast, which roused Lila from her sleep. Bacon and eggs could wake the dead. She soon sat on one of the barstools at the breakfast nook.

"You know I haven't had an orgasm with a man since Doug?" she admitted.

"What?" Jenny exclaimed in shock.

Lila signaled for Jenny to fill her glass with orange juice.

"I can't. Every time I get close, I think of Doug or that Peter guy, and I lock up. I feel guilty."

"So, it's not pleasurable at all?" Jenny asked as she poured.

"The sex feels good but would be so much better if I could orgasm. The best part is the end, when the guy comes and the burning stops. But it's not so much pleasure as it is

relief."

"That totally blows, Li. I'm sorry."

"Yeah, I don't create that magical lube I'm supposed to because I don't orgasm. That's why I've had so much trouble, you know... killing guys and almost killing myself. Shit, the whole thing takes a lot out of me. I am constantly trying to make sure I pick just the right male, which I'm still bad at, and figure out ways to get him off fast ... I don't know." She shrugged and swung from side to side on the barstool.

"Why didn't you ever tell me about this?" Jenny questioned, obviously offended that Lila had been withholding something so dire from her.

Lila put up her hands. "Look, it's not something I like to talk about. It's doesn't feel so great to say you've killed two people and now you can't get off because of it."

"Jesus, *Lila*. I would have been a lot more supportive about some of your screw-ups had I known that. You're supposed to talk to me. I'm your freaking family, for God's sake," Jenny said resolutely.

"I know. I know. I'm sorry. I am still new to this. I mean my mother was three hundred and sixty years old when I left home. I'm only six in Lilin years. Six years as a Succubus is a raindrop in the ocean. Don't worry about it. I'll figure it out." Lila gulped her juice.

"Don't worry about it? Whatever, Lila. Is there something we can do to help you get off again? You know, maybe I could help?" Jenny looked at her, eyebrows raised in mischievous suggestion.

Lila smiled. "I don't think so. We've been there, done that." She began drawing imaginary circles on the countertop with a fingertip. "Anyway, I'm used to it. It's just another obstacle in my already heinous life."

"You shouldn't have to be used to it. You should be happy. And I'm going to make sure that happens. The Den is the answer," Jenny promised as she shoved bacon into her mouth. "See you later, sister." She stole more bacon for the road and kissed Lila's cheek then waved as she scooted out the door for work.

Lila shoveled some food into her gullet, then went into her room to change clothes. So many things were troubling her, and a recurring thought crept up again. She would be alive when Jenny died. After that, she would be alone. She wouldn't trust any other human with her secrets, even if that human chose to believe them. Jenny had been her friend, her family and the medium through which she experienced love. Once she perished, there would be no reason to continue living.

Chapter 8

The intruder used a cloth-clad hand to break the thin, stained glass that adorned the sides of the main entrance to the house. He stuck his hand in the break and unlocked the latch, then quickly scanned the area for an alarm system but found none. He was infiltrating the home his boss had directed him to. His orders were to procure a young woman and her parents, alive.

The prowler passed the fireplace in the moonlight. He noticed a picture of the targets. The mother was on one side, the father on the other, and a stunning woman, twenty-something, stood between them. He paused for a moment when he saw the picture, because the beauty of the woman in the middle of the photo took him by surprise. Had he not been working for one of the most powerful demons topside, he would have entertained aborting his mission to run away with her just based on her gorgeousness alone. She was perfect. He touched the picture where she stood. Then he shook his head, forcing himself to refocus and set out to complete his task.

Slowly, he crept up the stairs and opened the first door on the left. It was the daughter's room, but her bed was empty. He lurked around, found a lamp, and turned it on. He scanned the feminine space, which was bathed in pink light. He felt a warmth in the room. The attractive female target had photos stacked on her dresser, and he looked at each of them carefully. She was stunning, especially when she smiled.

He should have left the room, but instead, he went through a few of her personal items and wondered what his boss wanted with her and her parents. He didn't understand his attraction to her. It's not like he could have a relationship with anyone. He smelled her sheets, but there was no trace of her scent, only fabric softener. He opened a drawer in her dresser that contained bras and panties. Holding up a white lacey thong, his dick threatened to tear through his pants. He dropped the undergarment and readjusted himself before the urge to masturbate right there became overwhelming.

He quietly left the room, closed the door and crept down the hall to the master bedroom. The door was already open. He saw bodies slumbering in the bed. He crept close to the sleeping elderly woman and shot her in the neck with a tranquilizer dart.

The senior man next to her jumped up immediately and rushed him. He swung and broke the old man's nose. The victim toppled over the bedside table lamp as he fell to the ground. Blood was splattered against the covers, on the bed, and the floor.

The trespasser picked up both of his targets, placing one on each shoulder. Opening the front door, he peeked out into the shadows, scanning for probable witnesses. Finding no one, he took long strides to his vehicle and dumped both bodies in the backseat.

On his way to take his bounty back to his employer, he smiled at his accomplishment. Then he thought of the beautiful young woman in the photos, and his smile dissipated. His boss was not the pleasant type, and he almost regretted taking her family away from her. They would surely never return home. He had never judged his moral character before; why start now? He just had to forget all about the girl and the strange fluttering feeling she sparked in his chest.

Chapter 9

Lila woke up screaming. She was on the couch and quickly rose on her elbows. Jenny rushed around the corner and sat next to her, cradling her in her arms.

"Are you okay, Lila?" Jenny lightly shook her. "You scared me to death. Are you okay?" She examined Lila's face, which was unusually pale.

Lila shook her head and pushed herself up the rest of the way, so she could sit upright. Tears streamed from her eyes, and she blinked rapidly to clear her vision.

"I had an awful dream about my parents," she whispered.

"What kind of dream?" Jenny whispered back.

"They're dead. My parents are dead. I saw it."

"What? What do you mean?"

"I mean they're dead. I know it." Lila stood up from the couch, pulling free from Jenny. "There were Succubi being tortured in cells, and my parents tried to escape, but they were murdered. I need to find them. I need to go back to Charlotte," she said, rubbing her eyes.

"Lila, Lila. Listen to me. There's no way your parents are dead. It was just a dream, honey. Go see them if you need to, but it was just a dream."

Jenny reached for Lila's hand, but Lila grabbed her head and began pacing. "I have a bad feeling. A really bad feeling."

"Then we'll go see your parents," Jenny said, standing up. "It's cool, we'll go check on them. Just calm down."

"Okay. Yeah. Okay. I just need a drink. I'm losing it. Been having a hard time lately. I wasn't cut out for this demon shit."

"You'll get the hang of it. Sure you want a drink this early?"

"Yes, please."

"Must've been some dream." Jenny was already on her way to the fridge. "Your favorite? Vodka and OJ?"

"Mmm hmm."

Jenny made two drinks and handed one to Lila. She slammed it back faster than Jenny could even take one sip and she held her glass out for more.

"It's gonna be one of those days, huh?" Jenny asked rhetorically as she took Lila's glass back to the kitchen.

After a couple of hours had passed, Lila was lying on the couch again with her feet in Jenny's lap.

"I really freaked out earlier, huh?" Lila asked, slurring her words.

"Yes. Yes, you did." Jenny patted Lila's leg.

"Thanks for being here—you know? Every time things get shitty. It's not that I don't want to see my parents, it's just been so long, you know? Like, what would we even say to each other? I ran out on them, and they probably hate me for it. I think I still hate them. But I think I love them. I guess none of it matters if they're dead." Lila lifted her arm, almost spilling her drink on her shirt.

"They just didn't want their only daughter to run away. But they should have told me everything when I was younger. But maybe I would have rebelled earlier if they had. You know, I was thinking how I'm glad that they scared me into waiting. How, if I was younger, it really would have been awkward trying to mate..."

"Lila," Jenny stopped her. "You're babbling sentimental bullshit. Your parents don't hate you. If you want to see them, go see them. If you don't, then don't. Think about it and make your decision later when you aren't absolutely plastered. Luke's going to be here any minute," she finished, setting Lila's feet on the floor. She got up from the couch to put her glass in the sink.

"Refill!" Lila yelled.

"I think you're done for the night, girlfriend," Jenny laughed, disappearing into her room.

Over the week, Lila went to and from her bartending job. Despite her feelings about her parents, she decided not to go to them. They had never attempted to find her, so she wasn't going to be the first to act. It felt petty to think that way, but she found a way to justify it nonetheless. Besides, she was only thinking of going to see them because of a stupid dream.

"Hey, Lila. What are you doing tonight?" Tony asked from across the bar. She knew her coworker had had a crush on her for a while. She refused to give into his advances, though. She didn't want to become involved with him. Too close to home.

"The same old shit, Tony. Why?" she asked, wiping down a wine glass.

"Because I want to take you out," he said as he moseyed over to her. He dipped down below her stomach, lightly brushing her hip with his shoulder, and grabbed a bottle of strawberry margarita mix out of the floor cooler. As he came rose, he smiled and locked eyes with her.

Why did his eyes have to be so pretty? They were hazel. Bluer some days and greener on others. They were greener tonight.

"Well? I'm getting really tired of asking you all the time."

Tony swept his dark hair out of his eyes and set to making a drink. The glitzy girl who ordered it eyeballed him and whispered something into her friend's ear.

"Why don't you ask the girl who ordered that drink? I'm sure she'd love to go anywhere with you tonight," Lila chuckled.

Tony walked over and set the drink in front of the girl, who tried to say something to him, but he never even looked at her. He just sauntered back over to Lila.

"Because I'd rather go with you. Quit telling me no, Lila. I know there's something between us."

"That's where you're wrong, Tony. There cannot be anything between us." She brushed him off and took a drink order from a burly man smoking a cigar.

"Well then, we'll go out as friends first. See where it goes from there."

"God, you're persistent tonight," she said in amusement. She was actually itching to take a mate. It had been five days. She'd suppressed her desire for Tony a few times before, and now he was wearing her down.

"Say yes, and I'll stop persisting," he said into her ear and pressed his body against hers as she poured a shot of Southern Comfort.

"Yes, Tony. Yes," she relented.

Lila walked into her apartment after two in the morning and dropped her purse to the foyer floor. She heard Jenny and Luke laughing in the living room. She sighed and thanked her lucky stars that Tony liked head more than he liked sex. After fifteen minutes of sucking him off, he slid inside her and came after three minutes. He was embarrassed, but she assured him everything was okay and made him promise that their next shift together would be normal and weird-free.

She knew that wouldn't happen though. Tony probably wouldn't remember some of what occurred between them. That was a common side-effect of hypnosis. He would wind up asking her questions, trying to clear his mind.

She wished her hypnotic influence lasted forever. She would have told Tony and every other man she had screwed that being with her was just a dream. It would have been so much easier that way.

Lila grabbed a glass of orange juice and then slid into the La-Z-Boy. She was almost drained after the long run she had gone on after the much-needed Tony-sex.

"What are you two laughing about?" she drawled.

"Just this movie. Jenny's about to crash though," Luke said. "You look exhausted. Rough night?"

"No. Just thinking about switching jobs again," she answered and took a sip of her drink.

"Damn, girl. You go through a lot of jobs. Sit tight for once," Luke said and then laughed at the TV again.

"Yeah," she sighed, finishing her juice.

Lila woke up late the next day and rolled over in her bed a few times, wishing she could fall back to sleep, but it wasn't happening.

She got up and walked into the bathroom to wash her face. She looked in the mirror, hoping to see a wrinkle or a grey hair when she heard a knock on the front door.

Completely unpresentable, wearing only a tank and short shorts, she figured she'd let Jenny get it.

Lila heard the door squeak open, and she listened but didn't hear voices. There was a strange silence, an intrusive silence, and it made her shiver. She peeked out of her room and looked down the hall. Not seeing anyone, she tiptoed along the floor. She peered around the corner to see a tall, big man in a dark hoodie standing in the foyer with Jenny. When she looked more closely, she noticed that the man had a knife pressed into her friend's throat.

Fucking great. She had just imagined her life without Jenny earlier that week, and here stood some prick in her apartment with a knife against her friend's jugular.

Jenny's eyes were wild with fear, and Lila protectively took a step forward. She was much stronger than any human man, and she was going to give this one the fight of his life. She might even kill him. How dare he threaten the only person in the world who sustained her life without a sexual exchange?

Lila composed herself, deciding that a dead man in her apartment wouldn't be favorable for anyone. Maybe she would simply take the knife away from the guy and then demand that he beg for his life. Maybe she would fuck him and drain him until he went into a coma. Decisions.

Decisions.

She crept toward them, pivoted, and planted her back foot into the ground. She pushed off, lunging forward, but the man quickly turned and dodged her advance swinging the knife at her. In the process, he threw Jenny to the ground. *Good.* He'd have to deal with her before he carried out whatever sick plans he had for her human.

As Lila swirled around to meet the villain head-on, Jenny scurried into a corner and muffled her ears with her hands. Lila immediately wished she would've covered her mouth instead, because she kept squealing like a stuck pig.

Lila glared at the hooded man with murderous eyes. He hunched, arms flexed at his sides, waiting for her next attack. She feigned left, spun around, kicked her leg straight up, and brought it down on the brute's shoulder. While the blow should have taken him to his knees, he barely budged and circled around with the knife again. He used his size to back her into a wall. She punched him in the gut twice, but he still advanced, and didn't stop until she was wedged between the drywall and his chest. She tried to push him away, but he had clearly overpowered her.

He smelled like a rainforest might, maybe with a little wild animal mixed in. She looked up at him. His eyes were hidden behind shades, and she almost went to take them off his face. She actually forgot that she was fighting the wall of man in front of her for a second and became irrationally lusty. Something about the man's presence and power made her knees give a bit. His lips looked soft and completely kissable, but she barely had time to fully appreciate them before he curled them up over his gleaming teeth and stabbed her in the shoulder.

When she didn't cry out, he slid the blade deeper until he had pinned her to the wall like a picture. He backed up, awaiting a response, for her to scream and beg him for mercy. Then he realized who she was. She was the girl from the picture on the mantle in the home of the targets he abducted a week ago. The moment he had seen her in that picture, he had wanted her; and now here she was. Right in front of him. His employer was picking her family off for some reason. He didn't want to do what he had to, didn't want to hand her over to his boss, but he didn't have much choice.

Lila whimpered, but pulled the blade out of her shoulder. She jabbed it at the bastard's face, nicking his jawline. The asshole stumbled back a bit and his hood fell off. She swallowed hard at the sight. He was the most amazing piece of man she had ever seen. The show of his brutal strength added to his appeal. He looked to be in his mid-twenties, a little young, statistically, to be a serial rapist. His hair was sandy blond and stylishly messy, and his face was freshly shaven.

He charged her again. Jenny screamed louder in the corner of the foyer as Lila side-kicked the guy in the face. She missed his nose but landed her heel in his jaw. He spat blood out onto the floor and then turned to smile at her sadistically—the sadistic part being that his jaw was clearly broken.

"What the ...?" she choked on a spiny lump of fear when the man didn't hit the ground. She scampered back, and he leapt out at her like a jungle cat. He caught her around the waist, and they flew through the air until they hit the hall wall, crumbling it before they fell to the floor.

They rolled and rolled like alligators do with their prey until she ended up beneath the intruder, losing the deathroll.

The beautiful bully examined her shoulder quickly. It had already healed. For a fraction of a second he looked confused and cocked his head to the side, like a dog does when it hears a high-pitched noise.

She writhed underneath him, but he was too strong for her. He couldn't possibly be human.

"What do you want?" she asked in a ragged breath.

"You're coming with me," the man snarled in a tone that matched his deadly tendencies. She should have been frightened, but instead, she was aroused. She wondered what was behind those sunglasses, and what was underneath that hoodie of his. She found herself getting wet thinking about it. She liked being dominated by a man for once. She always had to have control of her sexual escapades to avoid disaster, so she didn't know what a real man could be like. *Strip off my clothes and do me right here on the floor.*

"Where are we going?" she asked, still breathing hard. He was crushing her rib cage.

The man's grip tightened on her wrists. He stared her down, almost like he wanted her, and there was a silent moment between the two. A silent moment. As Lila realized that Jenny had quit screaming, she saw her come from around the corner with a cast iron camping skillet.

She swung it like it was a bat, and she was Ty Cobb, against the big guy's skull. The man collapsed onto Lila.

"Lights out, bitch," Jenny huffed.

"Jenny, did you give that little Internet creep our address?"

"No, I promise. I actually told him we lived in Charlotte. Nothing else. I swear!" She dropped the skillet.

"What the shit is going on, then?"

"I don't know, Lila. I'm scared. Is he a demon?" Jenny whispered the last part as if it wouldn't be true if no one heard her. Lila rolled the man off her and quickly stood on her feet. She paced the hallway for a moment, and Jenny started crying.

"Help me take him to the bedroom," Lila said as she bent down and grabbed the gorgeous stranger's ankles. She and Jenny dragged the man to Lila's bedroom and heaved his huge body onto her bed. Lila pulled off the guy's shades and placed them on her nightstand. She stared at him for a while and then panicked. She needed something to bind him with.

She ran around, flitting through the apartment, trying to locate something strong enough to hold him down. Then she remembered the chains. They had been in the back of Jenny's old Accord for a while. Her car had gotten stuck in a ditch, and Luke tried to pull it out with his truck. The chain broke, along with Jenny's bumper, and Lila laughed, knowing she could have just pushed the car out of the rut.

Jenny bought a new Lexus and threw the chains in their storage closet. Lila and Jenny each had a padlock for their gym lockers, so everything worked out pretty well in the end when it came to securing their hostage.

Lila pulled Jenny to her and held her head close to her chest.

"It's okay, Jen. I don't know what's going on, but I'll figure all this out. In the meantime, you need to get out of here. Go far away, and don't tell anyone where you are going. Not even me."

"What about you? What are you gonna do? What *is* he?" Jenny asked, pulling away and drying her eyes.

"I don't know, but it's you I'm worried about. I'm gonna find out who the fuck is chained to my bed, and then I'm going to kill him. I'll be just fine."

Jenny grabbed hold of Lila and hugged her tight, then she scurried into her room. After a few minutes, she came back out with luggage and her purse. She was crying again and hugged Lila one last time. Lila kissed her on the forehead then pointed to the door. Jenny flew out of the apartment without another word.

When the man woke, he struggled against his restraints. *Where the hell did she get chain this thick? Great Lucifer, my head hurts.* He stirred and opened his eyes, but his vision was blurry. He blinked several times before he focused on the woman standing in front of him with a hand on her hip. He had greatly appreciated the fight the firecracker had put up. It took all the self-control he had to force his erection down when she pulled the knife out of her shoulder. *Fucking hot.*

He liked the way her hair had fallen in her eyes when she had bucked him, and the way her body curved right now while she stood staring at him. She was tall and limber... sex on long, long legs.

"So how do you know Silas?" she asked, knife in hand. She knew the Internet junkie had something to do with the thing on her bed. No way was he human.

"I don't." The man closed his eyes before she came too close. They would surely reveal what he was.

"Wrong answer." She took two strides forward and stabbed the liar in the thigh with his own blade. He winced but didn't howl out like she'd hoped.

"I don't fucking know him. He works for my boss," the creature seethed through gritted teeth.

"So, you *do* know him. Who is your boss? And don't get this one wrong or I'll cut off your testicles and feed them to my neighbor's dog. She's a Chihuahua named Princess." She tapped the bloody knife against her palm.

"Fuck yourself, gorgeous," the man insolently answered, cracking his lids open just a bit.

She unbuttoned the degenerate's jeans and slowly unzipped the fly, driving her hand into the opening of his briefs. She felt sweaty dude-flesh, and then the thin skin of his sac. Yep, there they were. She gripped his balls and squeezed hard.

"Okay, okay!" the he yelped. "His name is Gaelon. He is the owner of The Den. He wants me to bring you to him."

"What on Earth for?" By the time she asked, the stranger's thigh had healed just as she had suspected it might.

"You're a demon." She hadn't had the chance to look for his shadow in all the commotion.

"And so are you." The large man-thing opened his eyes. His secret was out.

He tried to sit up, attempting to figure out what the woman was. He had looked for her shadow during the fight when he realized how strong she was, but it had eluded him, and he couldn't see it now, strapped to the hot bitch's bed.

She quickly moved closer to his bound body and shoved the blade under his chin. The captive tilted his head up in response and locked eyes with her. God, he was devastatingly handsome. And his eyes ... blue with vibrant violet flecks. Beautiful, strange.

She smelled the lust rolling off him. He was actually enjoying this.

"What does this Gaelon want me for?" She narrowed her eyes at the creature.

That, I don't know. I am a procurer." The words came out disjointedly, probably because of his broken jaw.

"Of demons?"

"Sometimes."

"What will happen if I refuse to go with you to The Den?" She pressed the cold metal harder against the monster's throat.

"Gaelon will kill me and come after you anyway. He's got a lot of pull in our world."

"Well, why don't I just kill you and take my chances? I'm sure my methods will be more pleasurable than your boss's."

That, he didn't doubt. "Gaelon is descended from Abbadon," he said firmly.

She had heard the name before. Abbadon was the original Destroyer, the fallen angel of the Apocalypse. This was a sticky situation.

"Interesting," she said, but she couldn't quite focus on the smell of the shit storm headed her way. She wanted to devour the beast before her. Never had her need been so great. He was unknown to her, yet so familiar. Even though he had fought her, stabbed her, and threatened her friend's life, she wanted to fuck him until she fizzled out. She climbed onto her bed and straddled the large expanse of muscle that was the devil. She looked at him and hated seeing his lovely face contorted the way it was, so she took his face in her hands and with a quick adjustment, set the demon's jaw back in place. It would heal more quickly that way. The minion sighed in relief and scanned her body up and down.

She unzipped his hoodie and used the tip of his knife to rip the thin cotton shirt he wore under it. She drew blood just above his belly button and smelled his lust, growing stronger now. There was also an impressive erection filling the space between her legs. She bent down and licked the blood from the demon's rippled abs, and he groaned deep in his throat. He tasted delicious, and as she swallowed his blood, she ground her pelvis into him and closed her eyes.

Lila had never enjoyed giving head and only did it when she had to, but now, a fervor washed over her. She slithered down the scoundrel's stomach and perched herself between his massive legs, ready to take him into her mouth.

"Stop," he rasped.

She slid her body up his, resting her breasts on his chest. "No," she whispered defiantly. She took in a deep breath against his sculpted pecs. He smelled like earth and rain and musk. His aroma comforted her, somehow. Made her feel at home—wherever that was.

"Lila, stop." The command was firm this time.

"You know my name, but I don't know yours. Now how is that fair?" She rose a bit so she could look into his blue-violet eyes.

"My name is Stirling."

"Stirling. Hmmm." Even his name was beautiful. "You want me, don't you?" she taunted.

"What the hell would make you think that?" he laughed.

"Well, Stirling Junior isn't good at keeping secrets. And I smell it on you."

He stopped laughing as soon as he heard her last words. He struggled against his restraints to sit up farther. He looked at Lila's eyes again and cursed. *Just perfect.*

Chapter 10

"What?" Lila asked as she placed the cool part of the knife blade to her forehead.

"Irony, that's all," Stirling huffed and shook his head.

She raised an eyebrow to him, but he didn't tell her what was so ironic. She peeled herself off him and walked into her bathroom. She washed her face, scrubbed her arm free of blood, and ripped off her torn tank, then walked back into her bedroom, wearing nothing but shorts and a lacy red bra.

"Put some damn clothes on, will you?" Stirling tried to say evenly.

"Why, I am bothering you?" she asked in a sassy little voice.

"You are putting us both in danger."

"By being half-naked? I think not, hostage." She sauntered over to where the god-like creature laid and said, "We have some things to clear up. What are you? And again, what does your boss want with me?"

She doesn't know what I am? His eyes should have given him away. "I'm a demon. I just work for Gaelon. I do what he commands, and I don't ask questions. I don't know why he wants you."

She couldn't help but put her hand over his erection. It had popped out of his briefs and jeans and poked up past his belly button. It was a masterpiece of satiny flesh and vein and manhood. She stroked it once and felt his heartbeat in her hand. She licked her lips and clenched her thighs together.

He thrashed in the chains and spat out more curses.

"If you want me, why fight it?" she asked benignly.

"You are going to get me killed. Get away from me."

His eyes warned her, but she ignored them.

"I'll get away from you as soon as you tell me what you are and what you want with me." She stroked his breathtaking erection in her palm again. She couldn't close her hand around his girth, and she shuddered when she thought about how good he must feel. Suddenly, she envied every woman who had had the pleasure of being with him.

He stiffened under her touch but didn't say a word. She suspected that he was torn between his loyalty to his boss and his loyalty to his cock. Tough decision. Maybe she should make up his mind for him. She pulled off her shorts and climbed back on top of the demon, but backward. She pushed her smooth ass and red thong in his face and then moved farther back until she felt his breath against her. She wanted him to smell her womanhood as she slowly took his erection in her mouth.

He pressed his face into her, and a couple rough breaths escaped his mouth, which was close enough to her pussy to make her heart palpitate. She worked him deeper into her throat, and he licked her, so close to her entrance. She hummed as she slowly pulled her mouth up to his head, and the vibration she created caused his eyes to roll back into his skull. She tasted some of the sweet nectar that escaped his slit, and it tingled in her mouth and then in her throat as she swallowed. The sensation traveled through her chest and rammed into her clit. The realization came to her just as the he-thing broke free of his shackles and pinned her underneath him.

"You're an Incubus," she breathed. Her eyes were wild, and her chest heaved with exhilaration.

"And you're obviously a Succubus." He angrily made the statement, and she would have thought he didn't want her for some reason had his erection not been stabbing her in the stomach.

He started at the base of her neck and inhaled her scent all the way up to the top of her head. He closed his eyes and rested his cheek on her forehead.

"I'm a century old, and you are the first. I was beginning to think of your kind to be a myth. And Gaelon wants you for himself." He laughed, but it was a bitter, harsh laugh.

"What the hell is so funny?" she demanded as she pushed him away with her head.

"Nothing. Absolutely nothing is funny about this situation." He looked at her adoringly for a moment. "I never imagined you would be so..." He bit off his words.

She studied his chest and picked her head up to breathe in his scent again. She wouldn't wash her sheets until his smell faded from the cotton.

He looked down at her breasts and reluctantly tore his body off hers.

"I have to take you to him now before I make a huge mistake."

"What mistake?" she asked, sitting up on the bed.

"The mistake of fucking you until you beg me to stop."

"And that would be so bad because ...?" She watched him curiously, as he stood from the bed. He tucked himself back in his pants and moved in front of her.

"Because I don't want to bond. Ever."

"Why the hell not?" she asked in sheer confusion. "I mean, I know we don't know each other, but we obviously want each other. We could get to know ..."

"We couldn't try if we wanted to. Not with Gaelon on your heels. Listen, I don't mind what I am, and I don't want to take the chance of being connected to the likes of you." He waved her off like she was a fly.

He tried on the surface to dismiss her, but the truth was, something inside him transformed the moment he saw Lila in that damned picture. She captivated him like no one else and when she fought him downstairs, he thought he might actually fall in love with her.

His grandmother once told him that when he met a Succubus, he should take her if they were compatible. She said that things would be so much easier that way. He closed his eyes and thought back to when she had lectured: *"You will immediately feel the void inside you close almost completely. Because we are sexual beings deprived of companionship, there is a thirst for intimacy in most of us, which we can't obtain until we are bonded. You can tell yourself you don't want to bond all you want, but it doesn't make sense any other way, son."*

Stirling had told his grandmother that she was crazy and didn't know was the hell she was talking about. She responded by touching his chest, then sent about two hundred thousand milliamps of electrical currents through his body. It was the first and last time he disrespected his grandmother.

The jezebel in front of him made him hotter than any human or demon had ever come close to. But she was also a walking death sentence. All Succubi were since they began disappearing. He didn't need it. Any of it. What he needed was to deliver her to Gaelon and force himself to forget he ever met her.

"Again, why the hell not? What would be so awful about bonding with the *likes* of me?" Lila stood up and challenged him with her lingerie-clad body.

"Well, first off, I don't know if I'm ready for the same piece of snatch for the rest of my long, long life, and second, if my lifemate died, so would I. If I stay single, I don't have to worry about either of those concerns."

"If a bond is made and a lifemate dies, the other does too?" she asked. Her mother had never told her that. Big surprise.

"You must be ignorant or an orphan not to know that fact."

"Both, in a way. But you won't bond?"

"I'm not willing to make that kind of commitment," the demonic ass replied.

"You'd rather live your life having sex that causes you to burn alive? Never knowing what love is? Never knowing what it's like to be normal?"

"The burning is nothing, because I'm really good at what I do. I don't feel the need to be loved. My momma gave me enough of that when I was young. And sugar, we'll never be normal." He smirked.

She wanted to spit at him. What an arrogant dick. He was such a typical male. She searched six years for an Incubus and ended up finding the biggest jerk-off of her life. What the hell did he want from her? And Jesus, Succubi were so rare that only she was born from a life cycle that produced fifteen males. He should have been chomping at the bit to secure a bond. Could he really be that rogue, that cold?

"Well, we have to figure out what to do," she said desperately.

"There's nothing to figure out, sweetheart. I'm taking you in." He grabbed her bicep, forcing her up from the bed. He dwarfed her five-foot-nine body. His shoulders were strong and broad, his chiseled pecs were sprinkled with light sandy hair accented by light brown areolas that she wanted to suck into her mouth. His stomach was a washboard of muscle, and down the leg of his pants, far down the leg of his pants, still throbbed his erection. It was the only erection she had ever come across that she would die to feel inside her.

"Pack some things. We need to get on the move," he said as he zipped up his hoodie.

"You're a prick." She tore her arm from his grasp.

"You would love to have mine, honey, trust me." He smiled, deriding her.

"I can't believe you would deliver your own kind into the clutches of some maniac."

"I don't have a choice. Gaelon will torture and kill me, or worse, if I don't. I could never challenge him. He could take my soul." Stirling made the statement spitefully.

Lila turned away from him and angrily pulled out her dresser drawers.

"And you are pretty sure he'll do the same to me, huh? Steal my soul?" she asked sharply, throwing clothes onto her bed.

"I never said that. I don't know why he wants you," he said quietly, praying to Satan that he wasn't going to be a part of razing this woman. Hell, he knew better.

She yanked on a tee and jeans, then stuffed her essentials in a duffle bag. When she was finished packing, Stirling approached, invading her personal space. The sexy goliath locked his thick fingers around her wrist and ushered her out of the apartment.

"So, Gaelon's a Destroyer. He can demolish souls?" Lila asked fearfully, struggling to keep up with him. His strides were much wider than hers.

"Yes, he is capable of that. Destroyed souls cannot return to Heaven or Hell. They are gone forever," he answered, his tone severe.

He dragged her to a black car parked just out front of her apartment. He opened the door and forcefully shoved her into the passenger seat. What a jerk. She was really going to have to work to get away from him. It would take brains because he beat her on brawn.

Once the sex god took his seat, he cranked up the radio volume so loudly that she couldn't even begin to have a conversation with him. She wanted to know more about this Destroyer. She shot Stirling a nasty look, and he smiled. It was so cruel that his smile was the most beautiful she'd ever seen. She slammed her head into the headrest and clamped her eyelids shut.

Three hours had passed when finally, the pair pulled up to a cheap motel.

"Where are we?" Lila asked.

"South Carolina. Don't get out of the car for any reason. You hear me?" Stirling cautioned, sliding on his pair of dark sunglasses.

"'*You hear me?*'" she mocked after he slammed the car door.

He strolled over to the bulletproof window that housed a small rental office. There was a woman behind the window, with hideous permed, bleached hair. *Great.* Someone of her caliber would definitely want to fuck the hell out of Stirling. Then again, who in their right mind would turn him down? *Men* probably begged to be with him. Jealousy stabbed Lila in the heart, and she looked ahead at the closed pool area, away from the two. She wouldn't know how to react if he led that woman out to the back of the building and did her up against the brick wall.

She thought about running but decided she wouldn't get very far on foot when he had nearly three hundred horses to chase after her.

After what felt like an eternity, Stirling hopped back in the car. He placed his sunglasses in the center console, paused and looked at her. "You really need to get control of that," he snickered.

Why do his eyes have to be so mystifying? Blue-violet irises. "Control of what exactly?" she spat.

"Your lust for me. It's stunk up the car."

"Then roll the fucking windows down!" she screamed, crossed her arms over her chest and puffed.

"What's wrong with you?" he asked, putting the car in reverse.

"Oh, nothing, besides the fact that you're taking me to God-knows-where against my will, you won't bond with me, and now I get the satisfaction of knowing that you may screw the lady who gave you the room key."

"Jealous?" He cocked a brow.

"No. You know why? Your kind outnumbers mine. When I get away from you, I'll just find another Incubus to bond with. One with a kind heart and a gentle hand."

"Well, good luck with that. We're pretty much all the same. And something tells me you don't want a gentle hand. You seem to like being roughed up." He grinned then licked her cheek.

She vigorously erased his saliva from her face with her forearm like she was in kindergarten and he had cooties. God, her mother wasn't lying about Incubi dispositions. They were downright unbearable creatures.

"Ugh." She buried her head in her hands and waited for the bastard to pull up to the right motel room.

Stirling parked the car then looked at her sincerely. "Lila, she wanted me, but I won't be taking a mate tonight. I can't be distracted or leave you alone," he said.

He grabbed his duffle bag and stepped out of the car. He didn't bother opening her door for her. For whatever reason, she felt better knowing he wasn't going to offer that motel window woman the best sex of her life. She took her bag from the backseat, got out of the car and followed him.

He opened the door to the roach motel and tossed his belongings on the only bed in the room.

"Can I call one of my friends?" Lila asked, setting her bag next to his.

"I trust you won't be calling the police." He said facetiously and handed her his cell phone.

She rolled her eyes while quickly dialing Jenny's number. On the second ring, Jenny answered. "Hello?"

"Jenny? It's me."

"Oh, God, Lila! Are you okay? That man was so violent! Did he hurt you? Where are you?" She babbled and babbled on before Lila could answer her questions.

"Jen, I'm fine right now," she interrupted. "The man who attacked us isn't a man. He's an Incubus."

"Oh my God! Well, what's going on? Will he bond with you?"

"No. He won't bond with me because he's afraid of being tied down. Big narcissistic piehole if you ask me."

Lila looked at Stirling and stuck her middle finger out to him. He just chuckled and pulled a pair of handcuffs from his bag.

"Then what does he want with you? This is ludicrous! Come home!" Jenny started crying on the other end.

"I can't, Jen. I'll try my damnedest to get out of this, but I don't know how I'm going to do that at the moment. I'll call you after I know more. When it's safe."

"But..."

"I love you, Jenny. Just do as I ask. Goodbye." Lila hung up the phone before she started crying herself.

"*Piehole*?" Stirling laughed, holding out his hand for the phone.

Lila slammed it into his palm and then watched as he stripped off his shredded clothing. When he was naked, he grabbed Lila by the arm and moved her forward into the small bathroom with him.

"What are you doing, may I ask?" She struggled in his grasp.

"Well, I was looking around the room. The headboard is flat. The TV stand is a dresser. The chairs and tables are too light, and there really isn't anything else in this room to handcuff you to. Unless you want to be strapped to the toilet. Your hair might get in the bowl, though."

He was smiling that smile. That deadly, wonderful, evil smile.

I'd rather not be strapped to the toilet."

"Then get undressed. Take a shower with me."

"Why don't you undress me?" She put her weight on one hip, pushing the other one out.

"With my fingers or teeth?" he asked seductively, meeting her eyes. He tilted his head to the side and lightly bit her neck.

She couldn't make up her mind. Goosebumps prickled across her entire body. Stirling's teeth were perfectly straight and white and nipped in just the right way, but his fingers were thick and long and strong. She wanted to feel them on her back, her breasts, her everything. She pushed him away.

"What are we doing here? You have refused to have sex with me, so quit playing games with me."

"Fine." He shrugged nonchalantly.

He took the cuffs he was holding and slapped one around her wrist. Then he shoved her to the dirty, cold floor and wrapped her arms around the toilet, cuffing the other hand as well. Her cheek smashed against the toilet lid.

"Fuck you," she strained to say.

"I told you no, sweetheart. Now this may take me a minute. I have to rub one out. You make me so hot I can't stand it." He laughed and turned on the water in the shower.

He began stroking his huge shaft in his equally huge hand and crouched down, placing his cheek against hers. "You know, this would be so much nicer if you would help me," he breathed in her ear. "I mean, we might as well fool around."

"You caught me at a bad time, big boy. I have shit stains on my arms at the moment," she grimaced.

When he stood, she observed his shadow against the shower curtain in the dim, yellowed light. It displayed the colossal ram horns that she had seen in her father's shadow, and ginormous, tattered wings.

"Maybe later then." Stirling and his raging hard-on disappeared behind the curtain.

Lila squeezed her eyes shut and tried to repress the vomit rising in her throat at the smell of the toilet. Stirling was singing some horrible Guns 'N' Roses song, his voice absolutely out of tune.

"I thought only women sang in the shower," she sneered.

"I thought only drunk people hugged toilets," he shot back.

She snarled in frustration and gritted her teeth. She tried to rip out of the cuffs that were now slicing into her wrists, but that only dug the metal in deeper. Then she contemplated pulling the toilet out of the floor entirely, but decided that would take too much time, and she'd still be cuffed. He'd surely catch her.

"Why can't I break out of these cuffs?" she asked, attempting to swivel her head into a less awkward position.

"I thought you'd never ask," he said and gargled some water loudly. She heard him spit, then he pulled the curtain aside. "I have a few witch friends." He winked at her and closed the curtain back.

He looked even better wet. She made up math problems in her head to suppress her hunger for him. She was *starving* for him.

About thirty minutes passed when Stirling decided to end his shower. Lila was half-asleep. So was her body. Her legs crawled with stinging pangs, and her arms were numb. Her neck hurt from being forced into its contorted position.

"Your turn," he hooted.

Her eyelids flinched as she opened them slowly. He was toweling off his hair. She watched beads of water glide down each of his hard muscles and fall to the floor. She yearned to lick that water off him, from his mouth to his balls. He wrapped the towel around his lower half then bent down to unlock the shackles that bound her to the shit bowl.

She rotated on a butt cheek and struggled to place one foot under her leg to prop herself up. She almost fell back, but he took her arm and steadied her. Looking up, she accidentally caught his eyes. For a moment, she thought she witnessed something inside him soften, but as quickly as she saw it, it disappeared. He turned and padded out of the bathroom silently.

She stripped off her clothes and stepped into the steamy shower, pondering her next move. She would have to sneak out while he was sleeping. But if he cuffed himself to her, there would be no way to escape. She'd have to trick him somehow, break down his walls.

While scrutinizing her quandary, she washed the toilet bowl stank from her arms and damned the motel for not having conditioner. Still feeling grimy, she rinsed, dried off, then walked into the room with the towel around her.

Stirling was nowhere to be found, and the door was ajar. She peeked out the window and saw him standing with his cell to his ear. She pressed her ear to the glass and held her breath.

"What does he want with her, Silas?" he almost yelled.

A pause.

"I didn't sign up for this. What the hell am I supposed to do now? You knew what they were, and you didn't tell me? You tracked them? We're like brothers, man! You should have warned me the minute you knew about the orders!"

Another pause.

"What is he doing with them? Are her parents alive?"

Lila stiffened.

Another pause.

"If this has anything to do with the recent exterminations … dammit! I want answers, Silas. This is my race we are talking about!"

Lila backed away from the window and scurried back into the bathroom. What did he know about her parents? Was her dream about them dying and the caged Succubi accurate? Dread flooded her body, and she felt she might drown in a sea of bewilderment.

She quickly flashed back to the last time she saw her mother and father. Back to six years ago when her father had scolded her, and her mother watched her walk out the door.

When she heard the motel door slam shut, she composed herself and walked into the room. Stirling sat down in a flimsy chair at the dinky table against the wall. His face was riddled with rage.

What the hell was *he* so angry about? It was *her* family that had been delivered into the clutches of evil, and she was next.

Ignoring him, she unzipped her bag and retrieved her panties. She turned away from the deviant, dropped her towel, and bent over to slip on the undergarment.

Stirling couldn't help but take notice. Her bare butt was pushed out, her luscious, irresistible lips visible between her thighs, taunting him. His eyes bulged, and his breath caught at the sight of her. He was frozen while he watched as her back muscles rolled under her ivory skin and how her ass flexed as she rose.

Before she could rifle through her bag for her night shirt, Stirling's strong arm encircled her waist. He had grabbed her so hard she couldn't breathe. He ground his stone-hard erection into her lower back through his rough jeans, then shoved a hand beneath her panties, cupping her sex hard. Her pussy was still wet from the shower, and he couldn't believe how soft her feminine curls were. All sanity evaporated as he plunged two fingers deep inside her. She gasped and flung her wet head back against his shoulder.

"I have a few things to figure out, and you're distracting me," he snarled lethally against her ear. "Get. In. Bed." He spun her around and threw her onto the bed so forcefully she almost collided with the headboard.

As she covered herself with the sheet, he sucked his fingers into his mouth, cleaning her juices from them. She felt like crying and sat there with a lump in her throat. He was the worst. She had to escape his captivity.

Seemingly satisfied by her taste, he slipped into the bed next to her. She rolled over, her back to him, and looked at the ancient clock on the nightstand. It was only eight.

"I'm hungry," she murmured.

"I doubt this place offers room service. Go to sleep. You're annoying me," he responded.

"I'm not tired. It's only eight o'clock, for fuck's sake," she shot back, turning to face him.

"Then just lay there and shut up."

He scrubbed a palm over his face. It appeared that an internal battle raged inside him. He was so sexy even while tormented, but she would tear his gorgeous head off the moment the chance presented itself.

"What's wrong, Stirling?" she asked softly, hoping she sounded concerned.

"I said, shut up. I need to think."

Okay. Confined, bored and in a state of flux, she took the remote off the nightstand and turned on the TV. The volume was a bit high, and before she could find the button to turn it down, Stirling had leapt onto her and forced her arms above her head.

"I said, I need to think! I can't concentrate with you walking around naked, with you rambling on, or with the fucking television on full blast!" He ripped the remote from her palm and shattered it against the wall.

"I was going to turn it down," she said in a small voice, nearly cowering.

He was clutching her wrists so tightly that her hands were growing cold from lack of circulation.

"You're hurting me," she whispered cautiously.

Her eyes met his, and while she saw fury in his purplish irises, his lust washed over her like a tsunami. Her breasts had become exposed during the struggle, and he looked down at them ravenously. His breath came out in hot bursts against her face. His nostrils flared, and his jaw clenched. He didn't move.

He thought about what Lila had said about wanting a normal life. About finding love. He had had never wanted a bond, yet now, as he straddled this rare and wondrous creature, his conviction crumbled. Suddenly he realized his loneliness.

He was born condemned to a life of fast, meaningless fucks and solitude. Never did he have the time to fully appreciate sex with his prey, and he hated introductions and the trite chit chat that followed. He had taken to hypnotizing women to bed just so he didn't have to hear them talk.

There was no way to sustain a relationship with a human woman, or with any species but his own. He'd accepted his fate at a young age and convinced himself he was better off alone. But now, with a potential lifemate beneath him, he wondered about the possibilities. Could she offer him the passion he truly desired, love he denied himself, deprived himself of?

He wanted to know everything about Lila. And wanted her to know him. She was the embodiment of beauty, a goddess whom he could make love to for hours on end. He could get used to her warm body next to his every night.

But he couldn't make that choice yet. Not with the potential death warrant Gaelon signed for her. He decided that for now he would stick to what he'd done the past hundred years. Fuck and duck.

"Stirling?" Lila asked, extracting him from the vortex of his mind. She tried moving her wrists in his grasp again.

He relieved some of the pressure he was applying. "I'm sorry," he said, merely centimeters from her cheek.

He brushed his lips across hers, and her mouth opened slightly. Her breasts rose and fell with each labored breath. This svelte demon straddled her, restrained her, and wanted her, yet he wouldn't take her. Just her luck. On top of it all, he had something to do with her parents' likely demise. She hated him but longed for him too. The yearning made her everything hurt.

"It's okay," she said, willing him to just kiss her. Maybe if she could seduce him, she could run later.

He sat up slowly, releasing her arms; when he did, his erection pressed against her mound. Her breath left her lungs in a rush. *I almost came!* She grabbed his bicep as he went to crawl off her.

"Wait!" Desperation saturated her voice. An impossible need overcame her, a need that trumped her desire to flee.

He tensed but remained still and looked at her hard.

"Remember in the bathroom? You said we could fool around?"

No answer. He was a glorious statue.

"Could we?"

"It's too dangerous." He averted her eyes.

"But why? Why have you changed your mind?" She tried to find his eyes again.

He moved a large hand to her cheek and brushed her dark hair away from her face. He looked at her puffy lips, remembering what they felt like wrapped around his cock. God, she was so perfect. So was that ass. Round and strong. An ass that could handle a few hard spanks. And her breasts, so heavy and creamy, with light brown nipples that were tight and hard right now. He was so consumed by the woman in front of him that he had forgotten what she'd asked.

"What?" His voice was gravelly, and he cleared his throat.

"Why have you changed your mind?"

"Because I may not be able to stop myself."

"Then I'll stop you. Can we, please?" she pleaded.

He tore his bicep from her grasp irately. "I can't. And you wouldn't be able to stop me. I am stronger than you."

He had to find a way to keep her from Gaelon. After he spoke with Silas, he was sure Gaelon was behind the Succubi disappearances. He would fix this somehow, and then he would contemplate taking Lila as a lifemate. That's if she would even have him after she found out the truth. He wasn't giving into her so easily, so soon. He couldn't think with his prick now. If he did, they would both suffer and die together.

He moved off Lila and grabbed the cuffs, securing one to his wrist and the other to hers.

She sighed heavily, irritated.

He grunted and shut his eyes.

Unable to shake her need, she stared at him, admiring his flawless profile. He had a strong nose, a chiseled jaw, and his lips... oh so luscious. The bottom one was a little fuller than the top, and she wanted to suck that lip into her mouth. She watched his stone-like pectorals rise and settle as he breathed. The light sandy hair on his chest looked soft, and she stroked it with her eyes, all the way down his rippled abs until it disappeared in a trail beneath the sheets.

"What?" he asked, annoyed.

"What, what?" she said innocently.

"You're staring at me. Stop it."

"Have you ever killed anyone?" she blurted out.

He slowly opened his eyes and turned to face her. "Where is this going?"

"I'm just curious. Have you?"

"Yes. I've killed many beings."

"By having sex, I mean, by accident?"

"When I kill it's on purpose, not by accident. What do you mean?" His brow furrowed.

"Well, can't you accidentally steal too much life force from a woman?"

Succubi. So rare they knew nothing about their opposites. "No. But they can sure as hell steal it from me. I learned at fifteen what to do in order to secure a life force without complications. It's demeaning as hell, but it works."

"What do you do?" Lila was honestly intrigued.

"I have to ejaculate inside a woman to secure a life force, right? So, imagine what it's like for me after a hundred years of boning. I have the stamina of a god. My dad taught me to hunt an attractive female, give her several orgasms, and have her suck me or tease me until I'm on the brink. Then I can enter her and come in time not to burn alive. While I'm very skilled in giving orgasms, women are still pissed about a five-minute fuck no matter how many times they come."

"Do you ever get bored? I mean a hundred years of sex..."

"Yeah. I have to mix things up. The rougher the play, the more fun I have. I like to take two or three women at once. Things stay more interesting that way, but the burning lasts longer when I'm screwing three different women in one sitting. I have to divide my attentions."

Lila pictured him with multiple women begging for a taste. Two would go down on him while he fingered another. Then one would sit on his face as another rode him like a cowgirl on a mustang. Why did the thought of him with other women bother her so much? She suddenly wished she never inquired about his sex life.

To her dismay, he kept talking about it.

"It's also amusing when I get off while a woman's blowing me. Then they don't know what's hit them." He almost laughed.

It took all Lila had not to tell him to shut up.

"They get all moany and touch themselves and rub themselves. Then I can slip away, escaping the ranting and raving about how they wished I had lasted longer and this and that. I often hypnotize women into keeping their mouths shut, but it would be ideal if I had power enough to make them forget me permanently."

Lila had felt the same way. She wished every man she had taken would have never remembered it. "That's hardly fair. You mean you can secure a force if she just tastes you?"

"She has to taste enough, sweetheart. Which is quite a bit."

"I have to obtain a man's seed for a life force, but you have to expel yours. How does that work?"

Stirling was shocked that Lila didn't know the basic dynamics of their curse. He wondered about the life she'd lived before she met him.

"If I release enough of myself into a woman, some of her essence leaves her body and I absorb it. I burn the minute I enter a woman, but I don't secure a force until I burst, and it's difficult to orgasm when your body's on fire. If I don't get off, I die. After a hundred years, I'm still trying to perfect the art."

You are the art. "Well then, I definitely say it's easier for you Incubi. You don't even kill women through sex? You just absorb what you need?"

"Just what we need. The humans get sleepy for a while afterward. But no. No death by sex," Stirling answered.

"I suck the life out of men the second they enter me and it's hard to make some of them come quickly."

"Sorry God punished you broads more harshly than us men, blame Lilith, but I refuse to believe you have any trouble making a man come." He laid his head back against the headboard and closed his eyes again.

Gee, was that a compliment? "Men are stubborn. They pride themselves on stamina. You should know that better than anyone. It's irritating, for Satan's sake," she complained.

"Well, that's what your orgasms are for, sweetheart. Use them, and it shouldn't be a problem. What are you bitching about?"

"I can't have them," she admitted quickly, and looked away from Stirling's marvelous face.

"Can't have what?" he asked casually, eyes still closed.

"I can't have orgasms," she whispered.

"What? You can't orgasm? Why not?" he asked, surprised, yet again. Who was this creature? What had she been through?

She still wouldn't look at him. She felt him shift in the bed, then he was messing with the cuffs. Before she knew it, her hand was free, and she exploited the freedom to turn away from him completely. She felt his eyes on her back, spearing holes into her. Perhaps she was one step closer to escape. Physically and sexually.

"Is there something wrong with you? Have you been... circumcised? I mean, I've heard of that happening to women… What, what is it?" he asked curiously from behind her.

"I killed a boy." Lila hated the way it sounded out loud. "The first boy I was ever with. My parents never told me the rules, and I unknowingly broke them all. I came a few times with him, and every time I orgasmed, so did he. It was amazing, and just as I thought I might like being what I am, my mother called me into the kitchen the next morning and told me he was dead."

When Stirling didn't say anything, she carried on.

"I took another man shortly after, and I was close, so close, but every time I got there, I thought about killing my first lover, my friend, and I couldn't focus. I lost my bearings and killed my second mate, too. He was a husband and father." She dropped her head in shame thinking about the past. She had tried so hard to suppress it.

"From then on, it's been something I can't overcome. I've learned to deal with it, but it's dangerous. I almost committed suicide after forcing a pizza delivery guy from me. I laid on the floor burning alive for hours before my friend coerced a drunk guy into having sex with me."

"Shit," Stirling commented sympathetically. "How long have you been going through this? How old are you?"

"I was twenty-two when I succumbed. I'm only six years into my curse."

He grasped her shoulders, turning her body into his. He examined her face in search of deceit. But no. She was wasn't lying. Her youth explained her ignorance about their species.

"Holy Hell, you're a baby," he uttered in astonishment. "I can't believe the strength it must have taken to hold back for so long."

She tore away from him and turned back around. She didn't need him telling her she was a baby. She knew it, and it embarrassed her. "It's been a nightmare. And then I find you, and..."

"You thought I was the answer," he finished.

He reached a hand out for her bare back and hesitated slightly before running a finger along her spine. Goosebumps broke out running across her skin. It felt right to touch her. He wanted to touch her more, to hold her, to kiss her.

"I hoped. But you're vicious and rude. My mother said bonding wasn't easy.... Listen, I don't even know why I just told you all that."

She hadn't meant to tell him so much. She'd meant to say just enough to soften his spiny exterior, but it just kept spilling out. It felt good to say those things aloud to someone who really understood, but in the end, it didn't matter. She and Stirling were enemies.

Stirling felt a sudden obligation to change things for Lila. She was delicate, a new Succubus, and had been tormented immensely. He wanted more than anything to take some of the burden away from her, but he had to tread carefully. One wrong move and he could be hers, and Gaelon could kill them both in one felled swoop.

He stood and shed his pants then brought his body down close to hers, sliding his muscular legs on either side of her slim ones. His erection pressed into her back and stifled a groan at the pressure. Tenderly, he brought an arm around her waist.

She couldn't believe he actually caved or that his touch pacified her. Soon, she found herself sobbing in his arms.

"Shhh, don't cry, *meine Flamme*. I'm going to take the pain away from you," Stirling promised in a hushed voice.

"Take off your panties. Please."

She rose slowly, did as he asked and sat back down, veins pumping fast.

He positioned himself behind her again and stroked his shaft until a bead of semen formed at the tip of his head. He swiped the shimmery liquid off with his first finger and brought his hand around the front of her body. She spread her legs without direction, and he placed his silken finger on her clit. Gently, he began to massage her.

Lila felt the tingle his semen caused immediately. In response, she pushed her hips back then brought them forward slowly as he applied more pressure and another finger to her sex. Still swirling her clit, he teased her entrance with a third finger. The torture was unbearable. Her breath was heavy and inconsistent. She dropped her head back against his hard shoulder as he kissed down the line of her neck. His technique was phenomenal. Without thinking, she lifted her arm, cradling his head between her neck and bicep, and grabbed his hair.

He opened his mouth against her throat. "Yes," he breathed and withdrew his arm from around her waist. He ran his hand up to her breasts, and across her nipples.

"Oh, oh, I want you," she cried. She did want him, in every way, but dead too if he had harmed her parents. The dream she had about them was still fresh in her mind. She had to force it aside.

"I want you, too." As soon as he said it, he knew it to be true. He had to keep this woman out of Gaelon's clutches. He had to be hers.

He rose on his knees behind her, leaving her breathless. He gripped her sides and pulled her toward the center of the bed, laying her on her back.

She propped herself up on her elbows to watch him as he spread her legs open with his thigh. Reflexively, her hips lifted off the bed, but he forced them back down into the mattress. The dominate move challenged her and she glared at him irately. A feral growl emanated from her throat.

He glared right back at her, hungrily stroking an incisor with his tongue. Palming his cock again, more of the magical liquid dripped from the head, down his knuckles. She observed his masturbatory skills intently then he began rubbing his velvety tip all over her mound.

The tingling she felt ramped and transformed into a sensation she could hardly describe. Every part of her body tightened. Her nipples were at full attention. Her toes curled, and her clit swelled with fever.

He lowered himself onto her, and she thought he might enter her. She couldn't bond with him now. Not without answers. She tensed, ready to buck him away, but he slid his erection between her lips, along her nub, back and forth. Melting and panting, her brain short-circuited, except for the part that managed this level of pleasure.

He moved faster against her.

"Yes, yes," she whispered. She was actually so close.

He touched his forehead to hers and parted her mouth with his. "Kiss me," he said, so softly.

She scarcely heard him, but his words made her heart stop. As if there wasn't an option, she entangled her fingers in his hair and licked his bottom lip.

He took her tongue into his mouth, where she explored the tips of his teeth, the sides of his cheeks, the roof of his mouth. He cupped her face and kissed her ravenously. Their tongues danced, intertwining, prodding and teasing. As the kiss became more intense, so did Lila's bliss. Liberation sat on the horizon, moving closer toward her each second, with the help of the most savage man she'd ever met, the most flawless man she'd ever met.

She closed her eyes. "I'm about to let go," she said against his mouth.

"Let go," he whispered.

As quickly as he slipped away from her heat, he thrusted two thick fingers deep inside her, prodding her spongy spot vigorously.

"Holy shit!" she screamed. Her chest and shoulders came off the bed, and her head fell back, straining her neck.

He felt her contract around his fingers and pulled them out of her as she ejaculated, dousing him in her mystical fluids. As her legs trembled, he got back on his knees and jerked himself off to the most mind-blowing sight of his life. He splashed out onto her quaking pussy and watched in awe as she shattered into pieces again.

She collapsed and tears streamed down her face. He thought that maybe he had gone too far. And he had. He had fragmented her world with betrayal and ecstasy. But it was worth everything he'd ever known.

"Lila?" Stirling ran his hand along her cheek and pushed aside hair that had matted to her face in her tears.

He would remember how she looked when she came, forever. The way her lips parted, and her eyelids fluttered. The way her breasts swayed, and her thighs quivered. The way she trusted him to offer her something she'd been deprived of for years.

She grabbed his hand and squeezed but said nothing. Her sweat cooled, sending a shiver through her she looked at him with esteem and hatred all at once.

"Well, I'd say that was about six years of tension released. Are you okay?" he asked, standing and surveying the sheets. *Goddam,* he thought.

She couldn't speak. Her breathing was labored, making her chest heave.

Looking around the bed, Stirling found her toppled bag at the foot of it. He bent down and pulled out the night shirt she had attempted to put on earlier. He helped her sit up and slipped the shirt over her.

"Oh my God," she said, her head spinning. She thought she might black out as she began to fall back in the bed.

"Easy there," he said and caught her. "I need you to go sit in that chair for a bit. I have to change the sheets or we'll drown in our sleep."

He helped her to her feet and led her to the chair, which she slumped in. *Did he just make a joke?*

She watched Stirling go around the room, tearing the bed apart, making it back up. He hopped in the shower again to rinse himself off after the seismic wave she had unleashed against him. Her sweat had dried, and so had her tears. She felt disconnected, like nothing around her was real. She watched him get out of the shower and dry himself off.

He peeked into the room to check on her, then wet a towel and strode into the space, kneeling before her.

Lila closed her eyes and rested her cheek against her shoulder. Emotions beat her mind, heart and soul with spiked clubs and she was too exhausted to battle back. She felt Stirling lifting her shirt and wiping her down with the warm towel. After he was done cleaning her, he picked her up and carried her to the bed, laying her down carefully.

She rolled onto her side and inhaled deeply. She was on the verge of tears. She was on the brink of turning and relenting to Stirling. She was on the fringe of losing her fucking mind.

He reached out and swept his hand down the length of her back, smiling. He had never even entered her but had the most intense sexual experience of his life. It was intimacy, which he'd never experienced before. His grandmother had been right. And to think he had actually considered not bonding with Lila. Now it was his only purpose. He just had to figure out how to keep her away from Gaelon. Also, if she found out that he had abducted her parents, there was a possibility that she would never forgive him. He'd have to convince her that he had had no clue of what he was being ordered to do. If Gaelon hurt her or her parents, he would find a way to kill him before her eyes and make things right in hopes that she may spend lifetimes with him.

He slid under the sheets and held Lila close, relishing her warmth. He would change everything for her, at any cost. He would be with her and fill the black abyss that encompassed them both.

Chapter 11

Stirling woke to the sun streaming in through a small slit in the stained curtains. His cock was hard as granite, and he hoped with every ounce of his being that Lila would help relieve the morning tension. He reached for her in the bed but felt cold sheets. He rolled onto his side, and she was nowhere in sight. Maybe she had gone to the bathroom.

He stood, stretched his muscular frame, and walked to the bathroom pushing the door open. She wasn't there either. Quickly, he tore back the shower curtain, then panicking, he stormed back into the room. Her bag was missing.

Hastily, Stirling shrugged on his pants and rushed out the door into the parking lot. His car was gone.

"Shit!" He stormed back into the room and paced the worn carpet. Where was she? Where could she be? There were only two places he knew to look. At her parents' place in Charlotte and her own place in Asheville. He decided immediately that she had no reason to go back to Asheville because she told her friend to flee from there. She was in Charlotte, at her parents' house, looking for answers. And by God, he would have to give them to her.

Lila parked Stirling's black Charger in her parents' driveway. Reminiscently, she stared at the house before summoning the courage to go to it. Finally, she stepped out of the car.

A strange vibe shrouded the property. She hadn't been here for six years, yet she remembered the feeling her parents' home had given her. It had always been welcoming, warm, and safe. It had a certain smell, like furniture polish and fresh cookies. Her mother had been quite the homemaker, whether she had wanted to be or not.

Today, while the street looked the same, business as usual, her childhood home did not. It was dark even in the sunny day, and it felt desolate. A chill ran along her spine, which had nothing to do with the cool, October air.

Slowly, she walked to the front door. She had always kept her key just in case she needed shelter. She slid the key into the lock but noticed a break right through the glass framing the door. The key wasn't necessary. The door was unlocked.

As she stepped inside, stale air punched her in the face. It didn't smell like the house she remembered. It smelled vacant.

She walked through the foyer and living room, then down the hall toward the kitchen. There was no sign of recent activity, no sign of anything. Everything was in its place.

She circled back to the living room, where an old quilt was lying on the couch. It was the quilt her mother had always wrapped up in to watch TV. She picked up a corner of it and deeply inhaled. It smelled like her mother's scent: Earth and sea, tinged with Red Door perfume.

Lila dropped the quilt and went to the fireplace mantel where she saw a picture of herself standing in between her parents. She had almost forgotten their faces. Her mother was beautiful and pale, like herself. Her emerald eyes shiny and alive. Grey hair, thick and wavy, fell to her shoulders. Her body was a sculpture of delicate curves. Lila hadn't realized how much she looked like her mother until she saw that picture now.

She hadn't inherited much from her father in the way of looks, or anything else, for that matter. He also had grey hair, but it was pin-straight, and his eyes were hidden behind blue contacts. She remembered her father's eyes as empty and cold, distant, despite masking them with lenses.

Lila had never loved her father the way she loved her mother. There was always a disconnect, but he was her father. And so help her, if Stirling was guilty of harming them in any way... If her dream about them dying rang true...She would kill him. Somehow.

She tore the back off the picture frame, then folded the picture in the center where she stood and slid it into her back pocket. With a sour feeling in her stomach, she ascended the stairs to her old room. The pink canopy still hung above her bed and her furniture had not been touched. Her bed was made. Her mother had waited all this time for her to come back home.

Tears welled in Lila's eyes, and she suddenly regretted staying estranged from her parents. She had misplaced her anger and ran from what reminded her of what she really was. It must have killed her mother to hope she would return, then wake each day to be disappointed that she hadn't.

Lila left her room and travelled down the hallway to her parents' bedroom. There, she found what she was looking for: signs of a struggle. The lamp that sat on her father's nightstand had been toppled over. The sheets were pulled off the bed, and small blood droplets stained the comforter and carpet.

This had Stirling written all over it. It was no coincidence that her parents were gone, blood had been shed in their home and he had abducted her. Bastard. Incubi were Incubi. Her mother had said it, and Stirling confirmed it. She was definitely not bonding with him, or any Incubus.

She smoothed out the sheet and comforter across the bed, picked up the lamp and placed it back on the nightstand. Maybe her tidying was her way of denying the truth, or at least hiding it for a while. She wasn't ready to face it. She slowly made her way back to the living room. She needed a plan but didn't have a clue how to start formulating one.

A couple of hours passed, and Lila still couldn't think of where to go, who to ask for help. She was alone in all of this. Stirling was the only link to her parents and the only link to the monster that hunted her now.

Just as Lila pondered that it might have been hasty to run from him, she heard the sound of squeaking brakes outside the front windows of the house. Quickly, she peeked through the blinds and saw a large man behind the wheel of a silver Chevy.

Any self-doubt about fleeing from Stirling evaporated when she saw him get out of the car. Rage bubbled up in her chest, and she ran into the kitchen grabbing the biggest butcher knife she could find. She stood alongside the frame of the front door and waited.

Soon enough, the door slowly opened, and Stirling stepped into the house sniffing the air. He paused and turned. Seeing her only shot, Lila drop-kicked him in the stomach with everything she had. He faltered and tried to speak.

"Lila," was all he could muster before she spun around and landed a kick to his chest, knocking him to the ground.

She was still coming for him, so he quickly ignored the pain in his gut and sternum and stood unsteadily. He backed away from her with a hand outstretched when he saw the size of the knife in her grasp.

"Lila, let me explain," he tested, but no way was she was listening.

"I heard everything, Stirling! I heard your conversation with Silas! What have you done?" she screamed at him.

She shoved him forward several times, threatening him with the knife, and cornered him in the kitchen between the cabinets and the refrigerator. With murder in her eyes, she jabbed her blade deep into his chest, narrowly missing his heart.

"What have you done with my parents?" she seethed, bloodthirsty.

The knife wound didn't hurt him nearly as badly as Lila's expression did. It was one of anguish and betrayal. Murder and hatred. He grabbed her hand, still tight around the handle of the butcher knife. Carefully, he inched the blade out and threw it to the ground.

Lila punched him in the Adam's apple and stalked away from him, disappearing down the hall.

Stirling slid down the cabinets and grabbed at his throat, gasping for air. After a few long moments, he gathered himself enough to look for her, his hand over his wounded chest. She was sitting on the couch in the living room, and she was crying.

"Lila, I will tell you everything that I know. Okay?" he winced as he spoke.

He stood, hunched and bleeding, yet still managed to look too perfect in only a black tank and jeans. How did he make simple clothes look so Armani? His sandy blond hair, messy from the morning, glistened in the sun that beamed through the living room windows. His jaw was set in a hard line, and his eyes were swimming in grief. With his arms cocked by his sides, biceps bulging, it was as if he was ready to take out an army. He was brilliant like the moon on a cloudless night.

She felt so small sitting on the couch, tears streaming down her face, wrapped in that old quilt, while he came close and hovered over her.

"Tell me. What did you do with my parents, and what the hell do you want with me?" she demanded, her voice laced with poison.

Stirling held his hands out, indicating that all his cards were on the table. He knelt in front of her.

She stared into the wall across from her because she couldn't look at his face and still hate him as much as she needed to.

"Gaelon found out about you and your parents through your friend's cyber buddy, Silas. Silas is a tracker for Gaelon. He finds things Gaelon wants, and I procure them. He ordered me to kidnap you and your parents at night about a week ago. When I arrived here, your room was empty. But I still had to carry on with my task. I hit your mother with a tranq dart, then your father struggled with me. I broke his nose before I put him to sleep. I had no idea you were Lilin. The dark hid the shadows. I haven't found out what Gaelon did with your parents. It's not my place to ask."

"What else?"

"My next order was to finish the job by securing you. When I tracked you to your apartment, I recognized you from the picture that was there, on the mantle." He gestured toward the fireplace. "I didn't know what you were, and I didn't care. I wanted to stop. I fell for you when I saw you in that photo, but you were still an assignment. I was commanded, and I obeyed. I didn't understand what was happening until I realized you were a Succubus.

"I called Silas at the motel for intel about Gaelon's intentions. Three Lilin in one week? And the rumors of others missing?"

"What?" Lila finally turned to him.

"Lilin have gone missing. But mostly Succubi."

"Well, what did Silas have to say?" she asked sharply, not yet trusting him enough to tell him about her haunting dream.

"Silas knows that Gaelon is kidnapping Lilin. He doesn't know why, though, and he's not even sure what Gaelon does with them afterward. Once the Lilin are delivered, they disappear.

"Gaelon used me to abduct my own kind, and I didn't even know it. He counted on my ignorance, my arrogance, and my thrill for the hunt. There is nothing I can say to you to make you forgive me but hear me now. If Gaelon means you harm, I will protect you. Even if you hate me."

"You'll protect me? What a fucking joke. You're the one who got me into this mess! Gaelon's a descendant of Abbadon, meaning he can destroy souls. He's probably destroyed my parents' souls, and mine is next!" she shouted as she threw the quilt off her and planted her feet on the ground.

"Lila, we don't know if that's what's happening. I can't say that he hasn't killed your parents, but to destroy their souls? I can't think of a reason for it."

He stood from the floor and reached for her, but retreated, shaking her head.

"And to say you *fell* for me a week ago? From a goddamned picture? Ha! This is the end of the line. Get the fuck out of my house. I will deal with Gaelon alone." She pointed to the broken door.

"Lila, you can't. He's too strong. You need me. I have connections. Think about it, Lila. Please." He took a step toward her, but she put her hand out defensively.

She looked at the hole in his black tank and was sorry she missed his heart. Well, almost. She knew she needed him. She just hated that she needed him and wanted him all at once. Dropping her hand, she allowed him to approach.

“Lila. I’m so sorry. And I did fall for you. I can’t explain it, but I did,” he swore, and opened his arms to her. Tears dripped down her porcelain face, and all he wanted to do was hold her and kiss her and make sweet love to her.

She wanted him too. She yearned for his comfort. But she couldn’t be with him. Not after this. She stepped forward and as he smiled, closing his eyes, she buried her elbow into his face.

Chapter 12

"Put this on. There's blood all over your shirt," Lila said as she came down the stairs slowly, thinking Stirling might ambush her. But he was on the couch, still holding his nose. She threw him one of her father's baggier shirts.

He pulled off his tank, and she looked away from him to avoid becoming aroused as he brought the shirt over his massive body. When he was changed, she cursed to herself, how well he wore blue.

"It's a little snug," he said passively. "You got something I can wipe my face off with? You broke my nose."

"Come here," she said apologetically, and grabbed one of his big hands. She led him into the kitchen, and they stopped at the sink.

"Does it hurt?" she asked, examining his face. She brushed the back of her hand across his cheek quickly.

"Not anymore. I reset it."

Stirling tried to catch her eyes, but she was already looking down, rinsing a washcloth.

She brought the cool towel to his face and dabbed where the blood had run out of his nose. Then she cleaned off his chin and neck.

"There, that should do it," she said, and he grasped her by the hand before she could pull away from his face. "It's on your hands, too," she said, trying to distract herself.

Stirling stared at her while she washed him. He loved the way her hair fell in front of her face, how delicate her hands were in his, how overwhelmingly beautiful she was.

She turned away from the sink and opened a drawer to retrieve a dry towel.

"Here," she said as she handed it to him. *Dammit. He's too much.* That blue shirt with that hair and those eyes...

There was no denying the sexual tension between her and the demon who stood before her. Every time she hurt him, she wanted to mend his wounds. Every time they grappled with one another, she wanted to wrap her legs around him and take him inside of her, and every time he touched her, she became weak with the need to become his.

Stirling dropped the towel to the floor and took Lila's face in his hands. She resisted for only a second then met his lips. There was only him in her world, her fucked up little world. He somehow gave her peace. Made her whole. His supple kisses, his earthy smell, his masculinity and vulnerability. She felt right in his arms and knew they should be together. Every ounce of detestation she had collected for him in a pretend jar escaped in that moment. Each minute together, they were consumed with one another. It was just as bad as her curse. She was irrationally in love with the one creature she wanted to hate.

She pulled away from him against her will. "Go get some pizza. There's a place just around the corner. Take two lefts out of here, and it'll be on the right, about two miles up the street. I'm going to take a bath," she said.

No way was he going to leave her alone, even after the kiss they shared. He still didn't trust her to stay put. "We can go together," he suggested.

"Or not." She shrugged and disappeared up the stairs.

In her parents' master bath, she ran chilly water in the huge Jacuzzi, and poured in sea-foam crystals. She shed her clothing and slipped into the water, exhausted and in need of sex.

Her temperature was running high, threatening to burst her into flames. After her soak, she would go out and find someone to take, but she'd have to wait until Stirling was asleep to sneak away. Technically, she was still his captive. Dread encased her when she realized he would have to take a mate soon as well.

After twenty minutes or so, Stirling paced behind the master bath door, and a few times, he almost opened it. What was he thinking? She hated him, didn't she? She was trying to break his guard by kissing him. It had worked at the motel, and it was working now. If nothing else, she didn't trust him. He was responsible for the potential destruction of her parents' souls. He couldn't imagine anyone doing to him what he'd done to her.

Guilt crushed his chest like a cruel vice, and his mind raced so fast it felt like his brain was running repeatedly into the sides of his skull. He had a headache, and his eyes were strained from stress. She'd have to forgive him at some point. She had to. It wasn't all his fault. *I'm such a fuck-up.* He shook his head in frustration. What the hell was he thinking? At six years old, Lila was shrewd, already a master manipulator, and dangerously captivating. It was ridiculous to think she'd ever have him in any way or form. She was messing with his mind.

He paced again. *Fuck it.* He opened the door to the bathroom.

"Lila," he began, and then took in the sight of her lying in the water, bubbles barely covering her nipples. Her head was leaning against a bath pillow before he disturbed her. He should have left her alone. This was her only solace in the past couple of days.

"I'm sorry to bother you, but I have to talk to you or I'll... I don't know." He looked down at the tiles on the floor. There had never been a time when he was at a loss for words or had to apologize for anything.

"It's okay," she said lazily. "Come in." She laid her head back on the pillow.

"You believe I didn't mean for any of this to happen, Lila? Had I known you were my own kind I never would have agreed to do what I did. I'm stupid. I'm blind. I'm impatient. I'm violent and immature...I'm also *aware* now. I've been careless and downright naive. I want to make things right, starting with you." He knelt at the base of the Jacuzzi.

"Stirling, you are all of those things, and it has caused both us and who knows how many others, suffering. You do the bidding of an evil monster without question. It seems, well, ignorant. You're a childish beast." Her eyes were closed, her voice, calm and even.

Well, that stung a bit, but she was right. Looking back, he couldn't justify most of his behavioral patterns.

"Lila, I found that job working for The Den decades ago. I bounced there, met women there, and then took work from Gaelon. The deeper I got, the more he required of me, and he threatened me numerous times. I know what he's capable of, so I was... I couldn't leave. I've seen his wrath firsthand. I've seen the souls leave the bodies and then... he takes hold of them."

Stirling clamped his eyes tight and furrowed his brow as if trying to forget a painful memory.

Lila raised her head and turned to look at him. Her vision spun a little, and she was feeling queasy. Even sick, she didn't want to miss anything he had to say.

"I have to protect you and our species. I promise I'll stop him."

"You think he's crushing Lilin souls?"

She didn't want to think about never seeing her parents again. She'd left them in her first life but knew she'd see them in the afterlife. Only, that wouldn't happen if Gaelon decimated them into oblivion.

"I don't know. He may be using us for some type of sexual experiment for all I know. He's a twisted son of a bitch. There's no rhyme or reason here. I don't know what to say, Lila. I'm so sorry."

Lila dropped her head to the rim of the tub. "Shit," she uttered.

"I know, Lila. Tomorrow, we'll go see someone who can help. I need advice." He kissed her head and rose from the floor.

"Stirling? You say you will stop him, but *can* you? You said yourself he is one of the most powerful demons topside."

"I will figure this out and make it right," he promised, and departed.

Lila didn't put much stock in Stirling's vow, but she had no one else. What could she do but wait for Fate to unfold? For now, she was going to try and sneak out, get food and find a mate.

She emerged from the bathroom after a while and went to her bedroom to change. She put on old jeans and one of her comfy throw-back tees. Her clock displayed seven thirty. She snuck down the stairs and saw Stirling sitting on the couch with his head in his hand. To her relief, he was fast asleep.

She needed time without him so she could try to process everything she'd learned. He clouded her judgment and made her unbearably horny. Thinking about his fingers inside her, his veiny shaft against her bud...*Fuck.*

She tiptoed back upstairs and shed her grubby clothing. She slipped into a low-cut maroon sweater, a black skirt, and knee-high boots. After a fluff of the hair and a glance in the mirror, she thought she looked sexy enough.

She crept downstairs again, successfully making her way out and to the car, undetected. Stirling's was snoring when she left.

Lila gently closed the car door, then released the emergency brake and coasted down the driveway silently. When she felt it was safe, she started the obnoxiously audible engine and drove to a little diner down the street.

The diner was a reminder of the good ole' days. Back when she was aloof and childish and happy. Tonight, she was the bipolar. All she really knew to be one hundred percent true right then was that she wanted a burger.

She sat at a table she and her mother would sit at frequently. By the window. The waiter, who she didn't recognize, came to the table and asked if she was eating alone.

"Yes, I am," she answered, locking eyes with him.

Handsome. He was tan and emitted a surfer vibe with light brown hair, light brown eyes, and a killer smile with dimples to boot.

"Well, what's a pretty girl like you doing here alone?" he asked in a backwoods country twang, tapping his pen against his notepad.

The dialect didn't match the mouthpiece, but Lila was okay with that. "Just broke up with my boyfriend and got a little hungry." She shrugged.

"Mostly when people break up, they're pretty upset and don't eat much," the waiter said. "They just come in and order a drink."

"No, not me. My ex is a big jerk, so I'm not upset at all. Just hungry."

"Well that's good to hear. Know what ya want yet?"

"I'll have the cheeseburger with fries, and I'll have you later. That is, if you get off soon," Lila said quietly. She actually meant the last part quite literally.

The waiter blushed. He placed his hand on the table and leaned into her. "My name's Dave. I'll get that right out to you, and I'll take a break as soon as you want me to." He smiled at her doltishly and strode off.

The burger was great. Lila hadn't eaten anything substantial since meeting Stirling. After savoring every bite of her meal, she sat at the table contemplating. She wondered who Stirling was taking her to meet in the morning. What answers would they have for her? Would they have answers? What happened to her parents? What would happen to her? The queries rushing through her brain were endless.

Stirling had brought nothing but strife to her. He was her bane. But, in all fairness, he'd revived her sex drive and given her the most sensational orgasms she ever dreamed to have. *Stirling.*

He consumed her. Each though she had somehow led back to him. He devoured her very being. She wanted to go back home and kiss, no suck, no...There were so many things she wanted to do with him. To him. It pissed her off. She almost drove her fist into the table when Dave, the waiter checked in on her.

"Miss? Um, ya done with that? Well, 'course ya are." Dave nervously gestured to her empty plate.

Lila snapped back to reality. "The name's Lila. And yes, I'm finished." She pushed her plate forward.

"Well, I'm goin' on break now. You wanna follow me out back?" The waiter used his thumb to point behind him at the exit door.

"What about the tab? How much do I owe you?" she asked. She didn't want to feel like she was whoring herself out for a cheap meal.

"Don't worry 'bout it," he said, waving her off.

She retrieved a twenty-dollar bill from the cup of her bra and placed it on the table anyway. Dave smiled and led her to the back of the diner.

The alley was lit by a dim yellowed bulb attached to the building. A Dumpster was present and a few empty cardboard boxes littered and trash littered the ground. *How romantic.* Dave took Lila's hand, pulling her further around the diner where the stench of the Dumpster disappeared, and the lighting was non-existent.

This was the first time her primal urge to mate was somehow stifled. Normally, sex was decent and the relief after was amazing. But now, she wished she were with someone else. *Stirling.*

Dave stopped and turned her into him. "How ya wanna do this?" he asked, already unbuttoning his fly excitedly.

"Get behind me and lift up my skirt." She tried not to sound despondent.

Without another word, he turned her around and hiked up her skirt.

She slid her panties down and bent over, placing one hand on her knee and the other against the brick of the building.

He shoved a finger inside her, as if to prime her, and slowly pushed inside her.

The stinging began. Lila shut her eyes and tried to concentrate on the empty sex she was having, but she couldn't. *Stirling.* She took a deep breath and tried to compose herself. She had to keep tabs on her burning, or she could kill... whatever his name was. Then, a new thought crossed her mind. Maybe she could try to have an orgasm now that Stirling had broken that dam.

She felt Dave's hand between her legs and became a little optimistic until he started rubbing around aimlessly between her folds. She gritted her teeth in frustration, and all she could do was wish that the man behind her was Stirling. *Stirling.* He was all she thought about because nothing compared to the way he made her feel. Nothing. He extracted every emotion she'd ever known and some she never knew she had. He made her crazy and calm and jealous and content. He was the most impossible aspect of her life despite it all.

She heard the waiter talking to her, but she wasn't paying attention. The burning under her skin was just starting to intensify when she felt him spasm inside her. She pulled up her panties and left the waiter alone in the alley.

She jogged around the block until she reached the parking lot. Loaded with energy, she hopped in the Charger, hoping she could get home and to the bathroom to clean up without Stirling catching her.

She sped back to her parents' house and slipped through the door. Stirling was still on the couch, still snoring.

Quietly, she rushed up the stairs and into her bathroom. She took a quick shower and washed the stench of that waiter off her. He had smelled like greasy fried chicken. She dried herself off as she went into her room and pulled a skimpy teal nightgown from her dresser. Pulling the lingerie over her body, she nearly jumped out of her skin when she heard Stirling say, "So you went out."

Lila shook her head and held her face in her hands for a moment then she turned to the sexy Incubus, whose face was saturated with something bordering rage and torture.

"Stirling," she said warily and took a step toward him. He took a step back.

"What would you have me do? I wasn't feeling well. You'll have to do the same in a couple days." She tried to reason with him, but he still looked so...devastated.

"Did you come?" he asked curtly.

She took another step toward him and he took another step back. He was in the doorway now.

"Stirling, what's wrong?"

"Did you come!" he roared and bashed the door frame with his fist. It cracked and gave out. Lila jumped. She thought that he might hurt her or that he might not want her ever now.

"No. No, I didn't," she answered quickly, tears threatening to free her eyes. She braved one more step, which backed him out of her room completely. She couldn't believe his reaction to the situation. It was sex. They survived on it. She looked into his eyes and his jealousy radiated through her. A tear finally slid down her cheek. She attempted to suppress the rest of the waterworks but found herself inhaling erratically. Tears kept gliding down her face. She became enraged that he could do this to her. It wasn't her fault that she had to fuck someone else, and yet he laid a guilt trip on her anyway.

She stepped forward again, but this time, he didn't move. There was nowhere left for him to go except through the wall.

"What was I supposed to do? Will you have me die? You knew I would need a mate! Why are you barging in here, in my home, questioning me? You have no right!" she screamed.

"Did. You. Come?" he asked evenly this time, yet fury blazed behind his blue-violet eyes, disintegrating her composure.

"I didn't come! Is that what you need to hear?" she yelled.

His grim expression faltered. He didn't want to upset her, but he had yet again. He was unruly, and let his instincts override his ability to process the situation properly. He was an animal, possessive over his claims. He reached for her, but she batted his huge arms away.

"I didn't come, Stirling!" She hit him in the chest as hard as she could. He placed his hand over where she planted her fist into him. "I thought I'd be able to. I even tried to, thinking I didn't need you," she ground out through clenched jaws and came at him again.

He turned his head away from hers and closed his eyes. He deserved everything she dealt out and he couldn't stand to see her so undone.

"Damn you! Damn you to Hell! I couldn't come, Stirling! I couldn't come before because of my baggage, and I couldn't come tonight because he wasn't you, and I hate you for it! For my parents! For making me fall for you! For everything!"

She beat him in the chest one last time then succumbed to her grief and crumpled to the floor. Her body trembled as she sobbed, cruel reality finally catching up with her. She was exhausted. Even the life force she had just taken wasn't enough to help her fight her sorrow.

Stirling knelt beside her. "I can't stop hurting you, can I?"

He ran his hand along her spine. When she didn't respond to his touch, he picked her up, took her into her room and set her in bed.

She curled herself into a ball as she cried. He crawled into the bed behind her and held her as tightly as he could.

"I'm sorry, Lila. And I promise I won't ever hurt you again." He kissed her shoulder and stroked her hair until she fell asleep.

Chapter 13

Lila woke suddenly with fear stuck in her heart. Where was she? What happened? She sat up, absorbing her surroundings. Oh. She was in her parents' house and in her own bed, lying next to the most perfect of demons.

She had fucked some random waiter then cried her eyes out when Stirling proved that he gave a shit about her. *Whew.* She needed orange juice, which she had none of, and she really needed to just get away from it all. But she knew that wasn't possible.

Stirling roused when she got out of the bed to get dressed. He stretched and yawned, watching as she went to her closet.

She grabbed her emerald green, velvety jumpsuit. It was so comfortable that she thought she could handle most of the bullshit that would inevitably come her way today.

"I'll be ready in ten. Then we need to get on the road. It's a twelve-hour drive from here to Ouachita Parrish, Louisiana," Stirling said, half-asleep.

"Twelve hours?" she asked in shock. "What's in Louisiana?"

"What's not?" he asked back.

"Well..." Lila looked in her vanity mirror, the mirror that had once reflected normalcy. That had once shown her a life of innocence and serenity. She became calm and composed in those moments that she stared at herself. Memories flowed through her. Memories of a time before Doug and Peter. A time when things had seemed right.

She turned her body this way and that, then she faced Stirling. "I guess you're not gonna tell me, huh?"

"You look stunning in green. Brings out your eyes," he said lazily.

"Thank you," she responded pertly. She her pulled on her sneakers, then went into the bathroom to do some necessary grooming.

"We're going to see my Oma," Stirling answered, looking down at Lila's pink comforter. He was tracing the floral designs on it with a finger.

"What? Your Oma?" Lila stepped into the doorway of the bedroom, brushing her teeth.

"Sorry. My grandmother. Oma is German for grandmother."

"What does your Oma know about the shit we're in?" Lila asked in disappointment. She expected that he would be taking her to see an immortal, or a brutal fighter, an expert demon slayer. But his grandmother?

"Lila, she knows things ...," he started.

"Like?"

He jumped out of the bed and brushed past Lila, into the bathroom. He did a little bit of cleanup but didn't use her razor. His facial hair had poked through his skin since she first saw him. God, he looked sexy.

Lila leaned down and opened the cabinet under her sink. "Here," she said, handing him a new toothbrush.

After brushing her hair and slathering on deodorant, she walked over to her bedroom window and pulled the curtains aside. She looked at the street she grew up on and wished she were ordinary, like the children running around playing tag, riding bikes. Across the way, a boy and his father were jumping into piles of raked leaves, and she sighed.

"She has connections. She can help us out. I know it," Stirling said with a mouthful of toothpaste. She heard him gargle and spit.

"Do you think she'll like me?" Lila asked, still staring out the window.

He came up behind her and kissed her neck, then he rested his head on her shoulder. His arms encircled her waist.

"She'll love you," he assured against her ear.

Lila relaxed her head against his and closed her eyes. Just as she was about to turn around and kiss him, to let her guard down, she heard a car pull up to the house. She snapped her eyes open to see a black SUV parked in the driveway.

"Stirling?" she whispered urgently.

"Hmmmm?" He was nuzzling her neck still and couldn't believe that she had let him for so long.

"Who is that?"

"Who is what?" He sounded drugged.

"Stirling, focus." She shrugged him off her. "Who is *that*?" She pointed out the window.

He looked and saw a girl getting out of the vehicle. She was one of Gaelon's. A Scavenger. Scavengers were nasty little creatures. They had gangrenous bites and poisonous claws. Once they killed a victim, they'd let them partially decompose before eating them.

Stirling laughed. One Scavenger was nothing against two Lilin.

"What are you laughing about?" Lila asked.

"Gaelon sent one Scavenger ..." He watched as two more characters he recognized exited the vehicle.

"And two others," she finished.

"An Assassin and a Consumer."

"A what and a *what*?" She turned to Stirling, who had morphed into the demonic form of Incubus she and Jenny had researched on the Web. His clothes were shredded, and he shrugged what was left of them off his massive new body.

"*What the ...*?" she breathed.

"Change, Lila. Now," Stirling demanded, spreading his expansive, tattered wings.

"What are you talking about, *change*?" Her voice cracked.

She was so astonished by his transformation. His eyes were glowing and beautiful, but the rest of him was terrifying. His nose had flattened out, and his nostrils flared. His brow was bony and greatly pronounced. She ran a hand down his forearm because he was now too tall for her to reach his face. He had a leathery feel, and over his skin were what looked like plates of armor, covering most of his muscle. Her eyes slowly travelled away from his body and up to the ceiling, where his impressive curling horns scraped.

"Lila, change!" he commanded again.

She scrutinized his face again, almost cross-eyed. *God, his teeth are sharp.*

"Lila!"

She snapped out of her trance. "I don't... I don't know how to," she stammered.

Again, she regretted leaving home so soon. There was so little she knew about her world. About herself.

"Stay here," Stirling demanded and pushed her back into the corner of the wall. He stomped out of the bedroom, turning sideways and ducking through the doorway, which he had broken out last night.

As Stirling made his way down the stairs, the Consumer hissed, "Stirling, the girl was supposed to be delivered yesterday. What is going on?"

He was wearing a white T-shirt and jeans over scaly yellow skin, black gloves on his hands.

"Things have changed a bit, Markus. I'll take her in when I'm ready."

Stirling came closer to the Consumer, who blinked his reptilian eyes and tilted his head to the side, not understanding Stirling's words.

The Assassin was oil-black and featureless. He stood motionless behind Markus, and the Scavenger was on all fours beside him, wagging her long green tail to and fro.

Stirling sized each of them up. Markus couldn't consume and use any of Stirling's power against him, unless he wanted a raging hard-on and an internal inferno of horniness ripping through him, so he wasn't a primary concern. He was the messenger. He was always the messenger, and Stirling had liked Markus up until now.

Getting around the Scavenger would be difficult, because she was quick and venomous. Lastly, dealing with the Assassin would be the worst feat. The black mass was silent and lethal. He moved like the shadows and when paired with weapons, was a force no one wanted to reckon with.

"Markus, get out of here. Go tell Gaelon to prepare for his funeral," Stirling warned, his eyes steely.

"I was hoping you would be more compliant. You were one of my favorites, Stirling. We will force her to come to us."

"Well, you've taken away her family. Not much is left for you to use as leverage."

"We'll find her weak spot. Everyone, and I mean everyone, has a fragile and breakable point." Markus signaled to the other two demons. "Guys, take him out, and look for the girl." He transformed back into human form and strolled out the door.

Change. Change. How do I change? Lila thought hard about anything her parents might have told her about her demonic form, but damn them; they had effectively sheltered her from her real life.

She heard things breaking downstairs and panicked. Leaving the false comfort of the corner, she ran over to her vanity mirror and looked at herself hard. She tried to clear her mind and concentrated on changing. *Changing into what?* Then she remembered her pendant. Lilith was a sleek black creature, with green eyes, wings, a long spade tail, and talons. She had perked-up ears, like a cat's.

Lila rubbed the pendant and closed her eyes, envisioning herself becoming Lilith. She blocked out the noises from downstairs and shut away her thoughts. She quickly became a Zen master.

After a few moments, she opened her eyes, and then her mouth, at the sight of herself in the mirror. She was exquisite. Her skin was formed of silken scales like a cobra's but pitch-black. Her ears were perky and cute, and she wiggled them back and forth. Smiling in wonder, she noticed her incisors were sharper and longer than when in her human form. She touched her mirror and saw her talons: long, razor-sharp claws on slim hands. Her whole body looked dainty and lethal all at once.

She explored each facet of her new skin. Turning side to side, she admired the claw-tipped wings that gracefully branched out from behind her shoulders. Her tail touched the ground, and she flicked it back and forth.

Still grinning like a child, she decided it was time to shred off what remained of her beloved jumpsuit, and help Stirling kick some demon ass.

One last glance in the mirror at her new exotic body gave her the courage and invigoration she needed to find her confidence. *Awesome!* She smiled again and then tore down the stairs to help Stirling battle the baddies.

Once Lila reached the landing, she saw Stirling struggling with a little green creature clad in what looked like a Hannah Montana T-shirt. A little girl. The thing was clawing at his arm, spilling blood all over the hardwoods.

In the near distance, a lean black demon hovered, clad in a partially unbuttoned white dress shirt and black blazer. His featureless ebony face gave away nothing, of course. He was just standing there. Waiting.

Quite suave taste for a demon, Lila thought. He seemed to sense her presence because he lifted his head and faced her. Creepy vibes exuded from him, nearly causing her to shiver.

Ignoring the demon, she skirted behind Stirling and the green thing that had its claws in his arm, just as he rammed it in the head with his horns. The Scavenger screeched an awful high-pitched cry, and Lila jumped back as it fell to the floor. It morphed into a little red-haired girl. Stirling stalked over to her and snapped her neck, which created a horrible sound; nothing like in the movies.

Lila gasped and looked at him in horror, as a throwing knife planted itself into the unprotected skin between his shoulder and chest. He grunted and tore the knife from his body.

Lila wheeled around and saw the Assassin moving in on them both. The oily-faced demon pulled two more silver knives from holsters strapped around his waist. He hurled one knife at her and it grazed her face as she turned her head quickly. The other knife hit Stirling in the neck.

Lila glanced at him. His expression screamed murder. He barged forward with his head down and rammed the trendy black mass in the stomach with unstoppable force.

The Assassin was lifted into the air and may have been stunned, but before Lila could properly make an assessment, the asshole stabbed Stirling in the back with yet another blade.

Stirling roared and planted his armored knee in the Assassin's stomach. The thing hit the floor with a bone-shattering thud.

Lila's fear almost exited her mouth in an unpleasant manner. She ran up behind Stirling, feeling completely useless, and pulled the blade out of his back.

He let his guard down and turned to her, assuring she was okay. When he did, the Assassin rose and stabbed him in the neck three more times, aiming for the jugular, then kicked him in the back, sending him to the floor.

It took severe strength to drop a monster as large and brutal as Stirling, but the wounds in his neck proved baleful. He pressed against the lacerations with a hand, attempting to staunch the blood flow. If he didn't heal soon, he was going to bleed out. *Shit, I should have taken a mate,* he thought.

Even though Lila was terrified, she rushed forward and power-kicked the Assassin in the jaw. He paused a moment, then threw a series of punches at her. She dodged a couple and landed a few herself. She was faster than Stirling because she was smaller, and the Assassin struggled to keep up with her.

They tussled around and around the room until she bumped into a wall. The black demon had her cornered and grasped her around the throat with a cloudy dark hand. He tilted his head and probably would have smiled had he had any facial features.

As Lila lost her breath, she clawed at the Assassin with her talons, spilling what looked like black sludge, but he stood there and took it. She brought her tail up and curled it around the thing's throat, tightening her grip as firmly as she could, strangling him like an anaconda. But he had about a minute more constriction time on her.

What felt like an eternity passed, and just as she thought she was about to lose consciousness, she was released and slid down the wall, collapsing on the floor.

"Lila, Lila." Stirling shook her.

Slowly, she opened her eyes, and as her vision came back, she saw a human-looking Stirling kneeling in front of her. He was caressing her face. She looked down at herself, in human form again too.

"What happened?" she asked, rubbing her neck and wincing.

"That Assassin almost killed you is what happened. Had you not been strangling him; he probably would've sensed me coming up behind him. They're weird like that. They sense everything, and they're freakishly strong."

"Yeah, I noticed," she quipped as Stirling helped her up.

To her side, she noticed the Assassin's body. Then she spied his head across the room. His human body had been of Asian descent.

Looking around her parents' house, Lila noted the numerous broken windows and picture frames. Candles were scattered around the floor and blood was splattered everywhere. She'd have to clean the hell out of the house before she put it on the market or lived in it again, whichever she decided later. God, her parents were dead. She didn't want to think about what to do with their home yet.

"Listen, get your stuff, and let's get the hell out of here," Stirling said urgently grasping her arm.

She was still a little unsteady and unbelieving. How many demons lived like this? No wonder her parents had sheltered her. She was beginning to understand them more and more, and regret crept slowly down her spine. She ran to the hall bathroom and threw up in the toilet.

Stirling stood outside the doorway. "Lila, honey? I know this has been a lot for you to handle, but don't lose it on me now. We'll be at my Oma's place in twelve short hours. It's ten already. We have to hit the road."

"Gimme a minute. I have to shower and get dressed. Demon fluids are all over me, and I need to brush my teeth again now."

Emerging from the bathroom, she stepped over the Hannah Montana Girl's body, and slowly walked up the stairs, gripping the railing for dear life.

Stirling giggled, watching her. She was a little squeamish, which he found cute, but she was also a soldier, and he admired her for it. When he was six in Lilin years. At that age, he'd had the support of his entire family and hadn't endured anything like what she was going through now.

After a ten-minute shower together, due to the sticky grime that adorned them, Lila quickly dressed herself, then noticed Stirling was still in the bathroom. He stood there, naked, and shrugged as he looked around him. His clothing lay in pieces on the floor.

"Get my bag for me?" he asked, stifling a chuckle.

Chapter 14

After Stirling donned another pair of jeans and a black shirt, Lila grabbed her duffle. She packed a green shirt, because he had said he liked the color on her. She also packed another pair of jeans she knew she'd still fit into. She hadn't gained or lost weight since her curse activated.

"Well, let's go," Stirling said, motioning toward her broken door.

Lila rubbed her forehead, sighed, and started for the stairs.

"Stirling? What the hell are we supposed to do with the bodies? It looks like a really gross crime scene in here. I mean, don't demons go up in flames or something once they die?" she asked, only half-kidding.

"No, we don't burst into flames. Think about it. Let's say we were in public and got in a bar fight. If one of us died and exploded, don't you think some humans would be asking a few questions?"

"Okay. Then how do you fix... *this*?" she asked, pointing at the Hannah Montana Girl, who's spine was poking out through the side of her throat.

"Oh, God," Lila said and ran into the hall bathroom again.

"Lila?"

"False alarm. I'm okay. Just get rid of them," she called.

"I need your phone book. I gotta call the local Cleaners."

She came out of the bathroom at looked at Stirling incredulously. "What?"

"The Cleaners. They take care of this kind of thing," he said, gesturing to the gore on the walls and floor.

"Wow." She shook her head and laughed. It began as a small, unbelieving laugh and then turned in to an uproar. As she held her ribcage, she pulled the old phonebook off the top of the refrigerator and tossed it at his chest.

"What's so funny?" he asked, staring at her, trying to decide if she was mentally stable.

She wiped a rogue tear from her eye and pinched the bridge of her nose but couldn't stop laughing. "You're fucking with me, right?"

"*Okay*... I'm just gonna make this call, and you go get in the car," he directed, putting his phone to his ear.

She squeezed her cheeks together with a hand, giggles coming out anyway, and winked at him before stumbling out the door.

By the time Stirling got into the car, Lila had quit cackling. None of it was funny; her mind had just refused to cope any other way at the time. She looked at Stirling, waiting for him to say something about what had just happened. He just looked back at her before sliding on his shades.

"Okay. We need to talk."

"About what, sweetheart?" he asked as he put the car in reverse.

"About what? About everything. Um, we can change forms?"

"Yeah. By the way, you look really hot in your demon skin."

"Yeah, but I didn't know we could change. My parents never told me anything. Why didn't my parents turn when you abducted them?"

"Like I said, I hit your mom in the neck with a dart, and I got to your father before he knew what was happening." Stirling's voice was low and regretful.

Lila slid back in her seat. She closed her eyes and breathed deeply.

"That little girl," she nearly whispered.

"What little girl?"

"The little vicious creature that attacked you. You didn't even pause before you broke her neck."

"Oh. You mean the bitch Scavenger that did this to my arm?" Stirling held up his forearm, and Lila grabbed it in horror. It hadn't looked like that twenty minutes before in the shower.

"Why haven't you healed? This looks awful! It's getting worse, Stirling!"

"It will take longer to heal than other wounds because those tiny bastards are poisonous. Their bites are contaminated with gangrene, and their claws are filled with toxins. She got me both ways."

Lila knew he should have recovered by now, no matter how skanky the bite was.

"When was the last time you took a mate, Stirling?" she asked, dreading his response.

"I need to take one soon," he answered, staring too hard at the road. He clearly didn't want to discuss the topic.

"As soon as we stop, as much as it will pain me, please take the first woman you see."

He was silent and obviously wasn't going to say anything to her about taking another woman, so she sure as hell wasn't going to push it.

He didn't speak for the next half hour. The silence was uncomfortable to Lila. She didn't know what he was thinking or feeling. She looked at him and went to say something, but just brushed his scruffy cheek with the back of her fingers. He took a hand off the steering wheel and placed it on her leg.

"Lila ... wake up." Stirling flopped a hand onto Lila's shoulder.

"Yeah, yeah. I'm up." She rubbed her eyes and focused them on the car clock. It was four in the morning. "We have six more hours in front of us, Stirling. Do you need me to drive?" she asked, sitting up in her seat.

He didn't answer her. He was slumped against the car door, breaths heavy and choppy.

Lila scanned her surroundings, unnerved. They were parked in a motel lot. Again.

"Stirling? Stirling. Oh my God, are you okay?"

Hastily, she unlatched her seatbelt and leaned across the center console. She grabbed his face and pulled him close to her. His eyes were opening and closing involuntarily. Completely frenzied, she scurried out of the car and ran around to Stirling's side. When she opened his door, he fell out onto the pavement. She looked around for anyone who might be watching, but the lot was empty with the exception of four cars.

"Stirling, get up." She tugged on his arm and pieces of rotten flesh came off in her grasp. She shrieked and stumbled backward. "Holy shit!" she cried. He was dying.

She was daunted but had to do something. She sat him up against the car, and his head fell to the side.

"Stirling," she whispered.

He didn't say anything. As she went to stand and figure out something useful to do, he reached out for her arm weakly.

"Get a room. Get me inside," he managed to say.

"Okay. Okay." She nodded quickly and ran to the office as fast as demonly possible.

She threw open the door and huffed, "I need a room. Any room on the bottom level."

The hideous, long-haired clerk just stood there gawking at her.

"Well?" Lila urged.

"Uh, sure," he said as if waking from a trance. "Okay, ma'am. Just fill out this paper, sign the bottom line, let me see your ID, and then I'll hand over the key. Ha, ha, that rhymed, didn't it?" The repugnant man laughed and scratched the side of his face with long, dirty fingernails.

Lila scrunched her nose in irritation and disgust. What was this? Bates Motel? It was sure creepy enough to be.

She filled out the papers as quickly as she could and dug her ID out of her pocket. The clerk took his sweet time making a copy of it and scribbled a couple of notes on her paper. She tapped her foot against the ground rapidly. She was about to snap the gross man's neck and take the key from him just as he dangled it in front of her.

She would have hypnotized him if she were thinking straight. As she cursed her stupidity, she snatched the key from the clerk rudely, and forced the door open.

She ran back out to the parking lot and dropped to her knees in front of Stirling. His car keys were lying on the pavement and she scooped them up.

"Stirling. Please. Please help me get you inside. It's just a few feet from here."

She was trying to be strong; but deep down, she knew if she lost him, she may never find her way out of this mess. She may never find her way at all.

With a lot of effort, she threw one of his arms over her shoulders and used all her strength to help him stand. He managed to get off the ground but still used her to crutch most of his weight. He must have weighed two hundred and twenty-five pounds, easy.

They hobbled together to the room, and Lila slid the key into the door lock. Once she got it open, she took four big strides and dropped Stirling onto the bed. Next, she hoisted his tree-trunk legs onto the mattress and came around the other side of the bed, sitting on her heels next to him.

"Stirling tell me what to do," she begged, flustered.

His arm was oozing pus and bleeding everywhere. Just as she went to get off the bed for a wet cloth, he managed to speak.

"I need a mate," he rasped. His eyes were closed, and he rolled his head from side to side on the pillow, attempting to refuse acknowledging his pain.

"Okay. Then I'll go find you one. But I need to go now. I don't even know where to look, though. It's too late for anyone to be out. Maybe a Waffle House? Did we pass one on the way here? How do I get a woman to follow me here? Shit! I could kidnap one," she blabbed on and went to get off the bed again, but he grabbed her by her leather jacket.

"Forget it. There is no … time, and who would take me like this? I couldn't even… will a woman at this point. I am too weak. The poison's spread… too deep." It seemed he had expended all his energy by just speaking. His voice sounded chafed.

"Well, I can't just let you die here. What do I do? I need you!" Lila wailed frantically.

"You can run. My Oma's place … is mapped out on my GPS. She will protect you. Did, did you get the keys to my car?"

"Yes, but ... I can't leave you."

"You have to. Go."

Lila couldn't have imagined Stirling could ever be weak. He had been the epitome of strength when she first met him, and now he lay dying next to her, and it was up to her to either save him or watch him slip away.

"I will take you," she said decisively.

"You will have me?" he asked, opening his eyes as wide as he could.

"Yes. I want you—but Gaelon; if he kills me, you'll die too. He'll have twice the opportunity to take us down."

"I don't care, Lila. I'll die bonded to you rather than live centuries without your soul as a piece of mine. There is no one for me except you. If I'd lost you unbound to me, I'd starve myself of life forces and burn until I died," he said as he touched her cheek with a shaky hand.

He struggled, but used his elbows to push himself into a sitting position against the headboard. "Come to me, Lila. Please."

Her heart liquefied. She forgot all about the danger they were swimming through aimlessly. Seeing him in this condition almost destroyed her. She realized then that she wanted nothing more than to spend the rest of her insanely long life with him. Between them blossomed an undeniable passion; not lust. Love. Even during their first struggle, she had thought fleetingly that he could be the one. He was everything and more than she could ever want physically in a man, and although he was a total Incubus, he had a genial side. A side he only revealed to her.

Gently, she removed his shoes and socks, then unbuttoned and unzipped his jeans. He grunted as he lifted his rear so she could pull them off his legs. She straddled him and wrapped her arms around his back, pulling him into her. Even though the situation was dire, a calmness swept over her as she touched him.

She slowly lifted his shirt and brought it over his head. He winced when the fabric scraped against his wound.

"I'm sorry," Lila said and cringed.

"Don't be."

Stirling watched her intently even though his lids were still heavy. Her eyes glued to his as she undressed. She tossed his shirt to the ground and shrugged off her jacket. Her shirt went next. Then she broke their gaze and dipped down, brushing her breasts along his chest and thighs, on her way to remove his briefs.

There was a static between them that rose the fine hairs on her body. She stood and shed her pants, socks and shoes, meeting his eyes again. His stare was enervated, but still fiery enough to melt her to the ground.

She crawled between his legs and took his beautiful penis into her mouth. He quietly moaned, but she hoped she was doing enough to arouse him. She opened her throat, coaxing him to go deeper. And he did, filling her airway, just to pull back enough to allow her a shallow breath again.

She felt his hand stroke her hair. That was a good sign. He wasn't too far gone to enjoy this.

Gradually, he grew inside her mouth as she sucked him harder and cupped his testicles, which were more than a handful, even taut. Slowly she milked him using her lips and tongue to apply pressure to the main vein in his shaft as she sucked him from base to tip. Then she played along the rim of his velvety head which was crimson with eagerness. His slit wept silky sweet semen and she took it down greedily.

"Lila," he whispered roughly.

"Mmm hmm?" She was still at work, wowing him with her tongue tricks.

"I want you. Now," he said more loudly.

She looked up at him, her mouth still locked around his cock. He continued stroking her hair so soothingly.

She sucked him one last time and he exhaled loudly when her warm mouth left him. He was the desert, and she was water. The drink of life that he physically needed now. He reached for her, his hand still trembling, reminding Lila that he was close to death.

She took his hand and he guided her onto him, sliding his amazing rock-hard erection inside her. The moment he entered her, she felt she may be too small for him. But he was gentle even in his state and allowed her to slowly lower herself inch by inch onto him. She pulled up and eased back down until she adjusted to his width.

Stirling listened to Lila's breathing. She held her breath each time she dropped her hips and released it when she brought them back up. His ego swelled along with his member when he realized he was the biggest she'd ever had. Her need to take him gradually turned him on in a way that it never had with other women, and he wasn't nearly as patient with other women, either. But Lila was definitely not other women.

Once he was fully buried inside her, she expelled all the air in her lungs and almost went slack with pleasure. He filled her perfectly as if he was made for her. Her lush walls molded to every ridge, curve and vein in his shaft. His head prodded her center with just the right pressure. The feeling of him triggered electric chills across her heated body, causing her to shiver.

She planted her hands on his chest, and lightly clawed at him as she glided up and down on his cock. Her eyes closed in contentment.

There was no internal inferno. No mind-fuck about Doug or Peter. No meaningless talk about nothing in particular. There was only her and Stirling. Peaceful and perfect. She moaned deep in her throat as she bucked her hips, grinding her swollen clit against his pelvis. She tried to suppress her moans, not wanting to be the noisy motel neighbor, but found that she only wanted to cry out louder.

Stirling took her by her sides and brought her into him, wanting her closer, needing her against his chest. She settled onto him and bit his neck, catching a thick cord of muscle between her teeth. He loosed a harsh breath in response.

"Did I hurt you?" she whispered into his ear.

He grasped a fistful of the back of her hair, guiding her head away from his neck, forcing her to look at him. Their eyes met, and the adoration between them swelled and exploded. Lila's eyes spilled tears which glided down her cheeks and into the hollow of her neck. There, they pooled and slid down her breasts. Stirling lapped them up with his tongue, from her nipples, which he took time to suckle, to her collarbone.

"Oh, Stirling," she cried, and leaned into him again. He kissed her tenderly but possessively. He tasted her tears, her fear and her strength, and he knew in that moment that he loved her, more than he thought he had already.

"Lila, I love you," he confessed against her mouth, then kissed her bottom lip longingly. He closed his eyes, praying to Hades that she loved him back.

Lila continued to clap her hips against his, but she fell apart at the seams. As she rode him for his life, she kissed his chest and his neck and the soft lobe of his ear. Then she took his mouth before she whispered, "I love you, too."

No way could she lose him after all they'd been through, after all they still had to endure. She held his face in her hands.

"Baby, I need you to come. I need you to stay with me," she begged between ragged breaths.

"I'll always be with you. Now, and forever," he swore as he splashed his seed deep inside her. His phallus pulsated violently as she ground out a few more slow, sensual thrusts against him. When his semen hit her core, she came apart, releasing his face, and death-gripping his shoulders. He held her through the intensity, and when the wailing, clawing and biting ceased, she gazed at him lovingly. As she slumped against his chest, contentment inundated him and he laid his head back against the headboard, eyes closed.

"Stirling?" Lila reached for his injured arm. The red swelling had gone down, and the pus-filled bites were sealing.

"Thank God." She put her forehead to his.

"What had you so worried?" Stirling laughed. But it wasn't his usual hearty laugh. It was inhibited and subdued. He was still sick but quickly recovering.

"Are you going to be okay?" she asked as she dried her tearing eyes. "I thought I had lost you."

"You can't be rid of me that easily, Lila. And I will be okay after I ravage you properly," he promised with a primal look in his eyes.

He drew in a few deep breaths, summoning strength, then lowered her onto her back. He glanced at his arm again. *Healed. Good.*

"Thank you, *meine Flamme*," he said, running a hand between Lila's breasts down to her dewy tuft.

"What are you calling me?" she asked, smiling like a child.

"*My flame*". It's German. You are the flame in my heart, the flame that has spared me a lifetime of burning."

"You said you loved me," she said softly.

"And you said the same."

He moved on top of her, pinning her down with his stare. "I do love you, Lila. I am yours now. And if you aren't convinced, I'll have to prove it to you with conviction this time."

"I don't know, Stirling. Maybe I do need a little persuasion." She smirked, comfortable beneath him.

He dipped his tongue into her sweet mouth. His kisses were faultless, but he soon left her lips, leaving her breathless. His mouth continued devouring her, down her neck and collarbone, to her left breast.

"Look my love," he whispered in astonishment.

Lila lifted her head. Where Stirling stopped kissing her, a blue tattoo covered most of her left breast, over her heart, and spread out across her shoulder. She sat up a bit for a clearer view. The brand was beautifully ornate. It delicately curled and twisted into gorgeous knots and ties and hitches. She looked to Stirling and gasped.

"*Wow*. Is this our bond?" She fingered the tattoo lightly.

"Yes, Lila. See." He took her hand and placed it over his heart, where an identical tattoo adorned his chest.

"We are one. A perfect match," he said. "Soulmates. I thought it was impossible."

"Soulmates," she repeated in wonder.

He continued kissing her breast, as she slid back down beneath him, eyes wide. *Soulmates.* She was dazed by the development.

Stirling fondled Lila's nipples with his skilled tongue. He trailed his hand down to her pelvis then grasped her thigh firmly, forcing her to focus on what he was doing to her. She spread her legs for him, and he roamed between them with his fingers, feeling every crevice, noting every response his touch elicited.

She grasped the sheets with both hands and arched her body against his.

"Stirling. I need you inside me," she begged.

He kissed her chest, down to her tight stomach, stopping just short of her manicured curls. Then he buried his face in between her thighs and slid his hot tongue into her slit, relishing the taste of her sweet nectar.

"Oh!" she yelped.

He lapped at her, teased her, rolling his tongue around her clit. He slipped two fingers inside her and sucked her bud into his mouth at the same time. In response, she thrashed her head from side to side wildly and squeezed her legs together.

"Now, Stirling! I need you now!"

"Anything for you, love." He sucked her into his mouth one last time, and she came hard against his face, writhing on the bed uncontrollably.

As she trembled with delight, he rose on his knees, sitting on his heels. Paralyzed by the explosion, she clamped her thighs tightly together while her clit spasmed. But he soon drove her legs apart forcefully. He took in the sight of her flower as he spread her labia open with his fingers. Slowly, he entered her.

"Oh, Stirling!" she cried out.

"Yes, *meine Flamme.*"

Lila's body was responding for the first time out of affection and love and not for survival. No more would she burn. No more would she worry about some poor schmuck dying on her behalf.

As Stirling moved precisely inside her, their tattoos shimmered and glowed, creating a blue halo between them. She wanted to cry out every time his hard, perfect flesh stroked her walls. They were making love. It was a first for each of them.

After a long while of soothing sensual entanglement, he pulled out of her, leaving her desperate. With a grin, he picked her up as if she were a feather and set her on his lap. Once he entered her again, she went limp and fell back. He braced her with a strong arm, admiring the way her breasts swelled with each labored breath. He slowly rocked against her, brushing her hair off her shoulders, kissing her sweetly between her breasts.

"Are you cold?" he asked. Her body was blanketed with goosebumps.

"No. You're doing this to me. You feel magical."

"This is magic, Lila. You and me together."

He pulled her hips into his securely, grasped her tightly around the waist and crawled off the bed with her. When he stood, she wrapped her legs around him with an iron-clad grip. He pumped his pelvis against her, palming her ass hard enough to cause a sting, but she enjoyed the pain as he stroked inside her at just the right angle.

"Stirling, I'm coming, baby!" *Again!*

"Come, lover. Come all over me." He drove into her over and over in calculated, firm thrusts until she erupted.

Enthralled by her pleasure and how gorgeous she looked when she came, he released inside her. After he attained a sense of poise, he tossed her onto the bed.

Lila watched as their juices trickled from his beautiful sopping penis. It was still fully raging, blushed, veins bulging. She was horny all over again. She propped up on her elbows and backed toward the headboard, smirking at him, taunting.

"I'm not done with you yet," Stirling promised.

The muscles in his chest and arms flexed as he grabbed her by an ankle. He dragged her to the edge of the bed as she giggled.

"On your knees," he demanded, his smile half-cocked.

She obeyed and backed her ass into him. He pulled her to his thighs and gripped the back of her neck, rendering her immobile like a predator would do with its prey.

"Change, Lila," he commanded, not to be denied.

Wow, this was going to be something. She had to concentrate hard for a moment then watched as her body transformed into the silken black creature she became at her parent's house. She was phenomenal and she peered behind her, smiling at Stirling, who was standing there gloriously.

His horns were magnificent, and his ebony-skinned body was indescribably stunning. His wings spread out wide like he was waiting to descend on her.

"You're breathtaking, my love," he said, rubbing a hand along her spine.

She flicked her tail along his shoulder and up to his cheek.

He chuckled huskily and reached beneath her, rubbing her clit with perfect accuracy. One of his claws poked her in the stomach, stinging her and tickling her simultaneously. Not a minute passed, and she arched her back like a cat, orgasming again. Her fluids shot against Stirling's pelvis, drenching his cock. Her chest and head fell into the pillows on the bed. Her wings deflated and rested on either side of her shoulders.

He brought her hips back and bent down to admire her glistening pussy. As he opened her up with his fingers, she wiggled her ass from side to side, waiting for him to inject her again.

He rubbed her, tasted her, and then buried himself inside her, pounding into her without restraint.

"You're so wet, so warm, so right," he purred with undertones of primal need.

She tried to speak back but couldn't. He felt too amazing for her to muster anything but a shout or howl. As his hips clapped against her, the headboard slammed the wall repeatedly. She wrapped her tail around his bulging bicep, and he pulled back on it, using the leverage to delve deeper. She was gulping air by this point and thought she may pass out. It was the most physical sex of her life. The rawest thing she'd ever lived through.

He spanked her hard, and she whimpered in response. He filled her with his sperm again, and as he pulled out of her, the warm semen slid down her leg, tingling against her.

Before she could catch her breath, he jumped onto the bed and rolled her on her side. He crouched on his heels at her feet. As he hiked her top leg over his shoulder, she slid her other leg between his knees. Bringing her close, he glided back inside her, caressing her silken tattooed breast. She tongued her fangs and settled her head on a pillow.

He moved a strong warm, clawed hand over her thin waist, down to her belly button, onto to her hip. Looking at her, he almost wept at her beauty. He couldn't believe he had been so harsh to her. So cruel. Then his thoughts evaporated, and welcome sexual consumption invaded.

With every ounce of his power and adoration, he dove into her. Her cries and pleas ramped his tension, but he wasn't ready to blow again. Buried deep inside her, he froze, closed his eyes, and basked in her wet warmth.

Lila picked up her head and looked back at him. "Honey, are you okay?" she asked, voice sex-saturated.

"There are no words to explain just how okay I am," he sighed.

"Well then, get back to work," she nagged, and plopped her head back down.

Holy Hell, she was immaculate. "Yes, ma'am."

He obeyed his Succubus, making love to her so voraciously, yet so passionately. She clawed at his chiseled abs, slicing into him with sharp talons. The sexual assault made his balls so taught, he thought he'd bust right then. Forcing the urge away, he continued gyrating against her.

"Yes," he groaned, pumping into her harder. "Do you like the way I feel inside you?" he asked, staring right through her.

"Yes, baby. Yes. I love how you feel." He hit her spot. "Right there. Right there," she directed.

Without realizing it, she was shredding the sheets with her talons. Stirling rotated his hips, forcing her over the edge again. As she screamed, he grasped her ankle, and pulled out of her.

Liquid Heaven flowed from her entrance, soaking her thighs and the sheets. She whined at his absence, so he entered her again. Teasing her, he withdrew slowly, and she screamed into the pillow, flicking her tail in warning. Enjoying her torment, he re-entered her and pulled out again. She wrapped her tail around his throat, tightening her grip. She was done playing this game.

"Okay, okay," Stirling laughed.

He took her like a wild beast, grinding against her, pounding her core. When her body tightened and the lustful shouts became whimpers, Stirling set his suppression free. They both orgasmed in unison, whisking them to a place they'd never been before. A place beyond the earthly realm.

He brought her leg down off his shoulder and situated himself atop her without withdrawing himself from her warm canal.

After shifting back into human form, he kissed her, massaging her tongue and nipping her bottom lip. He was as skilled with his mouth as he was with his manhood. His incredible manhood. Lila never imagined sex could be so extraordinary.

She transformed too and tossed her head from side to side while stretching her body. "I feel amazing!" she hooted.

Stirling laughed they rolled together in the bleach-scented sheets. She ended up on top of him and kissed him longingly. They had to be careful not to conjure up any more sexual energy or they would never get to sleep.

She left his lips. "I'm gonna hop in the shower, honey."

As she attempted to crawl off him, his arms flexed against her, forcing her back to his chest.

His eyes teared a bit as she looked at him. She reached out for his face, but he took her hand and placed it over his heart. It was racing under her touch.

"I do love you, Lila. The moment I saw you in that photo, I wanted you so badly it nearly drove me mad."

"I love you too, Stirling. The moment I chained you to my bed, I knew it," she giggled.

He smirked then held her around the waist burying his head in her breasts. For the first time, he was emotionally exposed. She stroked his shoulders lightly as he silently cried.

Chapter 15

Stirling stirred around nine. The sex he and Lila had and all the emotions he had released resulted in a hangover of sorts. He was exhausted and sore in muscles he never even knew he had. Marathon sex was new to him. He kissed Lila's cheek, then her neck and trailed a finger along her side. She shivered and rolled over, smiling, looking at him while he gazed at her as if he were in a dream.

"You're so beautiful, Lila."

"So are you." She hugged his neck and kissed him.

He caressed her back, and she closed her eyes at the feeling of his strong warm hands on her body. She ran her fingers through his messy hair, inching closer and closer to him, until his morning erection poked in between her legs. She dipped a hand under the sheets and grasped him firmly.

He groaned, then pecked her on the forehead, hopped out of the bed quickly and stood at the foot of it.

"We have to get out of here. As much as I want to make love to you right now, we don't have the time," he said.

"Not even a quickie?" she asked innocently and dragged the sheet off her breasts. She held her ankle and stretched her leg up to her shoulder, exposing him to an irresistible sight. She was spread out before him like an all-you-can-eat-buffet.

He shut his eyes and dropped his head back. "Ahhh," he sighed. "That's not fair."

"I know." She shrugged, and he jumped back in the bed behind her.

He took her raised leg in his hand and penetrated between her warm, splendid lips. She clutched his forearm and squeaked. Morning sex was amazing.

"You feel so good, love," he whispered in her ear.

"Oh, Stirling, so do you," she panted as he sailed in and out of her slowly and tenderly.

He dropped her leg, and she forced her backside into him, urging him to go deeper. He reached around her front and rubbed her pearl, which quickly made her climax and quiver. He came right after and held her close until the pulsating subsided.

She exhaled loudly as he pulled out of her. "You are so damned good at that," she said, brushing her hair back.

"Only with you."

Stirling got up and searched in his bag for fresh clothes. Lila watched his abs flex as he pulled on a grey long-sleeved shirt that hugged his Herculean body. He winked at her, then disappeared into the bathroom to take his long mandatory morning pee.

After he emerged, she reluctantly rolled out of the bed and proceeded to prepare for the remaining six-hour drive that would make her butt fall asleep. She swept her hair back into a ponytail and dressed in a red tank, which revealed some of her new tattoo. She adored the way it looked and found it hard to turn away from the mirror. She threw on her jeans and pulled a comfy grey sweater over tank, snagging it on her damned necklace.

"Honey, take this off me, please," she requested.

"What, that?" He pointed to the black jeweled demonic jewelry.

"It's magical. My mother gave it to me to remind me of my power. The only one who can remove it is my lifemate."

"You've worn that for six years?" he asked, moving behind her.

"Yes. It's like a huge weight now."

He undid the clasp, took the necklace off, and dropped it into her hand.

"Ahhh, thank you!" she sighed and rubbed her neck.

She looked at the necklace one last time before she buried it into a pocket in her duffle.

"You ready?" Stirling asked grabbing his bag.

"That's a loaded question," Lila responded with a roll of her eyes.

The two headed out into the chilly October air. It was an overcast day, and the atmosphere was ominous, almost like a warning of things to come.

Stirling pulled their car up to the office. As he went in to pay for the room, Lila squealed inside. She never imagined she would ever be with a man as perfect as Stirling, never saw herself with anyone, for that matter. Thinking she would be alone for the duration of her long life had depressed her for years, and she had forgotten what being happy felt like. It was indescribable.

As Stirling walked back to the car, Lila admired his…everything. His face was strong, and his sunglasses made him look arcane. His chiseled muscles threatened to rip through his shirt. He walked with the confidence of a god, and the smile he gave her now was bright enough to blind angels.

When he hopped back into the car, he pecked her on the cheek. Butterflies fluttered around wildly in her stomach but settled when she remembered that they were on a mission. A mission that may be deadly.

"Can we talk about something? I mean, anything? So, I don't think about what might happen to us?" she requested.

"What would you like to talk about, sweetheart?" he asked, pulling out of the motel lot.

"Well, I don't even know your last name."

"Fischer," he answered.

"My last name is Johnson."

"Where are you from, Stirling Fischer?"

"Germany. You?"

"I'm from here. Boring as hell." She waved her hand. "Tell me about Germany and how you ended up in America."

"My family and I left after World War II. Things were horrible for a stretch, and we just wanted out. America seemed like a logical choice. A safe choice. My mother had always dreamed of migrating to America because of how free it was, but it took the war to convince my father to budge and finally settle here. He was really set in his ways."

"Incubi," Lila said under her breath.

"Yeah, yeah." He squeezed her knee, tickling her.

"My mother casted a wide web to find others like us but only located a few Incubi. She made quite a few friends in Ouachita Parish, though. She loved it there. Loved the magic, the voodoo, the culture, and the food, of course. So that's where we settled. Even my grandparents took to Louisiana. We fit in pretty well there. Just seems like the right place for demons."

"So, why'd you leave?"

"Well, I travelled around a lot for kicks and met a demon who introduced me to Gaelon. Gaelon offered me a haven; a place that hundreds of other demons called home. I felt comfortable there, but gradually, I gave into my dark side. It was so easy to do under the influence of other demons. Now I regret all my reckless decisions. Look at the danger my choices have put you in." Stirling's knuckles turned white on the steering wheel.

"Stirling, you didn't know you'd end up in this situation and you should be glad you are. If you hadn't hunted me, another demon would have, and I'd be dead right now. And we wouldn't have bonded."

"You're right. I'm sorry. I didn't mean to undermine our bond. And I swear to you, Lila; you will not die." He looked her in the eyes with conviction.

She cupped a hand against his cheek. "Let's talk about something else, baby. You're getting upset," she said gently. "Tell me about your … Oma, right?"

He took a deep breath and relaxed his hands on the wheel a bit. "Yes. Oma. Well, she is eccentric, to say the least."

"How do you mean?"

"She's crazy."

"Crazy, crazy?" Lila asked timidly.

"Basically, but I think it's because she knows things. She consorts with witches, voodoo priestesses, and Straddlers."

"What are Straddlers?"

"They are the eyes and the ears of the afterlife. Ghosts and such. They aren't in Hell or on a plane beneath Heaven or Earth but in the middle somewhere. My Oma summons them mainly for clients but for herself also, when she needs information."

"Clients?"

"Yeah, she acts as a medium for those who want to contact their beloved ones. Oma has a psychic link to Straddlers, which I find creepy. I couldn't imagine knowing that spirits were lurking around me at all times. In the shower, on the shitter." He shook his head.

"So, there are Straddlers, and they talk to your grandma. You said they stay between Hell and Earth. Where is that, exactly?"

"Limbo. A place where souls are forgotten and in constant torment. Oma, or one of her kooky friends can explain it better than I can."

"So, all that time humans spend running around looking for ghosts is actually legitimate. Huh," Lila said thoughtfully.

"Yeah."

Stirling adjusted his seat and leaned back a bit, as Lila remembered her fifteen unknown brothers.

"Stirling, do you have any siblings?"

"I have three brothers but don't know any of them really well anymore. We all separated early on except me and Hale. He and I stayed together with my parents for a long time. Now, we all live in different states, which gives us even less reason to keep in touch. For a while, they would call on me, but when I stopped answering them, they quit calling."

"Call on you?" Lila asked. "Is this another Lilin thing I should know about?"

"Yeah. Our species can communicate telepathically."

"You mean like a conversation?"

"Not really. Our psychic connections are limited. The link for telepathic communication only lasts a few seconds and can take a while to reopen, so we usually just call each other by name or a phrase. Lifemate links can stay open longer with practice if the bond is strong. Oma and Opa are able to speak telepathically for almost a couple minutes now."

"Crazy!" Lila sat still and thought, *Stirling*, in her head.

Ha-Ha, yes, meine Flamme*?*

"Weird! Is that what a calling is like?" Her eyes lit up like fireworks.

"Yup. Pretty cool, huh?"

"Yeah, that's insane!" *I'm gonna bother the hell out of you now,* she thought and patted his thigh.

He picked up her hand and kissed it.

"You could never bother me, baby."

"I can't wait until we have time to practice this." Giddy, she smiled at him. "Well, how do you call a sibling?"

"Little concentration is needed in times of severe stress or happiness. It seems that the stronger the emotion behind the calling, the more easily the link opens. Then you just think their name, or a word and they hear it. Other times, a deal of concentration is needed depending on the circumstances. I think that over time, as technology progressed, we kind of abandoned the gift though. It's not necessary anymore to *call* another Lilin if you can pick up your cell and actually call them."

"Why did you stop answering your brothers?"

"For a lot of reasons, the most recent being my job with Gaelon. He doesn't exactly offer vacation time."

"Well, what if you had other siblings but didn't know them? Could you find them or call to them?"

"Yes, I don't see why not. You can track a sibling on instinct, without any clues, although clues would be helpful. Mamma and Papa explained to me that Lilin relationships have a gravitational pull of sorts. But I don't know if I'd look for unknown siblings without a damn good reason. Gravitational pull aside, Incubi don't mesh well. Why do you ask?" Stirling looked at Lila, feeling something curious inside her.

"I have fifteen brothers, none of whom I've ever met," she said. Then she thought about an incident that had plagued her for years. "I remember once, I choked at dinner because I suddenly couldn't breathe, and I pictured a dark-haired man in my mind, but I didn't know why. I didn't even recognize him. It was really strange, and it's happened since. I've glimpsed other men in my head, but never heard them. Could visions be a form of a calling?"

"No. The brief visions happen when a connection is severed. Fifteen brothers? Satan's red balls!" Stirling roared, throwing his head back.

"Wait, what? What does a severed connection mean?" She grabbed his bicep in alarm.

"Honey, I'm sorry," he said, composing himself. He cleared his throat. "Uh, severed connections mean death. You'll see who you're connected to and feel them and the more endeared they are, the more vivid the disconnect will be." He tried to restrain himself, but he snorted anyway. "Fifteen fucking Incubi brothers!"

Lila was taken aback by his easygoing attitude. Maybe living a hundred years numbed a demon to a lot of things.

"Why did they never call me, then? I've never heard anyone in my head. Is it because they don't know me?"

"They know you. They would've sensed your birth. Maybe they don't call you because they don't want you in harm's way. Incubi are troublesome creatures and loners to boot."

"Yeah, I've noticed. Maybe I'll try to find a few of them. It would be interesting now that I have no family left," Lila said sullenly. She was really intrigued by her brothers now and wondered if they ever considered finding her. "After all of this is over, will you help me? Find them, I mean?"

"Whatever you want, love. Of course, I'll help you find them. How old are they?"

"Way older than me, in human and Lilin years. That's all I know. They're old enough to have never been raised with me. My mother kept them a secret until I killed my first lover."

"I can't imagine. Sixteen children," Stirling said and scrunched his face up in disgust.

"Ha, I'm not gonna put my body or my mind through that, so don't worry. We'll stop having sex if it comes down to it."

"Oh no we won't. We'll just adopt a few out." He snickered.

She raised her eyebrows at him and started to laugh.

"Well, what about your parents?" she asked after they chuckled together.

"Died in a car accident. My mother was mortally wounded, so my father passed right with her. I didn't want to go to the service because of the pain, but I went anyway. That was the last time I saw my brothers and grandparents. That was when we boys dispersed from each other permanently. About twelve years ago now. There just wasn't any glue there to keep us together anymore."

"Stirling? You feel it with your lifemates. You feel it with your siblings. You feel it with your parents too, don't you?" Lila asked as blamelessly as she could. She didn't look at him when she posed the question.

His mood shifted, and she felt it. "Yes. It's a bond created between parent and child at the time of implantation of the fetus to the uterus. Parents and children have the ability to sense each other in the way siblings can."

Lila looked out the car window. "I felt them. I saw them in a dream. You told me that you had taken them a week before you found me. That was about the time I saw it happen. I really wanted to go check on them, but it just seemed irrational, so I stayed at home." She paused, guilt-ridden, and dropped her forehead into her hand.

Stirling stiffened. Remorse ripped through him as he thought back to shooting her mom and decking her father.

"I saw my father in a stone-walled room. He was enraged and in his demon form. Some hideous creatures had their arms wrapped around his biceps. There were barred cells with screaming Succubi behind them. My mother was being restrained, but she got away and tore off one of the creature's heads.

"The next thing I saw was my mother nod to my father right before she was decapitated. They never called to me though. Neither of them."

"They wanted you to stay away," Stirling said quietly, eyes fixated on the road. Then something she said registered. "Wait, you saw them?" he asked.

"Yes. They're dead."

"No. I mean, I understand that you saw your parents, but you saw the Succubi too?"

"Yes," Lila affirmed.

"They were alive?" He placed a hand on Lila's knee in anticipation.

"Yes," she answered again.

"I know Gaelon's behind the Lilin abductions. But I don't know why he'd capture them to spare them."

"So he's not crushing their souls?" she asked hopefully.

"Maybe not. But who's to say what's happened to them this past week. Oma will be able to help us understand this. I don't know what's going on. None of it makes sense."

"Maybe if I had stayed home, things would be different. I could have found my brothers. We all could have protected one another."

"That's great in theory, but Incubi don't really do playground time with others. We're all arrogant and confrontational. My grandparents always told me and my brothers that we needed to stick together; it just never worked out."

There was a long silence swelling, forcing Stirling out of his comfort zone.

"I saw my parents die too, Lila. I'm so sorry you had to go through that. It's something that stays with you forever. It's my fault. I'm so sorry." He spoke wistfully, and she knew he was thinking about his own torment as well as hers.

He sensed her grief and brushed his hand against her hair.

She was peering out the window again. It was starting to rain. The weather echoed her sorrow. They wouldn't be in Monroe until three or so and dire thoughts made her restless. She tried to process everything that had happened in her entire life within a few minutes.

Stirling looked over at her. "Lila, one day at a time," he said kindly, giving her shoulder a gentle squeeze.

"One day at a time," she repeated.

He turned on the radio, and a Stone Temple Pilots song was playing. She rested her head against the window, watching the raindrops against the glass transform into long streams, like rivers, due to the rushing wind. Even the sky cried.

After a pit stop, and a couple of shotgun changes, the ride went by somewhat quickly. By the time Lila opened her eyes, Stirling was driving down a dirt path surrounded by thick forest and marsh. The smell reminded her of a fish tank that hadn't been cleaned in months. Stagnant water and muck.

They pulled up to a house on stilts, a dilapidated old house that had been painted a bad shade of pink maybe a century ago. The shutters were either broken or had fallen. The whiteish staircase that led to the wraparound porch leaned more to one side than the other. The place was worn to hell by weather and time.

"Wow," Lila breathed, peering out at the abomination.

"I told you Oma was eccentric."

"To say the least."

Stirling put the car in park. Lila grabbed her bag from the back seat, and he was opening her door before she turned around. She got out and asked, "When did you become so chivalrous?"

"When you became my soulmate. A lot in me has changed, *meine Flamme*. The magical bond between us is the strongest of our kind's."

"I like it," she said, noticing three other cars parked in the dirt lot, and a Harley. "Who else is here?" she asked anxiously.

"Could be Opa's car, Oma's car, or some client's. The Harley is likely Cairo's. I should have known Oma would call my brothers. Don't be nervous, Lila." Stirling squeezed her hand.

"When did you talk to your Oma?"

"After you dominated me at your apartment. They're definitely here. I feel them."

The wind whipped around them, and Lila felt like she was surrounded by spirits, announcing their presence. The chimes adorning the porch clamored and rang, but their sounds were lost to the marsh.

"Come," Stirling said, and led her to the great pink house that promised secrets they would suffer without.

They ascended the steps, which Lila prayed didn't crumble beneath her feet. Once they made it onto the porch, her anxiety about meeting Stirling's family made her palms sweaty.

Stirling pounded on the door. There was no answer.

"Oma!" he yelled out and pounded again.

After a few moments the door slowly opened. A slender man, who looked a lot like Stirling, only with thinner features, answered the door. He had silky blonde hair, and it grazed his shoulders. His frame was lean and long, and his Incubus blue-violet eyes were exposed. He was expressionless as he opened the door further for the two to enter the house. Lila wondered about his true age. He looked to be in his early thirties.

"Beckett. It's been a long time," Stirling said, amiably enough.

"Yes, it has, brother," Beckett said back, hugging Stirling with a distant, manly one-armed hug.

Stirling and Lila stepped inside, as an old woman rounded the corner.

"My grandson. *My p'tit boug*!" she exclaimed beaming, with her hands held out.

She was gorgeous even though she may have been seven hundred years old. Her grey hair flowed down her backside like a glistening river and her piercing green eyes shone brightly. Small wrinkles gracefully crinkled her face, around her eyes especially. Probably from laughing a lot. Her vibe was charming. Lila smiled the moment she saw her. Stirling was all smiles too. Lila guessed Stirling's Oma's warmth was contagious.

"Stirling. You've come home! Here, sit down." Oma grabbed his hands and then gestured to a decaying old green couch.

Stirling looked at Lila and shrugged. He sat and she followed his lead.

Now his Oma hovered, making Lila uncomfortable. She clasped her hands together and stared at the seated couple.

"Who is this you have with you? A lifemate? Finally! But in such bad times, Stirling," his Oma said, almost disapprovingly.

"Yes, Oma, this is my lifemate. And I know that these are hard times, and we didn't mean for it to happen. The circumstances were just..." Stirling stopped talking, looked at his Oma and sighed.

"These things often happen when we least expect it, when we aren't even looking, *p'tit boug*."

Oma opened her hands and reached for Lila's. Lila hesitated, then relented and offered her palms. Oma paused and her eyeballs rolled to the side, over her shoulder, as if someone was speaking to her. Then her mouth dropped open, and she looked at Lila, stunned.

"A lifemate? Stirling? Ha! Now I've truly seen everything, brother," a man with short dark hair said as he entered the room, which seemed to shrink with his presence. He was older than Stirling in human years, but not many. Tattoos covered his arms, and he sported a piercing in his septum and his eyebrow. He smiled a perfect saintly smile, and Stirling stood to greet him. They embraced tightly.

"So, you finally made the leap, huh?" the shadowy man asked as they parted. He placed his giant hands on either side of Stirling's neck.

Lila couldn't help but notice Stirling's brother's brazen beauty. His lips were full. The angles of his face were hard. His frame was as large as Stirling's and the rest of his features were almost equally as sexy as her soulmate's. His eyes were hidden behind dark brown contacts and she wondered how much more stunning he'd look without them.

"Yes, Cairo. I made the leap," Stirling said, playfully punching Cairo in the gut.

"Well, son, I can say you've chosen one who is particularly beautiful. I never expected anything less from you, *p'tit boug*. But there is something you do not yet know," Oma chimed.

"What is she calling you?" Lila stood and whispered when Stirling made his way back over to her.

Cairo winked at Lila and bowed. When he smiled, her heart skipped a beat, and she hoped Stirling didn't notice.

"Her '*little boy*,'" Stirling answered, flushed.

Oma stood there, still staring them down. The short silence made Lila crack.

"I'm sorry." She extended her hands again to Stirling's grandmother. "I feel totally out of place here. And what do I call you, ma'am?"

"Darling, my name is Maggie, and you should feel right at home here. You are now part of the family." Maggie cupped her feeble palms around Lila's knuckles.

"Okay, Maggie. We just came because we need answers to some questions, and we need them quickly. This wasn't exactly supposed to be a homecoming. I apologize," Lila said as politely as she could.

"Yes, I know. Stirling and I spoke. He told me what he knows, and I've done some research. I called the boys and told them they must come home for this."

"Oma, what is going on with the Lilin?" Stirling pressed.

"Straddlers tell me that Lilin are being kidnapped and tortured and killed. Some of the souls don't make it out. They are destroyed. We all live life in hopes that there is something after this pain and suffering. To completely decimate a soul is the ultimate insolence. A whole life lived only to become nothingness. Appalling." Maggie shivered.

"It's mainly Succubi. Why?"

"A Succubus apparently fell in love with Gaelon's son. She had to continue to take mates to sustain herself. Gaelon's son took other mates also, but with selfish reason, or maybe just to spite her.

The situation greatly upset the Succubus, and she killed Gaelon's son while he slept. He was Gaelon's only offspring.

"Destroyer offspring are so few that you can count them. Only three have been born from Abbadon, and only Gaelon, of the three, procreated. So Gaelon is on a revenge hunt to exterminate our race as a whole," Maggie explained.

"Killing you ladies will ensure the end of our race, so picking you off is priority since your numbers are so low. He'll kill Incubi as well when he gets his hands on us," Cairo offered casually. "But personally, I think the dude's a pussy."

"This house is shrouded in magic. You and your lifemate can hide here, where it is safe," Maggie insisted.

"Oma, we don't want to hide. We want to stop this," Stirling argued.

"Son, there is honor in that, but there is also death. Diffusing this situation will be left to your brothers."

"I don't follow. Lila and I are in this, too."

Lila nodded her head in agreement.

"Do you know the prize you nurture inside of your lifemate?"

"What prize? What are you talking about?" Lila asked, stepping in front of Stirling, anticipation in her voice.

"Yeah, what are we talking about here?" Cairo asked suspiciously, standing and

folding his lumberjack arms across his wide chest.

"A spirit tells me that one of her eggs has been fertilized. Implantation will take place between four and six days from now, and then you will know the sex of the baby." Maggie's eyes were wide, and she wrung her hands excitedly.

Cairo snorted, then slapped his forehead. "Oh, man."

"My child, you must hide. Especially if it is a female. Neither of you can be part of this war," Maggie said and grabbed Lila's hands again.

"I need a minute," Lila croaked, her mouth suddenly dry. "Bathroom?" she asked, and Cairo pointed down a hallway.

She ran in that direction.

"To the left!" Cairo called.

Lila found the bathroom and slammed the heavy door shut behind her. Grasping the sides of the ancient sink, she ran the water cold. She splashed her face and looked at herself hard in the mirror. Pregnant? Her mother would have been ecstatic. And Jenny would be the happiest aunt, but how did *she* feel about it? There weren't really any downsides to the situation other than the timing.

She dried off her face, turned to the side, and pooched out her stomach.

"You'll look radiant."

Lila jumped. She hadn't even heard the door creak open. "Stirling."

He turned her around and into him, placed a hand on her womb, then knelt to kiss her belly. He embraced her hips as she ran her fingers through his hair.

"Come back out. We'll rest here a few days and figure out what to do next." He licked just above her belly button. "This is amazing."

"I don't know Stirling. I mean, with everything that's happening," she whined, rubbing her eyes. "I mean … I'm getting beat up here."

He looked up at her. "Honey, my brothers will handle whatever needs to be done with Gaelon. Let's go eat with them and then we'll take a bath and make love. We're going to have a baby. You should be pleased."

Stirling stood and placed an arm around Lila's shoulders. She felt a surge of happiness emanate from him. He was delighted about being a father, which she never would have suspected. Watching him, she wondered what he'd look like cradling a tiny baby in his burly arms.

He beamed at her and kissed her forehead as they walked back into the living area. They took a seat on the green couch again, and Cairo sat on the arm of a mustardy-colored chair. He appeared amused by the whole situation, and Lila felt like pummeling him for it. She heard Beckett rummaging around in the kitchen, but there was no sign of the third brother. She wondered if he was here and how beautiful he could possibly be.

"You all right, dear?" Maggie asked Lila.

"Sure," she answered, totally lying.

"Oma, we've had a long day. What's for dinner?" Stirling asked.

"Well, I'm making fried chicken, greens, carrots, mashed potatoes, and corn on the cob. Beckett's already started cooking. You two take your old room, and I'll start the wash for you if you need fresh clothes. Just pile 'em in the laundry, and I'll take care of it."

Maggie unleashed an awful cough. Stirling stood urgently, put a hand on her back, and bent down to look at her face. "Oma, you all right?"

Lilin didn't get sick unless they weren't taking life forces.

"It's nothing, boy. I'll be in the kitchen," she said sternly and turned away.

"Uh, Maggie, before you go, can I ask you something?" Lila stood and walked toward her.

"Yes, child?" she answered, turning back around.

She looked at Lila lovingly and Lila almost cried when she saw her expression. It reminded her of the way her mother used to look at her at times.

"My parents were murdered by Gaelon. Stirling tells me you connect with the dead. Do you think you could find them?"

"I'm so sorry about your parents, dear. I'll call forth my conjurers and tomorrow night we will cast a circle. If they are straddling, we will know," Maggie said. She smiled, then slowly made her way into the kitchen.

"Maggie, do you need help with anything?" Lila called.

"No, dear. Beckett is the real cook of the family. He tells me he went to culinary school," she giggled proudly.

"I have my own restaurant, too. In Manhattan," Beckett bragged as he popped his head out from behind the wall of the kitchen. His silky blonde hair fell into his eyes, and he smoothly brushed it back before disappearing behind the wall again.

"Impressive," Lila said, raising her eyebrows. "How do you manage that?"

"I have a lot of regular aging demon employees. I work behind the scenes so I can keep things going without giving myself away," Beckett called.

"Fucking show off," Stirling murmured under his breath. "How in the hell did you get here so quickly, anyway? And don't tell me you used a Transporter. Oma told me that you've put your demon habits behind you," he said, loudly this time.

Beckett answered sourly, poking his head back out from the kitchen. "I had to nab two tickets from two unsuspecting and unfortunate women. Wasn't one of my better moments. Took a flight and then a transfer flight, Stirling,"

"I didn't ask you to come. *'Better moments'*. Hmpf. Mr. Perfect," Stirling mumbled.

"Oh, Stirling, you're just harboring a grudge because you never used that law degree of yours. Instead, you roam around aimlessly. Oma told us how hopeless you are," Cairo chided.

"Watch your mouth, Cairo! I never said he was hopeless. Just lost," Maggie interjected from the kitchen doorway.

"A law degree? You never told me that," Lila said to Stirling, looking at him with proud eyes.

"Ha! So, what is it you do now?" Cairo asked as if he were on a really high horse. Lila wished he'd fall off and bust his face.

Stirling ignored Lila and responded to his brother instead. "I never used the degree because I'm not as crafty as Beckett concerning business, I guess. I'm a bouncer at a demon club and Gaelon's personal assistant," he admitted gruffly. "Thanks for bringing it up."

"What the *fuck*? You work for that slime-bag? Stirling, man, how'd you get messed up in that?" Cairo asked, revolted.

"Let's just save that part for later, please," Stirling answered, looking away from his big bro. "You're already starting to piss me off."

"It wouldn't be brotherly if we got along," Cairo laughed. "What do you do, Lila?"

"Not much. I've only been cursed for six years, and I've just kind of moved around a lot. I was a paralegal for a while but switched firms due to my obvious slowly aging face. Then I realized I couldn't take on such serious work with this...affliction, so I just take odd jobs and bullshit. It's depressing. Not really worth talking about."

"You never told me you were a paralegal," Stirling said, in shock. "It's weird that we...."

"What *do* you two know about each other?" Cairo asked, condescendingly.

"Enough. We know what matters. The rest will come later, brother."

"Wait. Did I hear you right? You're only six? You look like you're twenty in human years. How did you hold off so long?" Cairo asked Lila in astonishment.

"She's twenty-two in human years and shut your mouth for now. Please," Stirling requested, tiredly.

He rubbed his temples. Lila crossed her legs and rested her elbow against the couch arm, placing her head in her hand. Silence crowded the expansive room, and then Cairo slapped his hands against his legs before standing.

"It's been real, bro," he said, and disappeared down the hallway.

"Hale! Dinner!" Maggie yelled.

A splendid man descended the stairs. He looked like Stirling's twin. Sandy-blonde hair, the Incubi eyes—yet he was a bit smaller-framed than Stirling. He was near Lila's age in human years.

Stirling sprinted to him and hugged him tightly. They did the whole back-patting bit as well.

"Hale. I've missed you, my brother," Stirling beamed.

"And I, you. It's been too long. I see you've brought company. Is she yours?" Hale asked. Lila could have sworn she saw longing in his eyes as he looked at her.

"Yes. She is mine, and with child. And she is in danger." Stirling's voice had lost its spirited tone.

"Oma has told me of the danger. Your lifemate is pregnant?" Hale's brow rose.

"Oma says we'll know the sex of the baby in less than a week. She has only just been fertilized."

Lila felt like they were talking about her like she was a cow pasture and her fetus was a mushroom.

"Well, congratulations, brother," Hale said and clapped Stirling on the arm. "But with good news, there is always bad. You know that Opa is not well? I was just watching over him." Hale's expression turned grim.

Stirling looked to Maggie, who was peering out of the kitchen into the living room so she could eavesdrop.

"Oma?" Stirling questioned.

"Yes," she confessed, abashed. "We are coming to our end," she looked down.

Cairo walked forward and brought her out of the kitchen, holding one of her hands. Lila understood. If Opa died, so did Maggie.

"How serious is it?" Stirling asked quietly.

"Opa is ill. I am struggling with him. When he has coughing fits, I double over, and his fevers make me sweat. I have burning bursts; I am tired all the time but cannot sleep. I scarcely have the energy to help you, but I must. I made an herbal tea to give me strength, but I still need plenty of rest at night."

"Shit," Stirling replied.

Lila felt his overwhelming grief. She touched his shoulder, but it brought him no relief.

"Don't you 'shit' me, boy. We'll get through this. Right now, we have more pressing matters. I need to assist you while I can,"

Maggie said curtly. “C’mon in here and eat.” She summoned them all with sweep of her bird-boned hand.

Stirling gestured for Lila to enter the kitchen before him, then he pulled a chair out for her, leaned down and kissed her on the cheek.

Cairo, who had already taken his seat said, “When did you turn into a pussy, man?”

“Cairo,” Maggie warned. “You know the rules about that kind of talk at my dinner table.”

“Sorry, Oma,” he apologized quietly.

“You’ll never find a lifemate with the life you lead, so just shut it,” said Beckett. “It’s something you’ll never understand,” he continued while placing a basket of warm rolls on the table.

“Like you know what it’s like, Beck,” Cairo sneered, ripping a roll apart and shoving it into his mouth.

“I know what it’s like to be in love, to have partnership,” Beckett argued, then set a large bowl of mashed potatoes on the table as well.

“And have some respect around my woman, please. Must you be so crude all the time? You’re always trying to overcompensate. For what, I don’t know, but it seems like a personal problem,” Stirling stated stalely.

“Well, *woman,* didn’t you say you were a mere six years old?” Cairo asked, loading his plate up as Beckett set the rest of the food out.

“Yes, I did,” Lila answered stiffly, staring down at her plate. Slowly, she scooped some carrots onto it.

“So, you’re a total newbie,” Cairo laughed.

Lila raised her head. “You’re very easily amused aren’t you, Cairo?” she asked, shooting darts at him with her eyes.

“I just think it’s funny that Stirling’s a hundred years deep, and he snags a piece of ass like you.” Looking at Stirling he finished, “What luck, man. I never had it, that’s for sure.” Then he shoveled more food in his mouth.

"It has nothing to do with luck. What Succubus would subject herself to your abrasive ass? Pardon me, Maggie," Lila mumbled, and Stirling laughed sinisterly as he shoved himself from the table.

Lila felt his mood and what he was about to do. She grasped his arm, but he pulled away.

"Never you mind; well put, darling," Maggie responded. "This one has no hope of settling down." She pointed at Cairo with her fork. "He'll live a life of unfulfilling sex and darkness. And he'll deserve every minute of it," she declared in between mouthfuls of food.

She was completely relaxed even though a fight was clearly imminent. Lila, on the other hand, was totally on edge.

Stirling rounded the table and pulled Cairo out of his seat by the back of his neck. Cairo turned and pushed Stirling, who pushed right back.

"Take it out of the kitchen, you mongrels!" Maggie commanded, placing some chicken on her plate. Seemed this was business as usual.

"Is this a common occurrence?" Lila asked, severely concerned.

"No, it's not common, because we don't commonly see each other. This is why we don't stay in close quarters with each other," Hale answered.

Beckett just shook his head and continued eating. Lila leaned back in her chair and peered into the living room just as Stirling landed a punch to Cairo's face. Then Cairo landed one to Stirling's ribs. They grappled on the floor for a couple of minutes, then Cairo wiggled his way out of Stirling's chokehold by elbowing him in the stomach.

Both men eventually separated, sweating. Cairo bent over, placing his hands on his knees, inhaling deep breaths of air.

"You respect my lifemate, and you don't call her a piece of ass or make cracks at her at all, you shithead!" Stirling yelled at his brother. His chest heaved.

"I get it, man. Chill the hell out. I'm hungry as shit. Let me go sit down and eat," Cairo whined.

Lila couldn't tell who had won the fight. They were matched in strength and size.

Cairo finally stood and tried to put his hand on Stirling's shoulder in a brotherly gesture, but Stirling shrugged away.

"Don't fucking touch me," he seethed.

"Well, Satan's red ass. You're in a foul mood," Cairo laughed.

"Yeah, Cairo. Kinda got a lot on my plate right now." Stirling shoved a hand through his hair.

"That's what we're all here for. For you. For her." Cairo pointed toward the kitchen while he spat the words at Stirling, finally being serious.

"Then be here for me and her and keep your demeaning little comments to yourself. That'll help me out a ton. Think you can handle that, big brother?" Stirling asked rhetorically, but Cairo answered anyway in a subdued voice Lila had not yet heard.

"Okay, man. Understood."

The men took their seats back at the kitchen table. Blood dripped from Cairo's nose and Stirling's lips. There was blood all over Stirling's shirt and jeans yet again. He pulled off his shirt to wipe his face, and everyone at the table almost choked on their food.

"My boy! She is your soulmate? I haven't seen this in my entire time! We search our whole lives to find what you have!" Maggie exclaimed. "You must test your telepathy. I bet it's endless. I cannot believe this!"

Soulmate or not, Lila had dealt with enough for the night. "You know, I've lost my appetite. You'll have to excuse me. Maggie, Beckett, thank you for the lovely meal." She smiled falsely and stood from the table.

"You go rest, child. You must be exhausted emotionally and physically. I'll make you a plate and put it in the fridge for you, yes?" Maggie smiled widely.

"Thank you, Maggie," Lila said back.

“I’m going to apologize in advance for any more of our brotherly squabbles, Lila. Good night, and I hope you sleep well,” Beckett said, in a gentlemanly manner.

“Thank you, Beckett.”

Lila turned her back without acknowledging Stirling or his childish, yet delectable, brother, Cairo. She felt that Stirling was compelled to follow her, but before he stood from his chair, she raised her hand and said, “Eat your food, Stirling.”

She left the kitchen, and on her way into the living room, she heard Hale say, “Cairo, The King of Crass. Good job, buddy.”

Lila went upstairs to Stirling’s room with her bag and pulled out her dirty clothes for Maggie to wash. She found her comfy nightshirt and laid that out on the bed. For a moment she sat and worried herself sick about everything they were going through. The situation hadn’t been so bleak before she found out about the baby. Now everything was even messier. While Stirling said his brothers would take care of Gaelon, she couldn’t escape the nagging feeling that something would go wrong.

She looked around the small room where only quaint antique furniture adorned the space. The once white curtains were tinged yellow with age and dirt. The distressed wood floors were cold; the throw rug was worn to hell, and a musty smell saturated the air. The room had a sort of charm though. It was simple and had been Stirling’s once.

She half-smiled on her way into the claustrophobic hall bathroom, but her smile faded when she saw the makeshift shower. A curtain hung 360 degrees around an archaic cast-iron tub and only a small shower head poked through. Not what she was used to.

Looking in an old-fashioned cabinet, she discovered lavender pearls in a small plastic container, then she opened the narrow closet door and retrieved a towel. She pulled the shower curtain aside and ran a steaming bath, stripping off her clothes.

Slipping into the tub, the hot water felt good against her sore muscles. She closed her eyes, letting her head fall back, wetting her hair. The lavender beads melted and filled the room with a lovely, soothing scent.

There was a knock on the door, and Lila woke with a start. The water was almost cold.

"Honey? You've been in there quite a while. You ever coming out? I miss you and I'm sorry about fighting with Cairo," Stirling said.

"Uh, yeah, I'll be out in a minute," she answered as she sat up and pulled the drain plug. She shivered as she got out of the tub, stepping onto the freezing, cracked white tile floor.

Quickly, she dried off and wrapped herself in the towel.

She opened the door to see Stirling standing there with an arm resting over his head, elbow against the door frame. He was admiring her, staring her up and down. He walked into the bathroom as she looked up at him with burden in her heart. He knew just what she needed. She needed to forget everything for a while.

"You're sexy when you're wet. Here," he spoke quietly and touched her hair. "And here," he finished, slipping a hand under her towel.

He stroked her wet curls, then circled her entrance with a finger, barely dipping it inside her. She pressed her body into his and he lowered his mouth to hers, gently kissing her. He swooped her up and carried her across the hall into his bedroom.

"Don't even think about getting dressed. I'm gonna take a shower and then take care of you," he said, dropping her onto the bed.

She giggled and slid under the covers, feeling at home. After a few minutes, she drifted back to sleep.

Lila felt warm and wet between her legs. She slowly opened her eyes to see Stirling's head between her knees. The feeling of his hot tongue stroking between her valleys registered immediately.

Moaning, she grabbed his hair, pulling him deeper into her sacred cavern.

He growled like a ravenous beast, delving his tongue inside her, caressing her sensitive tissue in an upward motion.

"Ahhh!" She squeezed his head with her knees.

"I love fucking your pussy with my tongue," he said, his voice muffled by her sex. He sucked her bud in between his lips until she pulsated in his mouth. When her trembling legs fell to her sides, he lapped at her one last time, drinking more of her sweet ambrosia.

He raised his head and got up on his knees, grasped his hard length and began to stroke himself vigorously. Groaning loudly, he watched as she writhed on the bed, focusing on how her nipples peaked, just begging to be suckled. He orgasmed, drenching her tuft in his potent semen.

She arched her back and thrust her hips up, willing him to enter her. His stimulating cream caused her to come again before he had a chance to fill. She was incapacitated with bliss. He laid on top of her, and she thought how wonderful his weight felt against her body.

"Bite me, Lila. Hard," Stirling commanded, his tone dripping with heady lust.

Obeying, she lanced into his neck with her teeth. Warm, sweet blood filled her mouth, and her connection to him deepened, flooding ecstasy to every part of her body. She clawed his back deep, pulling him closer, drinking him until she felt crazed.

"That's it, baby, come again for me," he whispered, and she did. "I can't get enough of you coming on me." He drove into her as her jellied legs unwillingly unwound from his waist.

Sitting up, he pulled her into him. He palmed her breast; the one partially adorned with their bond tattoo. Then possessively, he secured her hip with his other hand, and thrust into her sensually and slowly, yet deeply and firmly. After giving up on trying to hold out, and noticing Lila was nearly drunk on lust, he allowed himself gratification. With his orgasm building, he lowered himself back onto her body seeking the closeness he craved.

"Look at me, *meine Flamme.*"

Lila's eyelids were fluttering. She opened them slowly, meeting Stirling's gaze. Panting, he drew her even closer. They were nose to nose and kissed fervidly as he released inside her. His orgasm struck like voltage, starting at his toes, running through every centimeter of him, stretching out the tip of his tongue. Lila felt his satisfaction in the way his kiss deepened. Sweat-drenched and exhausted, he buried his face into her shoulder while trying not to crush her under his dead weight. Her lead-heavy arms dropped away from his back as she sighed in contentment.

"Are you as tired as I am?" he asked, mouth nuzzled in her neck.

"Yes, I am. You wear me out. You are simply perfect in the sex department," she said, breathlessly.

He smiled. "And you are simply perfect."

Chapter 16

Lila woke, looking through foggy eyes at the ancient clock sitting on the nightstand. It was four thirty in the evening. Rolling over in the bed, she noted cold sheets and no Stirling. He'd probably risen hours earlier. As she sat up, rubbing the fog from her eyes, she spied a clean, neatly folded pile of clothes atop the dresser.

"Thank God," she said to herself.

Swiftly, she got out of bed, grabbed her jeans and a black long-sleeved shirt. She dressed, then dug her toothbrush out of her bag. After grooming herself, she walked down the hall and peered over the banister, which overlooked the living space.

Below, she saw a loosely gathered group of people; out of the group, Stirling looked up at her, also wearing jeans and a long-sleeved black shirt. He motioned for her to come down the stairs.

When Lila reached the bottom landing, she nervously looked around the room. All her brothers-in-bond were present. Maggie was speaking to some older ladies who were all wearing outlandish dresses with lace or floral patterns and stockings and gloves. One elder sported a white Easter hat adorned with brightly colored flowers. All grey-haired, the women turned simultaneously to look at her. She shrank back, as Stirling came forward, wrapping his arm around her waist.

"These ladies are part of Oma's summoning circle. They're here to help reach your parents. Get enough sleep?" he asked sarcastically.

Lila shot him a look. *Fuck off.* She had needed that long rest.

Ha-ha-ha. Okay.

This bond thing is pretty cool.

Yeah, and look how long we can talk.

The women in the room closed in on Lila at once.

"Oh. Hello, ladies." She smiled as awkwardly as she waved.

"I'm Helga," the first witch to approach said. She was African American and wore the Easter hat. Her dark eyes were big, and her smile was wide, forcing her cheeks into round lumps on her face. She grasped Lila's hand and said, "I'm a voodoo priestess. Honey, you are very anxious. I can make you a tea for that. Rest assured, there is no reason to worry about my religion. It's nothing to be afraid of. I don't practice black arts. You can trust me to aid in bringing your parents forth." Gently, she patted the top of Lila's hand then made her way to a huge round table.

Next, a short, plump lady barely wrinkled with age came forward. Her thick hair was pinned back into a bulbous bun. "Lila, I am Lisa, and I am a medium like Maggie. After the summoning, your parents will converse with you through us both." She touched Lila on the shoulder and then turned away to chat with Maggie and Beckett.

Lastly, a tall, twiggy woman stepped before her and offered her a frail hand. Lila took it, almost scared she'd break her. The woman's voice was kind, as were her deep blue eyes. She smiled, exposing perfect dentures. Her face was a map of wrinkles, and Lila callously wondered how long she had left to live.

"I am Hazel and I'm a Wiccan witch. I will be putting our mediums under a spell, or a trance-like state, so that they may speak for your parents. I will also assist in the conjuring."

"If my parents are in Limbo, you *will* be able to find them, right?" Lila asked.

Hazel placed a finger under Lila's chin, forcing Lila to meet her eyes.

"From what Stirling has told me, I assume they loved you dearly and probably locked themselves in Limbo to look after you or to deliver a message. So, if they are there, we will surely find them. We'll help them see the path to Hell and cross them over."

"Actually, I have a few questions about that. How does crossing over work? I mean, what exactly is Limbo and why pass them to Hell?"

Hazel responded, "Well, for demons, there are only two places to wait until after Armageddon and Judgement: Hell, and Limbo. Right now, Hell is a sort of safe space for demons, offering awareness and basic clarity to them. If the path to Hell is refused, or unseen, Limbo is the only other option. Demon breeds born with souls, such as breeds from angel bloodlines, often find their way back to Hell if they wish to. Though, if the soul resides in Limbo too long, its energy fades and becomes trapped. Forever."

"Why would my parents risk Limbo to communicate with me?" Lila asked, feeling a lump form in her throat.

"Limbo is the only dimensional plane demon souls can communicate through. Hell is not accessible unless black arts are used to open a portal, which is extremely dangerous for humans."

Lila swallowed hard, nearly choking on the throat lump. "Stirling said that Limbo is a place of suffering. While I'm not sure I want the answer to this question, is that accurate?" Now she was chewing the inside of her lip.

"Well, Limbo is a lonely place. It's a place where no entity has domain, so in essence, it's a state of chaos. Therefore, the souls can't communicate together or recognize each other's energy. We may be able to summon your parents at the same time, but they won't realize the other is there with us."

Hazel stopped and inhaled a wheezing breath. "Excuse me, dear," she apologized, patting her chest.

Again, Lila wondered how much longer she had left.

After a small cough, Hazel continued, "Also, time is not a concept in Limbo, which further adds to the torment and sometimes causes souls to lose their way to the path out."

Lila dropped her head. "They don't deserve that, especially not on my behalf. I have to bring them back," she said with a tremor in her voice.

Stirling rubbed her lower back with a warm hand and held her close to his side.

"We'll find them, Lila. No worries," he said confidently.

"Thank you, Hazel," Lila said, looking up with teary eyes.

Hazel smiled solemnly. "Dearest child, you must understand that we may not be able to get your parents to the other side in a day or even in a couple of days. You must help us and be patient. Above all, have faith. Without it, we're lost anyway."

Lila nodded firmly, nearly choking on fear and tears. Hazel nodded back and then took leave of her.

Maggie approached Lila and Stirling with a sympathetic smile. She was perfection in old age, and Lila could only hope she'd be the same way for Stirling.

"Lila, we ladies know how these things work. We can only go so far though. You have a big part to play. Whatever we ask of you, you must do and do it with conviction."

"I understand, Oma," Lila responded.

Maggie beamed when Lila spoke her German name and embraced her tightly. She spoke assuredly into Lila's ear. "We will start tonight when the moon rises and the Goddess is listening, when the candles and our voices will become your parents' light along the path out of Limbo."

A tear slipped from Lila's eye, and she quickly wiped it away before anyone could see, yet Stirling felt her sadness and guilt.

Pulling back and holding Lila firmly by the shoulders Maggie said, "Go eat, child. I made you a plate, and it waits for you. You must be strong for this ritual, as we will all need to expend some energy tonight."

"Yes, Oma, and thank you for doing all of this for a stranger."

"Not a stranger, love. A part of our family." Maggie released her with a smile.

Lila regarded each of the women before Stirling led her into the kitchen.

"I'll be back, love. I want to talk more to Oma about Opa and their 'burning bursts.' I don't like the sound of that at all. Once the bursts get too bad… never mind, sweetheart. You have enough on your mind already. Eat, okay?" he asked.

She smiled weakly, then softly kissed him. Once he left, she sifted through the refrigerator, finding numerous cellophaned and foiled items until she located a plate with "Lila" scrawled across the foil in black Sharpie ink.

Hale snuck up behind her. She nearly shrieked when she turned and saw him, almost dropping her dinner.

"I didn't mean to frighten you, Lila. I apologize," he said hypnotically.

On edge, Lila tapped a hand against the plate numerous times. She felt Hale seducing her with his eyes, but if he was aroused by her, he was good at masking his lust. She didn't smell it on him. Not yet anyway.

"Here, let me warm that for you," he said, gently taking the plate from her.

"Thank you. I've just been so discombobulated lately. I am two days pregnant, my parents are probably in Limbo, and my life is in danger because of a cruel Succubus and a crazy soul-crushing bastard. I'm not holding up too well."

Hale popped Lila's food into the microwave, then turned around and forced her into a corner with his lean body. She lost her breath. Why did Stirling's brothers have to be so smoking hot? She was driven by sexuality, which made it hard to turn off. She focused on the sound of the microwave and clenched her eyelids shut.

"What do you want, Hale?" she asked quietly.

He leaned in and brushed the tip of his nose against hers. That's when she smelled it: roses and almonds.

"I wish I had what my brother has. I wish I had found you first. You are a diamond," he admitted secretly.

"I thought you would be the gentlemanly type," she said back, about to break through the counter to get away from him.

If Stirling caught them, and she was turned on, he'd know it. She looked down at the floor and composed herself.

"Well then, you misunderstand me, Lila. Beckett is gentlemanly. My disposition lies somewhere between Stirling's and Cairo's." Hale breathed her in.

Stirling strode into the kitchen. Hale immediately backed away from his brother's soulmate, who defensively had both of her hands gripped on the countertops.

"Hale, I expected more of you," Stirling cautioned, and the glimmer in his eye told Lila that he was raging and about to pounce.

"Stirling, he was just being polite. Telling me his wishes of finding a lifemate. Please don't fight. I need to focus on finding my parents."

Lila brushed Stirling's cheek when he came close to her, and he immediately melted. But no sooner than she calmed him, his rage boiled back up. He shot his favorite brother a noxious glance. He just might have to adjust his loyalties.

Stirling wrapped an arm around Lila's waist, smirking hatefully at Hale, who slinked away on cue.

Stirling pulled Lila's plate from the microwave and set it on the table. The two sat down, and she forced herself to eat. Mostly, she just picked at the food. She wasn't hungry. Her weakness and depression surged through Stirling and he slid the plate closer to her.

"Once you've had Oma and Beckett's cooking, you'll find that all other food is less than satisfying," he promised.

Lila stabbed at the chicken again, then took a small bite. She didn't realize how hungry she was until she swallowed.

"It's really good," she confirmed quietly.

Stirling rested his elbows on the table and watched her eat. Once she was done with her plate, he took it to the sink, hand-washed the dish and set it on the dry rack.

"Come. We'll summon your parents soon. All is well, *meine Flamme*. Everything will be okay." He took her hand and led her back into the living room.

The women who would hopefully summon her parents' spirits stood around, talking and laughing. They had each brought a different food dish. Fruits, vegetables and herbs were placed on the table in the center of the living room.

Lila asked Stirling, "Why is there a huge round table here with food and junk on it?"

"This is the room where the ladies perform their rituals, spells, and séances. It's the largest room in the house, allowing them space to place their voodoo dolls and gris-gris around, their Wiccan books of rituals, and everything else needed for reaching into different realms. The food provides an invitation into the world as the spirits knew it. It's a worldly offering. The candles are placed for guidance. In this case, to help your parents see the path they need to find their way out of Limbo."

"Okay," Lila said unnerved. She was thinking the worst. What if the coven didn't find her parents? What were they suffering through? If they weren't in Limbo, had they been crushed by Gaelon? She wasn't prepared for any of it.

"Lila," Stirling said. "You must have faith. Faith in me, faith in the women my Oma has brought here for you, and faith in yourself. Without that, your parents will be lost to darkness."

"I understand. It's just that I left them. I made myself an orphan. And now I'm really an orphan. I have no legacy."

"That's where you are wrong. You will have me and our children and their children's children. We will create our own legacy."

He ran a palm up and down her spine. His hands felt so comforting on her body.

"I'm sorry, Stirling. I'm not thinking that far ahead. I'll catch up after this is over. I promise. Thank you for all you've done to try to make things right." She hugged him hard, and he firmly embraced her back.

"We will find them, Lila. We'll find them and cross them over."

She kissed his neck. "What do we do until dark?" she asked.

"Well, we have to actually wait until the moon rises, which isn't until about twelve thirty tomorrow morning."

"What? I thought the moon came out when it got dark," she questioned. She had definitely seen the moon before twelve in the morning before.

"Yeah, it's out there," he chuckled lightly. "But we have to wait until it's at its highest point. So, what do you want to do?"

“What’s there to do ‘round these parts?” she drawled in a southern accent, trying to make an attempt at normalcy.

“Well, let’s go fishing out back and then watch the sunset,” he suggested.

“Sounds like a good idea, love. I haven’t been fishing in a while. When I was little, my parents used to take me camping along the river, and we’d catch trout and bass and horny heads,” she reminisced, smiling.

“See, you’re in a better mood already.” Stirling grinned.

He gently squeezed her before he let her go. She followed him out to the back porch, which was screened in to keep all the bugs and critters at bay. Along one wall was a mess of fishing supplies: waders, boots, fly rods, reels, those goofy fishing hats, nets, and several tackle boxes.

Stirling bent, grabbed a green tackle box and set it to the side. He inspected the rods and picked two. One was longer than the other, and he handed the shorter one to Lila. Next, he opened the tackle box to examine their haul. Closing the box back, he said, “Gimme a sec. I need to grab some livers. Oma and Opa fish a lot, so there’s always fresh liver in the fridge.”

He popped into the kitchen, just to pop back into the porch before she could even miss him. “Let’s get going, baby,” he said grinning widely.

She felt his boyish enthusiasm, and it streamed through her, filling her with joy. She grabbed his hand, and they shuffled down the stairs that led to wet, sandy sludge.

“Should’ve brought the boots,” he said, but soon they were out of the muck and walking through dewy grass toward a long dock.

“So, what’s to catch out here?” Lila asked, checking out her rod, getting a feel for it.

“There are lots of catfish and a few bass. I caught a twelve-pound catfish once in this lake. That’s not huge, but it’s a record on this lake. There are also gators to bait for. In the summer, you can see them on the shores basking in the sun,” Stirling answered.

"Also, lots of snakes. They glide across the water and spawn in it. It's really active out here during the warm months."

"Ewww, I don't do snakes," Lila declared as she shook her head.

"But we're demons, honey," he chuckled.

"I'm still young. Only six, remember? Maybe when I'm one hundred years old I'll be ready to wrangle a gator and skin a snake."

There was a bench at the end of the dock, and they both parked themselves on it, staring up at the sky. Crickets chirped loudly, and owls hooted in the surrounding trees. Lila took in a deep breath, then shivered a bit.

"You cold, honey?" Stirling asked sweetly.

"Yeah, a little, but mostly I'm just nervous. I don't know if I'm strong enough for all this. My parents, the baby. Gaelon. I don't want to think about your brothers going to bat for us."

"Lila, I saw you pull a blade out of your shoulder. You stabbed me in the chest, and then you kicked an Assassin's ass. You are very strong."

She winced. "Yeah, sorry about stabbing you."

"It's okay. I deserved everything you dished out. I strapped you to a toilet bowl, remember?"

"Yeah," she laughed, nudging him in the chest, then she settled for his warmth and leaned against him.

After a few comfortable silent moments, he kissed her cheek, then got up and tied a hook to the end of her line. "Well, what do you want to fish for, bass or catfish?" he asked her cheerily.

"Catfish. I wanna beat your record twelve-pounder," she answered haughtily, standing and placing a hand on her hip.

"Oh really? Not gonna happen, sweetheart. Not in the fall." He shook his head blithely.

"We'll see. Hand me those livers," she demanded with her hand outstretched.

"You're going to touch these things?" he asked, surprised.

"Yeah, I've done this before," she replied.

"Okay, babe. Scared of snakes but will fondle livers. Makes total sense."

He handed her the container of livers. She grabbed a large piece out and hooked it through the sides, and again for good measure.

"You sure you don't wanna fish for bass? If we find a school, it'll be easy to catch them this time of year," he suggested.

"I think I'll stick with what I've got. There's a nice big log over there." She pointed to her left.

Lila casted her line perfectly, landing the bait right beside the log and missing the branches protruding from it. After her bait hit the bottom, she tightened the line and waited.

"You're so fucking hot," Stirling commented, while attaching a spinner bait to his line.

He casted on the other side of the dock.

"This is just what I needed, honey. Thank you," she said.

"You feel better."

"For now. It's the small moments that really count and add up in the end. I know that first-hand. So again, thank you."

"Anything for you, *meine Flamme*."

The sun began setting and painted the clouds orange and pink, with undertones of purple.

Stirling had reeled in and released two small bass, and Lila had casted out three times, still patiently waiting for a bite.

Stirling set his pole down and came up behind Lila, nuzzling her neck. "Looks like you won't be catching anything tonight, beautiful."

"I like your scruff. It tickles," she giggled, trying to stave off the inevitable onslaught of goosebumps he was summoning. "Look at the sky. Isn't it lovely?" she asked, entranced by the beauty and sounds enveloping her.

"I'd rather look at you. Nothing is as lovely as you. Let's go inside and make love," he urged, nipping at her earlobe.

"Just a few more minutes. I feel it coming," she predicted quietly, concentrating on her line and the water flow around it.

“You feel what coming?” he asked, amused. “The catfish that’ll beat my record? Ha! Wouldn’t you rather feel me coming?” He rubbed himself against the back of her jeans.

“Of course, but... I got it!” she exclaimed.

She felt a hard tug and pulled up on her rod to set the hook. Then she started reeling. The fish fought pretty hard, and Stirling stood back in anticipation.

“You’re nervous, aren’t you?” she teased. She knew her fish would be heavier than his. She just knew it.

“Fat chance. You caught a sleeper in October, Lila. Don’t get your hopes up,” he deflected.

She reeled steadily. “Then why are you so worried?”

“I’m not,” he protested.

“Honey, our bond says differently,” she stated truthfully.

Stirling shut his face and waited as Lila brought the fish up to the side of the dock. It was surely large and real feisty. It thrashed back and forth, making it difficult for Lila to grasp the line. Once the fish calmed a bit, she brought it over the top of the dock railing.

Stirling grabbed some rope, then reached out and carefully grasped the snagged blue catfish. “We have to take this one up and weigh it.” He released the hook from the fish’s upper lip and nostril, then he strung the rope through its mouth, and pulled it out through its gills.

“Aren’t we gonna let him go? Why are you stringing him up?” Lila asked.

“Well, if we don’t take him up and weigh him, how will we know if you beat my record? You want me to let him go *now*?” he asked slyly.

“No. As long as he’s cooked properly.”

“Oma will want to fry this one for sure,” he said and winked at her.

“We’ll then, let’s go!” Lila clapped her hands together and hopped up and down a couple of times.

They gathered their equipment up hastily and Stirling tossed the catfish over his shoulder.

Swiftly, they walked along the dock, back to the house, and once inside the screened porch, Stirling threw everything back against the cluttered wall.

After a quick scan of the available inventory, he plucked a digital scale from a hook and swung the fish to his front. Lila stood there with a smirk on her face and her arms crossed over her chest. He glanced at her and then sighed.

She felt his ego bruising and she was almost sorry that she was about to beat his record catch. Especially on her first time fishing his lake. She watched as he clamped the fish's lower jaw to the weighing apparatus. He waited impatiently for the result, which only took about five seconds, then dropped his head in defeat. While he was hunched, she stepped forward and peeked at the reading on the scale.

"16.2!" she hollered. "Woo-hoo!" She danced around and then slapped him on the butt. "I beat your big bad record, baby. How do you feel about that?" she sassed.

"Maybe the scale is broken. We should weigh him again."

She gave him a thumb down and grinned. He whined as she moved toward him and cupped his face in her hands.

"Aw, wittle Stirwing. I'm so sowry," she said in a baby voice before kissing his lips.

He snatched her around the waist with one arm and swung her around. Then he laid her down on the ground and hopped on top of her. They both stopped laughing as he met her eyes with his fiery irises. Seductively, he brought her arms above her head, grasping her wrists with a hand. She closed her eyes, expecting a kiss, but instead he pinned her down by forcing his head against her shoulder.

"Stop it!" she screamed.

He was digging his fingertips into her ribcage and she couldn't fight him back at all.

"Stop, please! Please!" she cackled.

She had always hated being tickled, especially on her feet.

Oh shit.

Your feet, huh?

Please don't.

He sat up abruptly and reached back for her sneakers as she tried hopelessly to bat him away.

"What's going on out here?" Cairo asked, filling the doorway, distracting Lila completely.

She quickly looked at Stirling again to remind herself that he was sexier than his older brother.

"Lila here, just beat my catfish record by four pounds. I'm really depressed about it so don't rub it in, Cairo," Stirling joked, standing and helping Lila to her feet.

"Fuck that, you pussy. You got beat by a girl with no fishing experience at all! This is some funny shit. Lemme take a look at this thing." Cairo stepped into the porch.

Stirling held up the catch and then punched Cairo in the bicep.

"I have plenty of fishing experience, I'll have you know," Lila retorted, offended by Cairo's assumption.

"Take it in to Oma, and tell her to freeze it for cooking," Stirling said.

"Yes, sir, inferior fisherman, sir," Cairo shot back, saluting and turning on his heel.

"I hate my brothers so much. And you think they're hot," Stirling acknowledged.

He nudged Lila. The chagrin that washed over her face was priceless.

"I'm sorry, honey. They just all... well, they all look like or remind me of you. I can't help it." She looked down and made a semicircle with her foot.

"Lila, it's okay. It's natural. There will be times when we find others attractive, and it will mean nothing. I don't smell any lust on you. And you won't ever smell it on me for another woman. We're soulmates. And speaking of lust, stay far away from Hale, unless you want me to kill him. I think he desires more than just to be your brother-in-law."

"Yeah, he kind of freaked me out earlier."

"I know. I sensed your concern."

"Let's get inside," Lila proposed. She didn't want to discuss Hale at all.

She and Stirling went into the kitchen to wash the smell of fish off their hands. Cairo was still laughing as he chopped off the record fish's head.

"Shut it, you jerk-off," Stirling said and planted his foot in the back of Cairo's knee.

Cairo almost collapsed to the floor but quickly recovered, turned and socked Stirling in the stomach. The two wrestled and grunted and cursed at each other. When Lila realized they were playing, she finished drying her hands and went into the living room.

"Nice catch, my granddaughter. I know you've hurt my *p'tit boug*'s pride," Maggie giggled and patted her on the back.

"I don't know about that; he seems to be handling it just fine," Lila chuckled and dodged Stirling and Cairo as they came hurtling toward her in the form of a gigantic bowling ball of testosterone.

Stirling untangled himself from his brother's hold and quickly collected himself. Hiding a smirk, he casually stood, while Cairo popped up from the floor as well. Cairo kissed Maggie on the cheek like an innocent child and disappeared back into the kitchen.

Stirling shook his head, laughing under his breath, then tucked a strand of Maggie's silver hair behind her ear. The shit they put her through.

"I'm proud of Lila's catch. She's an amazing woman. And patient, too. It took her quite some time to catch that fish."

"I'm proud too, boy. Of both of you." Maggie pinched Stirling's cheeks and joined Cairo for the filleting.

Stirling blushed. "Is it wrong of me to hate when she pinches my cheeks? Hey, take a bath with me?" he whispered into Lila's ear.

"Of course, you dirty boy," she whispered back.

The couple walked past the summoning group which was blessing the food on the round table in a strange language that Lila though might be French Creole or something like it.

Once upstairs and inside the bathroom, Stirling ran hot bath and slowly stripped Lila's clothes off, then she watched as he undressed himself. She caressed his bond tattoo, and he returned the gesture as he leaned into her. Backing away from him teasingly, she bumped into the sink and lost her breath when the cold porcelain met her skin.

Stirling closed in and smoothed his hand across her breasts. She moaned softly and grasped his warm shaft, stroking him firmly.

"I can't wait to take you," he told her.

"Then take me," she insisted and nipped his bottom lip.

He bent down and tore her panties off with his teeth. Slowly, he spread her open and teased her with his tongue.

"Now, Stirling."

Her commanding tone made him hornier. He picked her up as she wrapped her legs around him tightly and he moved to the far wall, pressing her back against it. Once he positioned her with his brawny arms, he slid himself inside her zealously. She clutched his rocky back muscles, digging her fingernails into his flesh, causing him to growl hungrily.

Stirling grunted like a primordial animal each time he thrusted into her and Lila had to give it her all not to scream out in sheer pleasure. She didn't want everyone in the house to be aware that she was getting banged against the bathroom wall, so she buried her face into her lover's shoulder and bit down hard. The taste of his blood was honey on her tongue.

"You are amazing," he breathed, scooting her farther up on his hips.

She was sliding down his body due to the sweat building between them. He almost pulled out of her to readjust, but instead, he lingered around her spot. The spot he had hit before they were bonded and caused her to ejaculate buckets all over the bed. He ground into her there, and she threw her head back against the wall, biting her bottom lip hard enough to break the skin. Drops of blood trickled down her chin.

"That's what I like to see. I love watching you come," he rasped, and licked her throat up to her jaw.

He covered her chin with his mouth, where her blood settled, and savored her taste. It was of salt and wind and of something sweet, something he couldn't quite pinpoint. Maybe honeysuckle. He figured that if love had a taste, it tasted like Lila.

As she finally drooped in his arms, he became enthralled at the sight of his exhausted mate. He embedded himself in her as deeply and firmly as he could without hurting her, and then he came, which brought him to his knees. He held her on his lap as she detonated again, this time not bothering to muzzle herself. His cock made her love-drunk.

After she stopped trembling, he gently withdrew from her, stood with her, and slipped her into the steaming tub.

"This feels so nice," Lila said with her eyes closed as Stirling searched the ancient cupboard for soap and a washcloth.

"You didn't say that while I was inside of you just now. I'm hurt," he pouted as he stepped into the tub. There was barely enough room for them both, but neither seemed to mind.

"Honey, you feel better than nice. You feel like... like Heaven, I guess, if I knew what Heaven felt like."

She moved a leg up and rested her heel on his shoulder. He ran a hand over her silken skin and closed his eyes too. It had been quite an active day. He was exhausted.

With the water finally cooling and Stirling still resting, Lila washed her hair and body. Afterward, she straddled her man, even though her knees crunched against the sides of the tub.

As he lightly snored, she bathed him. He exhaled long breaths in response to her soothing touch. Gently, she rubbed his head with shampoo and wiped his face with the washcloth. He roused a bit, smiling slightly, as she moved along his other parts, taking tender care of each. After he was clean, she forced him under the water to rinse his hair, and upper body.

Satisfied, she hopped out of the tub and grabbed their towels. Stirling shook his head violently, dispersing water droplets all over the room.

"You look like a big puppy dog," Lila laughed, handing him his towel.

After they dried off, they scampered down the hallway, and into his bedroom. Once in the room, Stirling hit the mattress hard. Lila crawled into the bed next to him and rested her head on his chest. He fell asleep fast, and soon she did the same to the rhythm of his heartbeat.

There was a soft knock on the door. Lila turned on the nightstand lamp and found her towel on the floor. She draped it over her front, then opened the door a crack.

"Dear, it is time," Maggie said quietly.

"Yes, Oma. We'll be down shortly," Lila said.

Lila went to the bed and watched Stirling sleep for a few moments. She remembered how much she had hated him when they first met. Well, she never really hated him. He had been so hard and so mean, but she took comfort in him somehow and the demon in him mystified her. His eyes, his lips, his hard... everything..., set her ablaze.

Now, asleep, he looked like a peaceful human man; for an instant, Lila felt like a human woman. She wanted to forget about the conjuring that awaited her now and the Destroyer who was hunting her. She wanted to fly into the skies with her soulmate and their child. She took a deep breath and lightly nudged Stirling's shoulder.

"Baby?" he asked, eyes still closed.

"We have to go downstairs. Oma called on us."

"Oh, shit, what time is it?" He sat up alertly.

"Ten till moonrise."

"Okay. Okay. Are you ready to do this?" he asked and hugged her around the waist.

She ran her fingers through his hair. He looked up at her, and she nodded, but he knew she was feigning.

"I'll be there for you. Any way you need me to be. Lean on me as hard as you have to."

"I'm scared, Stirling."

"I know. Your dread is almost drowning me. I hate feeling you this way."

"I'm sorry," Lila said, and rested her forehead against his. "Let's get dressed. We only have a few minutes."

Stirling released her from his embrace and pulled on a pair of black pants and a white tee. She shimmied into tight, black leather pants and a snug black tank.

As they stepped down the stairs, he held her hand like he'd never let it go. In the living area, they entered the circle of bodies formed around the round table adorned with fruit and food, wine, candles, and two voodoo dolls. There were strands of herbs spread about, and in the center of the table, was a large pentagram, made from what looked like salt. All the lights were dimmed, and the candles created dancing shadows against the wall.

"Dear, do you have a picture of your folks on you?" Helga, the voodoo priestess, asked.

"Actually, I do. I grabbed it before I left home for the final time. It's in my bag upstairs."

"Hurry, go and get it," Helga said, shooing Lila away.

Lila bolted up the expansive flight of stairs, reached the bedroom and rummaged through her bag. In the side pocket, she found the only picture she had of her parents: the picture that had drawn Stirling to her. She looked at it quickly, but sentimentally, then rushed back down to the coven.

"Here," she said as she handed Helga the picture, who immediately ripped it into two halves.

Before Lila could voice her protest, Helga put up a hand to silence her. "This is necessary, child."

Lila suppressed her tears as she watched Helga pin the half that was her mother's picture on the female voodoo doll and the half that was her father's picture on the male doll. Lila thought the pins were meant to hurt people, but Helga explained that the ritual brought life into the dolls and would help in summoning her parents.

Hazel stepped forward, holding out a beautiful silver dagger. She took Lila's hand and pricked a finger with it, drawing blood. She then brought Lila's hand over the table and squeezed her finger until a droplet of blood fell into the center of the pentagram.

"All join hands," Hazel instructed ominously. "Let the circle be cast."

Everyone moved into position.

Lila held Stirling and Maggie's hands as Hazel spoke: "I conjure thee, circle of worship and power. We have created a meeting place of love and trust as we seek a truth. We banish all wickedness and evil from entering this circle but summon those between the boundaries of the Earth and of the Darkness. We ask for protection, Almighty Mother, and hope within our hearts that we shall call upon these lost souls with your aegis. Blessed be.

"Our beloved Pearl and Perry Johnson, we bring you gifts from life into the after. Commune with us and move among us. Come to our light."

Hazel broke the circle to touch Maggie and Lisa on the forehead with decrepit fingers. She whispered something that Lila could not hear. Immediately, Maggie and Lisa began uttering words that had no meaning to Lila. Then, their voices came together in unison, and the words became a chant. The candles on the table began to flicker wildly.

Lila took a deep breath and closed her eyes. She felt a strange sensation overcome her, like static electricity, causing the hairs on her arms and neck to rise. Stirling shook her hand, and she opened her eyes.

Floating in front of her were vague images of her parents. They oscillated in tandem with the candlelight. Her mother was looking around, like she was in the dark; her father was almost invisible.

Hazel looked at Lila and nodded. "Speak, child," she whispered.

Lila cleared her throat and softly said, "Mom, Dad, it's Lila. I miss you, and I'm ready for your message."

Pearl smiled sadly as her eyes focused on her daughter. Lisa spoke, "Dear daughter, I hear you. You are with child and very worried."

Lila looked at Lisa, whose eyes were rolled back in her head. She was speaking her mother's words, sounding like her mother exactly. *Creepy*, Lila thought. She slowly looked away from Lisa and back to her mother's projection.

"Mom, you must tell me why you refused to go to Hell. It's not safe where you are. I have to cross you over," Lila insisted.

She looked back to Lisa, but this time, it was Maggie who spoke, "I missed you. I needed to see you by any means. Lila... have to tell...," Perry said through Maggie.

Memories whizzed back to Lila. Old memories of love and affection, and although her eyes swam in tears, she held it together. "Daddy, what do you need to tell me?"

"There are more. They need help," Maggie said.

"Hurry, Lila, I'm losing them," Hazel urged.

"Do you see the light? Come to the light," Lila begged.

"Lila," Lisa said.

The ghosts of her parents began to swirl and fade, and then, as fast as they had come, they were gone.

Both Maggie and Lisa abruptly woke from their trances.

Lila gasped sharply and buried her face in her hands. Stirling immediately gathered her and held her close. He palmed her head as she cried silently into his shoulder.

Maggie turned to her and gently rubbed her back. "Go back to bed, sweetheart. This is a process. The connection we made was quite good. Keep your chin up and have faith. I do."

Lila sniffled, and dried her eyes. "Thank you, Oma. For everything. I know you aren't feeling well, and I feel horrible about burdening you." She reached out and touched the beautiful old woman's face.

Maggie placed her hand over Lila's. "Daughter, you are no burden. You are an angel. You've brought my boy home and given him a family." Maggie pressed Lila's hand to her lips and kissed it softly. "We will try again tomorrow night. We will receive their message," she encouraged. "They won't cross over until they deliver it."

"Again, thank you all. For everything," Lila said, wiping again at her tear-stained her face.

She squeezed Stirling's hand and left him. Stirling wanted to go to her, but he knew she needed to be alone. He flipped on the lights in the living room and watched Lila slowly walk up the stairs. She paused on the balcony and weakly smiled at him. He half-waved at her and then placed a hand over his heart. She mimicked the gesture. Once she disappeared, he joined everyone, who was now eating from the food on the table, but he didn't have the stomach to take anything in because Lila was heartsick.

Around two in the morning, Stirling quietly crawled into bed with Lila, who was slightly snoring. He took that as a good sign and turned slowly in the bed so he wouldn't disturb her. He closed his eyes but still felt her lingering remorse for leaving her parents the way she had. He wanted to hold her but didn't want to wake her. Instead, he settled for falling asleep with his back against hers.

Lila woke early in the morning but refused to get out of bed. At some point in the night, she had lodged herself against Stirling's chest and into his arms. She was safe when he held her, so when he reluctantly let her go a couple hours later, she felt desolate.

While Stirling forced himself to eat breakfast, Cairo tried cheering him up, to no avail.

"C'mon man. She'll bounce back soon. Once we cross them, she'll start talking about nursery colors and baby names," Cairo said encouragingly.

"Yeah, it's just hard to feel your own feelings when you're bonded. Everything gets muddled. I should go talk to her, even though she wants to be alone. She's torturing herself."

"Don't let her do that. Go to her, boy. It's your job to take care of her. To be strong when she is weak," Maggie said, as she scrubbed the bacon pan.

"I know." Stirling excused himself.

Lila was sitting on the floor. Her butt had gone numb about an hour ago. She longed for her parents now; being so close to them, yet so far away, was excruciating. She was still upset with them about Doug, but she was even angrier with herself for not swallowing her pride enough to forgive them. Now they'd locked themselves in Limbo on a chance they would be able to speak with her. They'd never stopped loving her.

Lila heard Stirling coming up the stairs, and she opened the door for him just as his phone rang.

"Hello," he said, shutting the door behind him.

Trepidation shot from Stirling into Lila's heart. It pierced through, all the way. She grabbed his arm.

"I'll be there. Yes. Tomorrow night." With a blood-thirsty look on his face, he dropped the phone to the floor.

"Stirling?" Lila whispered. His jaw was clenched so tightly, she thought he may break his teeth.

"Hale, Cairo, Beckett!" he roared.

Lila stumbled backward onto the bed. She couldn't even be embarrassed about only wearing panties and her nightshirt. Whatever was happening was killing Stirling inside.

"Yeah, bro?" Cairo said, opening the door. The other brothers were right behind him.

"I have until tomorrow night to turn myself into Gaelon," Stirling said resentfully.

Lila couldn't speak. Her heart threatened to stop beating.

"Fuck him. The boys and I have been making some calls. We're getting some troops together before we go anywhere. And you can't tag along. Not with a baby on the way. Female or not; you're bonded," Cairo responded.

"I'm afraid there's no choice unless Lila decides otherwise." Stirling turned to Lila, whose eyes were glazed over. "He has Jenny. She is three months pregnant. Gaelon wants me to bring you in by tomorrow night. He's using your friend as leverage."

"Then I'm going in!" Lila exclaimed, standing up from the bed.

"No, you aren't," Stirling said firmly.

"What?" She was completely bewildered.

"If you go, he will destroy your friend in front of you and kill you anyway. Then her baby will die, our baby will die, and I will die. We will all die. If I go alone, I can try to negotiate Jenny's release."

"How do you plan on doing that?" Lila asked as her stomach turned over.

"I will offer myself and you as collateral. Gaelon wants me just as badly as he wants you for disobeying him. I will tell him that you are close by and that I will make a phone call to have you brought in the moment Jenny is released."

"What makes you think he'll believe you?" Beckett asked.

"Gaelon will know that I am being truthful about trading myself for Jenny once I pass the Reader at the gate. Beckett, you will pick Jenny up, if I'm successful, and bring her here where she will be safe."

"What is a Reader, Stirling?" Cairo asked.

"It is a safety mechanism. A Reader delves deep into the soul. The entity can sense deceit and true intentions. Lila being close by me is true, considering we've bonded. And I will make a phone call to have her brought in, but no one has to answer it."

"Oh shit." Cairo rubbed his face then ran a hand through his jet-black hair. Hale looked at the floor and Beckett leaned against the wall with his arms folded across his chest.

"Stirling. What are you going to do? What are you talking about?" Lila asked in horror.

"I am going to reveal my bond to Gaelon. Then he will think he has me and you. It's the only chance we have to save your friend's life and keep you safe."

"Shit, shit, shit," Cairo murmured, pacing with his hands on his head.

"Cairo, keep assembling troops. Beckett, get ready to leave."

Cairo came forward and hugged Stirling hard. He also kissed him on the cheek, and Lila swore she saw tears dropping from his eyes before he left the room. Beckett followed Cairo out as Stirling instructed.

"Hale, you stay here."

Hale closed the door behind his brothers.

"What are you saying, Stirling?" Lila caught his forearm.

"I'm saying that you are going to break our bond. Gaelon will never suspect a thing."

"Never! If you die, I will die along with you!" she crowed.

"And what if he takes my soul, Lila? I will not allow that to happen to you or my child. If you refuse to break our bond, I will refuse to save your friend," Stirling threatened coldly.

Lila looked up at him, but he looked away from her.

"But this can't be," she whispered in disbelief.

"There is no sense in everyone dying because of your inability to rationalize, Lila."

Feeling like the awkward third wheel, Hale took to staring at the ground again.

Lila released Stirling. She felt like she had been struck by lightning.

"You will take Hale tonight."

"No way! No! And you don't have to leave until tomorrow morning," Lila cried.

"Beckett and I are leaving as soon as we're done here."

Lila didn't recognize Stirling externally or internally. He didn't even want to hold her. He was ice inside. She slapped him across the face, trying to extract some type of emotion from him. He picked her up and tossed her onto the bed.

"Don't move again," he fumed, still not meeting her eyes.

Her mouth opened in shock.

"Hale, I'm giving you this task because I know how badly you want her."

"Brother ...," Hale started.

"Don't. I saw you with her in the kitchen. I'm not a fool. You will protect her, obey her, and love her. You will raise our child as if it's your own. And you will tell our child of my sacrifice when the time is right."

Hale nodded. "Anything you want, Stirling." He eyed Lila briefly and left the room.

Once Hale was gone, Stirling finally broke down. He hefted up his solid oak dresser and then brought it down on the ground. Part of it went through the ancient wood floor, and the rest of it splintered and cracked open.

"What if it doesn't work and he kills Jenny anyway? Maybe you should just stay here with me," Lila sobbed.

Stirling went to her and wrapped his arms around her.

"I will do whatever you ask of me. But let me ask you this. Would you be able to live with yourself knowing you never tried to save her? What if Gaelon tortures her? She is

pregnant. What if he destroys her soul? I can live with all of that. But can you?"

Lila didn't even have to think about the answer. If she didn't know Stirling was her soulmate, she would have thought Jenny was. The girl had been the only one with her since the sandbox and Barbie doll days. Jenny's life and all the lives connected to her were worth more than all the demon lives in the world. Stirling was right. There were worse things than death, and Lila couldn't sit back and do nothing to try to save her.

"That's what I thought," Stirling whispered.

His shirt was drenched in Lila's tears. She couldn't catch her breath.

"Shhhh, *meine Flamme*. Look at me. Look at me," he pleaded, pulling her hands away from her face.

She was breathing erratically. Despair slowly perforated her heart, and it hurt more than the burning she had felt the day she'd laid on the floor for hours, blazing, until Jenny had saved her.

"I need you to kiss me," he implored.

"I ... I can't. I ..."

"Calm yourself, sweetheart. If you don't kiss me now, you may never get to again."

Studying her face, he prayed that Gaelon would spare his soul. He wondered if he'd see Lila again in the afterlife. He pressed his lips against hers, and she wrapped her arms around his neck as tightly as she could. He allowed the world around him to disappear, losing himself in her completely.

Lila had no choice but to do the same. Stirling slid a hand up her body and cupped her soft breast. She grabbed at his shirt desperately until he tore it off and went back to kissing her. They kissed for long moments that were far too short.

He shoved her night shirt up until it reached her collarbone. While she helped remove the garment, he flicked his tongue across one of her nipples and then sucked on it gently. His hands moved down to her panties, and she sat back so he could pull them off. He finished undressing himself and climbed back into the bed, in front of her.

Lila watched him and swore that she would remember every curve of his muscles, every angle of his face, the very shade of his hair, and the softness of his lips. And she would never ever forget the way he felt inside of her.

His thigh separated her legs, and he lowered his head, inhaling her scent. He brushed his tongue against her jewel, and in between her valleys, tasting her one last time. Slowly, he kissed every centimeter of her body until he ended up back where he started—at her lips.

As he inched inside of her, he absorbed her stare. Their bodies molded and flowed as one. Each time Stirling exhaled, so did Lila.

Every time her heart thumped, so did his. Their tattoos shimmered brightly and reflected in each other's eyes.

Reluctantly, almost against her will, Lila came, and Stirling held her so close, kissing her intensely, almost angrily, as his orgasm infused her.

"I don't want to let you go," she whispered against his mouth.

For a moment, she contemplated killing herself after her child was born. *Cairo and Beckett would be excellent uncles.*

"Don't even think it, Lila," Stirling said sadly.

She started crying again. "If Gaelon allows your soul freedom, promise me you won't choose to go to Limbo," she begged.

He buried his face into her shoulder. "I have to go."

"Stirling," she tried again, but he peeled himself off her and grabbed up his clothes. "Stirling, promise me," she pleaded, sitting up in the bed. She snagged her shirt and pulled it over her head, then hastily yanked her panties back on.

"I can't," he answered roughly, looking down, shrugging on his pants.

"That isn't fair," she cried, trembling.

"None of it is. Come here."

He held his arms out to her. She flung herself into them and he embraced her, almost convincing himself that he would selfishly let Jenny die. But Lila would never forgive him. There was no solid exit strategy to be entertained.

"*Meine Flamme*, I love you, and I'm grateful that you know how strong that love is. Pass on my love to our child."

He kissed her lips, which were wet with tears.

"I love you," she breathed, while trying to catch a solid breath.

"I love you, too. And you know how deeply that love runs."

He knelt so he could press his ear against her belly. He closed his eyes, lifted her shirt, and kissed her womb. Standing, he brushed a hand across her cheek. Tears streamed down his face. She felt his misery. It was longing, jealousy, self-persecution, regret and loss all at once.

His last words were strangled by grief. "Name her Deva. It means divinity."

Before Lila could process anything, Stirling had kissed her forehead hard, grabbed his duffle off the floor, and fled from the room.

Deva. Divinity. Deva. That's a girl's name. It's a girl. How does he know already? Wait, wait, wait!

"Stirling!" Lila screamed, tearing out of the room and down the stairs. "Stirling! Wait!"

She booked through the living room and out the front door, just as Stirling and Beckett were backing out in the Charger.

"Stirling!" she screamed again and took off down the porch stairs, running after the car, which was now quickly rolling out of the drive. "Stirling!"

She felt arms around her waist and was lifted off the ground. "No! No! I can't do this without you!" she wailed.

"Lila, Lila, calm down," Cairo said against her ear. She beat on his arms and kicked her legs out wildly. "Lila! He's gone!"

"No," she cried hopelessly, wilting in Cairo's arms. "No."

He cradled her. "I've got you. I've got you, sweetheart."

By the time he got her inside, she had blacked out.

Chapter 17

"Lila, Lila," someone was saying, from so far away. "Lila, wake up."

Lila opened her eyes to see Hale and Maggie hovering over her. Quickly, she sat up, realizing her head had been in Cairo's lap. He held out an arm, preventing her from standing.

"Not so fast. You'll get dizzy. Give yourself a minute," he cautioned.

Lila grabbed her head. It was throbbing. "What happened?" she asked.

"You were upset and blacked out," Hale answered.

He went to touch her face, but she shrank back into the couch. Maggie patted Hale on the chest, and he followed her into the kitchen.

"Look at me. I'm a mess. I need to get cleaned up," Lila said, slowly standing up, pulling at her shirt.

"I'm not leaving you alone. Sorry. You want me to get Hale?" Cairo offered.

"No. Don't get Hale. I don't want to see him until I have to," she declined curtly.

"Well, let's get you cleaned up then," he said and followed her up the stairs.

Lila went into Stirling's bedroom to get her things. Her bag had fallen off the dresser when he heaved it across the room. After shoving her scattered items back into the duffle, she looked at the shattered dresser that was literally in the floor. What a mess life was.

"You okay?" Cairo asked.

"No," Lila answered.

Cairo went into the bathroom and ran the tub water. Lila was feeling spiteful, self-destructive, and downright defiant. She snuck into the bathroom with Cairo and closed the door behind her.

He turned and looked at her quizzically. She cringed before she spoke, but she didn't have much time.

"Look, I really don't want to do this. I don't even know if I'll be able to, but if I have to, I'd feel more comfortable with you. Cairo, will you bond with me? Hale creeps me out. I hate him."

"Uh, Lila," Cairo stammered, scratching his chin. "I don't know if I could do that. Stirling chose Hale. He's more responsible; he wants you. Not that I don't—you're hot and all, but I'm not lifemate material. I'd probably lust after other women all the time and then beg you to break our bond at some point. I can't really be tamed."

"Please! I don't trust him. He tried to seduce me behind your brother's back. What if he's awful to me? To my baby?"

"Lila, I am older and stronger than Hale. I'd never let him hurt you. I will stay in Monroe, close by, if you want, until things calm the fuck down."

"I'll break my bond to him. Someday," she promised hatefully.

Cairo reached out and hugged her. He felt like Stirling but smelled wilder.

"Don't talk like that. Is it because they look so similar?"

She buried her head in his chest. He had figured it out before she had. That's exactly what was wrong. She wouldn't be able to move on at all bonded to Stirling's virtual twin. Bonding with Hale meant eternal damnation for her sanity. She hated Hale because she was terrified of him. She looked up at Cairo.

"Why do you wear your contacts at home?" she asked vacantly.

"I go out a lot. Can't sit still for long."

"Got a touch of ADD?" She moved her arms up around his neck and brought her mouth close to his. She didn't know what she was doing, really. Numbness and madness had taken over. No matter what it took to stay away from Hale, she was going to do it. She was in survival mode.

"Lila, I can't do this. Don't make me," Cairo whispered in a raspy tone.

"I think I would have so much more fun with you, though. Just imagine. You could chain me up, strap me down, blindfold me, whip me..."

"Shit, you're gonna give me blue balls, Lila. Stop." Cairo grabbed at his groin. He pulled her arms down from his neck, while noticing that the tub was almost full. Pulling away, he reached over to turn off the water.

"Well, I can fix that for you," she said, yanking off her shirt and catching his eyes.

Cairo had seen hundreds of women naked and still wasn't desensitized to their beauty, but very few women were as beautiful as Lila. His eyes shifted from her eyes to her breasts. He dragged a finger from the hollow of her neck all the way down to the top of her skimpy panties. Then he looked up to her eyes again, as though asking her permission.

Lila slightly nodded, and without hesitation Cairo hastily grabbed her by her ass cheeks and picked her up. She wound her legs around him tightly, and he slammed her into the wall.

"I have no fucking self-control, you know that?" he growled.

"Neither do I," she answered.

Just as she went to kiss him, there was a hard knock on the door. Cairo dropped her immediately. Had she not been holding onto his neck she would have crashed to the floor.

Well, I tried. Lila pulled down her panties, went to the tub, and slipped inside, sending brimming water all over the tile.

Cairo opened the door hesitantly. "Hale. Uh, I was just running a bath for Lila."

"Like hell you were," Hale spat and stalked into the room. He noticed the wall; there was an indentation where Cairo had crashed Lila into it.

"No wonder Oma hates it when we come over. We're always fucking up her house." Cairo scratched his head, trying to pull aloof off the best could.

"It reeks in here. Did you bond with her?" Hale tried to ask as evenly as he could, but his tone was savage.

"You know, I'm in the room, Hale. You can address me directly," Lila said without turning.

"You've got your hands full with that one. She's the fucking devil," Cairo laughed and strode out of the bathroom.

Hale came around the tub and glared at Lila. He scanned her body for another bond tattoo and relaxed when he didn't see one. The absence of a sex halo should have registered, but he had been too pissed to process that.

Lila couldn't bring herself to look at him.

"Why do you hate me so?" Hale spoke quietly.

Lila looked at her hands under the water. She zoned out and wondered what it would be like to be a fish. *My fins would glide through the water effortlessly.*

"Lila?"

The water current would carry me to wherever I needed to go.

"Lila?"

The world would be free and vast, and...

"Lila?"

Then I'd swallow a hook, get dragged upon land, get my head chopped off, and ...

"Lila!" Hale splashed her in the face.

She looked up at him, finally. He was staring down at her with those beautiful Incubus eyes. Yep, she hated Hale.

"Get out," she threatened.

He didn't argue with her and left without another word.

Her eyes spilled tears. She rested her head back against the rim of the tub and thought of her brothers. *Please, find me.*

Lila donned some thin black sweatpants and the green shirt she had packed for Stirling, when he told her green brought out her eyes. She laid in the bed and rolled in the sheets, which smelled like her soulmate.

Stirling, I can't do this.

You must.

"Knock, knock," Maggie said, cracking the door open.

"Oma."

"The ladies and I are going to try to contact your parents again tonight. I know you have, uh, business to attend to, so we'll understand if you may not be fit to join us."

"Oma, I saw my parents before they died, and they were in a dungeon, with screaming Succubi behind bars. My parents basically killed themselves just to get away," Lila said.

"Interesting. I will ask your parents about this. This may be good news, child. Very good news. Maybe the Succubi are still alive. Come down to eat," Maggie coaxed, taking Lila's arm.

"I'm not hungry, Oma."

"Then come socialize. You can't sit up here all alone dwelling on things to come. C'mon now," Maggie insisted, pulling her forward.

Lila relented and followed her down the stairs. Hale was sitting in the yellowish chair watching every move she made. She wanted to stab him in the eyes.

Cairo was sitting on the couch again. "Oma, you really need a TV," he said.

"Nonsense, boy. That noise will rattle your brain." She shook a finger at him.

Lila went out onto the front porch to get some air. After a few minutes, Hale came out and stood next to her.

"I'll never understand why Oma painted this place pink," he commented.

Lila was silent.

"I'm trying to play nice, Lila. I'm trying, and you're making it so hard."

"Playing nice huh? This isn't a fucking game, Hale. And what makes you think you'll want to be a lifemate and father for the rest of your life?" she asked.

"I'm ready for it, Lila. I want it. I want you." He reached for her cheek, but she recoiled.

"You're a lot like Stirling. Same taste in women, too, right?" she quipped.

"I guess so. Lila, look at me," Hale said, turning her into him.

"I can't. It hurts too bad," she said and walked back inside.

She plopped down on the couch next to Cairo, who slipped an arm around her as the front door slammed shut. Before Hale walked out to the back porch, he glared at his brother. Cairo just shrugged and rubbed Lila's head.

Chapter 18

"Lila, get up," Cairo spoke urgently.

She woke with her head in Cairo's lap. Again.

"I gotta take a wicked pee," he whined.

"Sorry, I didn't think I'd fall asleep," Lila said as she sat up.

"It's okay," he said back, hobbling off to the bathroom.

Maggie was sitting in the yellowish chair now. She looked at Lila sadly.

"What time is it?" Lila asked, rubbing her eyes.

"It's that time, dear. Hale is upstairs waiting for you."

"Oma, I can't do this," Lila whispered hopelessly.

Maggie stood and walked over to her. She held out her hands, and Lila took them. Maggie pulled her off the couch and hugged her tightly. "You must be strong for your daughter."

"Stirling told you it's a girl?"

"He didn't have to," Maggie said, releasing her. A tear fell from her shiny eyes.

"Hale is a good man. He will take care of you both," she sniffled. "I am so grateful that you will carry Stirling's name and the best part of him, your child."

"Deva." Lila swallowed hard.

"Deva. It's perfect," Maggie whispered. She reluctantly left Lila crying and shaking.

Lila felt so alone. Her parents were dead, Jenny could be next, and her other half was surely going to be murdered all because he fell for her. Then, she would be bonded to a demon she could never love.

She turned and walked up the stairs, hating herself more and more with each step. Her stomach churned as she peered into the bedroom at the top of the stairs to her left. It was empty. She almost threw up she was so unnerved. Next, she passed Stirling's vacant room. She reached the end of the hallway and slowly opened the last door. Hale was sitting on a twin bed. He stood when he heard the door shut.

"Lila."

Chapter 19

Stirling hadn't breathed a word to Beckett the entire six hours they were on the road. Finally, after the solemn drive, he pulled his car up to a towering and impressive Sheraton Hotel in the center of Atlanta. Once he parked, he killed the engine, shoved on his shades and stepped out of the car with his duffle. Beckett followed his brother into the simple but elegant lobby.

While Stirling knew he wouldn't sleep at all tonight, he wanted to spend his last night alive in the complete opposite environment he'd been so used to of late. Sleeping on an old dirty mattress in a hundred-and-fifty-year-old house had been acceptable until he met Lila. She had brought light into his dark world, and that light shined on a part of his soul that he had never realized existed. He had free will, and he had used it grudgingly, foolishly, and murderously. Lila made him understand that things could be different.

Even though demons were plagues to those around them, they didn't have to inflict more suffering than they were cursed to deal out. They didn't have to live like heathens in the shadows and condemn themselves to solitude like Stirling had.

Beckett checked in with a lady at the front desk.

Stirling almost doubled over when he felt Lila's apprehension and disgust. It was all he could do not to communicate with her. He hoped she didn't call to him. No way could he answer her back. It was over. He had to let her go.

Beckett motioned to Stirling, and they stepped into an elevator occupied by a lone young woman. She had dark hair, and from behind, she could have been Lila. Well, that is if her ass was rounder and she was a bit taller. Maybe if her hair was a little longer and wavier.

The smell of lust filled the elevator and Stirling almost gagged. The woman turned and smiled seductively at him, but he snarled at her in response. Wide-eyed, she backed into the glass of the elevator wall. A horrified expression contorted her pretty face. Beckett placed a hand against Stirling's chest as the elevator bell dinged. The door opened, and the woman almost fell out onto the shining floor. She scampered down the hallway, looking back to ensure the beautiful but frightening men weren't following her.

Once the elevator door closed and stopped at the eighth floor, Beckett and Stirling stepped out and followed numbered plaques leading them to their room.

"I'm glad there's a balcony," Stirling said.

"Me, too," Beckett responded as he slid the key in the door lock.

Beckett tossed his small bag to the floor and looked around the room. It was quite comfortable, but a little too romantic for brothers to be sharing.

"You should see the size of the tub in this bathroom. It's obscene," Beckett called, but Stirling was silent.

Beckett walked around some more and spied the sliding glass door that led to the balcony. It was open. Stirling was already outside, sitting in a chair, sipping out of a bottle.

"Where'd you get the booze?" Beckett hoped his brother would open up a little now.

"I stopped when you were asleep. I only bought two bottles. I figured you didn't drink," Stirling said.

"I don't usually, unless I'm having dinner. Then I prefer a Merlot or a Pinot Noir." Beckett sat next to Stirling.

"Are you sure you aren't into dudes, Beck?"

"I'm not into dudes. I am domesticated." Beckett chuckled as he shrugged.

"*Mr. Perfect.*" Stirling swigged from his bottle.

Beckett snatched it from him and took a long pull of bourbon. "I'm far from perfect. I just don't live the way most of us do."

"You can't live that much differently unless you're bonded."

"No, I'm not bonded."

"Then you must be just as lonely as the rest of us. Living in a two bedroom house, stalking women at night. Denying that you may have just given someone herpes or HIV." Stirling shook his head subtly.

"I met someone who needs me to assimilate. I have to live differently than what is natural to me." Beckett swigged from the bottle again and handed it back to Stirling.

"Who could possibly have that kind of influence over you if you aren't bonded?"

"Well, I figure I may as well take on another curse, since I'm already afflicted."

"What curse is that?" Stirling asked.

"Love. It's enticing, all-consuming, and then it eventually dissolves you completely," Beckett answered, staring out into the sky.

"What species is she?"

"Human."

"What? Beckett, that's just got to be a major crush. I mean, what? Does she work for you? Is she one of your caterers?" Stirling chuckled, downing the rest of the bottle. He opened the second, finally feeling a buzz. "Beck? How do you know her, man?" Stirling asked again, backhanding his bro's shoulder.

"She's my wife."

"Ha-ha! Okay, okay. You almost had me. Seriously, is all of it bullshit, or just the human part?" Stirling tipped the bottle back while watching Beckett from the corner of his eye. His brother wasn't smiling. "You're fucking serious, aren't you?"

"I know what you're feeling, Stirling. I cannot be with her forever or offer her the things she truly wants in life, yet she stays with me. It's an agony I can't bridle."

"You mate with her?" Stirling asked in astonishment.

"Yes."

"Jesus, Beckett. How can she stay with you? She must think you're a total freak!"

"She knows what I am," Beckett answered curtly and took the new bottle from Stirling.

"Aren't you scared you'll infect her with something?"

"No. We use protection. She's also aware that I need to have sex with other women."

"She must be an amazing girl to put up with that, and to actually believe you're an Incubus." Stirling shook his head in disbelief.

"It's hard for her, but she knows sex with other women is just a medicine of sorts. And she didn't believe me about being an Incubus until I transformed in front of her. She refused to speak to me for days after that, but then showed up at my house about a week later. My contacts weren't in, and she stared at my eyes forever. The next thing I knew, she threw herself at me and told me she loved me."

"Wow," Stirling responded. He couldn't believe what his brother was telling him. He was in love with a human? It must have been torture. For both of them.

Silence breached the conversation, and the brothers drank their whiskey without the need to say anymore.

Stirling was glad he had asked Beckett to accompany him on the journey to his demise. Beckett understood his quandary and knew just what to say, and when and how to say it. He didn't try to force Stirling to convey his feelings, which he was thankful for. He didn't want to convey feelings about anything tonight, because none of it would matter the next day. Tears fell from Stirling's eyes, and he didn't bother to hide them or wipe them away.

Beckett handed him the last of the whiskey. Stirling took it down quickly, then stood up and slowly shed his clothing. Beckett did the same and stood beside his little brother, surveying his tormented face. "I'll miss you, Stirling," he said.

Stirling nodded once and pulled himself onto the balcony railing. He shifted into the monster that he was and flew off; the flapping of his wings blew wind through Beckett's blonde locks. After a nostalgic sigh, Beckett followed him into the moonlight.

Chapter 20

"Hale," Lila said icily.

He quickly stood from the bed.

"You weren't planning on me sleeping in here," she stated, pointing to the mattress. It wasn't large enough for them both to lie on unless they were stacked on top of each other.

"Oh, I made us a place on the floor. Yes. I'd like for you to stay with me tonight," he answered, as she came around to face him.

He had made quite a little spot for them. Pillows were piled in the corner, and numerous intricate quilts lay spread out just below the only window in the room. Moonlight danced over the space. Candles were lit throughout the room. The setting would have been romantic had the situation been completely fucking different.

Hale held out his hand to Lila. She looked at him, and his eyes glowed blue-violet in the shadows. Moonlight emanating through the window kissed his hair and the side of his face. She reluctantly took his hand, and he led her down to the palette on the floor.

"We can talk first if you'd like," he suggested.

"It's a girl," she said quietly.

"The baby?" Excitement oozed from his voice.

"Her name will be Deva."

"Lila, that's incredible," he murmured against her hair after pulling her close and placing a hand on her womb.

She tensed immediately.

Hale sensed her discomfort and leaned away from her. "I'm sorry. I know this is difficult for you."

"Do you? Do you really care? You just met me. How could you care for me?" she asked almost hysterically.

"From what I understand, you and Stirling didn't know one another long. He told me you hated him when you first met."

"Stirling and I are soulmates. I never hated him. I loved him the moment I saw him. I just didn't know it at the time," she argued.

"He mentioned that, too. He loved the way you fought him. Actually, he said he loved you before that, when he saw you in a picture. I can't compete with that. I can't compete with him in any respect when it concerns you. I can't replace him. I can't be your soulmate. But I can be a good lifemate and an even better father. You can learn to love me in some way." He reached out and touched her face.

She pulled away. "I can't."

"Your friend will suffer. Her child will die," he reminded her.

"You look just like him. How am I to ever let him go?"

"Pretend I am him for the night if you must. After that, we will take each day at a time. I won't press you."

He ran his fingers through her hair, and she closed her eyes at his touch. *How can I bring myself to do this?* she thought desolately. Then he was closer to her. Instinctually, she moved back from him again.

"Lila, what do you want me to do?" he asked, pleading with her.

"I don't know. I don't know. I don't know how to do this! I'll die inside!" she sobbed and stood up from the pallet.

"Well, it has to be done, Lila," Hale said firmly, standing as well.

He used his body like a deadly weapon to back her into the wall. Quickly, he stripped his shirt off and move himself against her. His warmth was too familiar.

"You don't smell like him," she whispered, eyes averted.

"Because I'm not him!" he yelled and put his fist through the wall, next to her shoulder.

Lila didn't flinch. She couldn't deny Hale's sheer beauty, his power, or determination. And ultimately, she wouldn't be able to deny him anything.

He pressed up against her again and brought his mouth as close to hers as he could.

"What's it like not being able to take me, knowing that I have to decide to break my bond?" she tormented.

"It's very uncomfortable. Submit, Lila, or I will leave you and you can deal with the consequences," he warned.

She knew she was stalling. Finally, she looked back into his eyes, and they bored right through her. The breaking of her heart nearly brought her to her knees. *Stirling. I love you.* She inhaled deeply, then threw her arms around Hale's neck. She kissed him, and the reciprocation came without restraint.

Hale grabbed her shoulders and pulled her to the ground with him. She left his mouth briefly, taking another deep breath as his lips and tongue trailed her neckline.

Stirling.

He was pulling her shirt over her head and kissing the tops of her breasts. She felt like the veins in her body were twisting, threatening to suffocate her. She felt like a light bulb two flicks away from burning out. She was shutting down.

"Lila," Hale whispered. "Lay with me."

Mechanically, she did as she was told. He slid her pants off and moved on top of her. His chest was smooth, not sprinkled with soft, sandy hair like Stirling's. He nuzzled her neck, and his face wasn't scruffy like Stirling's.

Stirling.

"Dammit!" she shouted in frustration and forced Hale from her body.

"Again, what do you want me to do?" He was struggling to stay calm, but she was eating away at his pride. "What. Do. You. Want?" His eyes were fierce now. Lust rolled off him, invading her senses as he propped himself up on an elbow and eroded her with his glare.

Finally, after several sad, quiet moments, she succumbed. "I want you to tear my panties off. I want you to grab me as hard as you can around the waist until I can't breathe. Force my shoulders down and fuck me for as long and hard as you can. Be as mean as you can. Make me feel something other than what I'm feeling right now," she wept uncontrollably.

Hale watched her fall apart and sighed. Her wondrous breasts shimmered in the candlelight. The moonlight illuminated the tears sliding down her cheek. He had thought taking her would be so easy, but now his own heart threatened to break for her. He envisioned her smiling and laughing in his big brother's arms. Soulmates. There was nothing he could ever do to make her as happy as she could have been with Stirling. It was the worst possible situation he could be in. He had lusted for Lila the moment he saw her, but now that he had her, it was almost impossible to take her. In this moment, he needed a reason to do what she claimed she wanted from him.

He cupped her face and forced her to look at him. "Tell me you hate me," he whispered.

"I hate you," she ground out with ease.

"Tell me you'll never love me."

"I will *never* love you." She clawed her nails into his chest, drawing blood.

He gritted his teeth. "Tell me I'll never be good enough."

"You'll never be good enough," she said heartlessly. "You'll never ever be good enough."

He lifted her off the ground. Securing her by the waist, he tore the panties from her sex. He grabbed her ass as hard as he could, and she gasped loudly in response.

"Am I getting through to you?" he asked, his hot lips to her ear.

When she didn't answer, he tightened his stronghold around her middle. She wiggled in his grasp, but he restrained her. He reached between the back of her thighs and felt her heat. Her breath caught and his cock grew harder in response.

"There we go. Finally," he panted and thrusted two fingers deep inside her.

"Ahhh," she moaned against her will.

She imagined being with Stirling and wrapped a leg around Hale's waist. He bit into her neck until he tasted her blood and she wailed.

"I am going to take you over and over and over again until you learn to love me," he promised.

He threw Lila onto the palette face down, shoved her shoulders deep into the quilts, and pulled back on her hair after straddling her luscious frame.

He bent over and pressed his cheek against hers. "And you *will* learn to love me."

It sounded like a threatening promise.

He released her hair, and her head smashed onto a pillow.

As Lila turned slightly, she watched him shed his pants and stalk around her, moving like a stealthy predator.

"Now," she whispered in defeat. Her voice was gone, swept away by sorrow. Tears spilled from her eyes, creating a river of pain that ran across her cheek, down her nose, soaking the quilts beneath her.

Hale situated himself behind her. She felt his firm hand on her lower back and closed her eyes. In that moment, she thought that maybe demons had every right to hate God for their curses.

Stirling, forgive me. For after this, I will never be the same.

Stirling's voice rang through her mind as if he were right next to her. Meine Flamme, *I love you. Goodbye.*

Chapter 21

The lights suddenly sparked to life, and Maggie was leaning in the doorway, breathless.

"Oma?" Hale asked, horrified. He felt like he was in college and just got busted trying to fuck the dean's daughter. He grabbed a pillow off the floor, covering himself, and jumped up in confusion.

Lila rolled up on her heels in a daze. She didn't understand what was happening either. She squinted because of the abrasive light and her stinging tears. Maggie rushed to her side.

"Lila," Maggie shook her and slowly Lila met her eyes. "I spoke with your parents. They bring good news. Gaelon is weak!" she cried triumphantly.

"What do you mean, Oma?" Lila touched her arm.

Bells and whistles rand out in her head. Had Oma found a way to prevent her from breaking her bond to Stirling? She quickly stood and found her clothes. "What is it?" she asked desperately as she yanked on her pants.

"Gaelon cannot destroy a soul without becoming very vulnerable. The process makes him so feeble that two of his loyal minions have to him lock him away from all others until he recovers. That's why most of the Lilin are still alive! He tortures them before he murders them, decimates a soul, rebounds and starts the course all over again. This changes the dynamic a bit, don't you think? There's a chance we can exploit his weakness. I thought you should know before you broke your bond to Stirling. Looks like I may have been too late?"

Maggie was hunched, bless her heart. Her face was beautifully concerned, and Lila hopped forward and kissed her.

"No, you aren't too late. And yes, Oma, this changes everything! We need a different plan. If we can hit Gaelon while he's down, Stirling doesn't have to storm his castle alone. I must go to Stirling and tell him we will fight with him for Jenny, for our race. For the souls that have been lost. But timing is everything."

"What about Deva? Lila, if you go to battle, Gaelon will have twice the chance of killing you and Stirling. Stay here with Oma where you are hidden," Hale tried to reason.

"Hidden," Lila repeated.

"Yes, dear. The shadow spell I cast over my property will shield you," Maggie said.

"That's why my brothers can't find me," Lila realized. "You warded this place. Hale, put your clothes on, we need to go!"

Lila sped down the stairs and bumped into Cairo.

"There's a lot of ruckus up there. Is Hale alive or did you eat him?" he laughed.

"Cairo, I have to find my brothers," Lila stated urgently.

"I was just on my way to Stirling. Wait, you need to find your brothers? Why?" He held her shoulders possessively.

"I'll explain later," she said.

Hale jogged down the stairs, and Maggie trailed slowly behind.

"Let's go. Now!" Lila demanded.

"Okay, okay," Cairo responded with a bewildered look. He grabbed his leather jacket and rushed out the door.

Hale shrugged on his leather and followed.

Lila looked to Maggie once they were alone. "The shadow spell; can it work on me?"

"Yes, daughter," Maggie said, coming to the landing.

"I'm sorry, Oma. I know you wanted Stirling to have a good life. I know you are excited about our baby. I can't promise you any of those things now. I have to save my friend and our kind. We might die fighting, but Gaelon won't be able to destroy our souls. Not during a battle, when he can't afford weakness."

"Stirling has you and your child now as he will have them in the afterlife if that is the fate of it. There is no reason for you to hide here. Go beautiful girl. Go and save us all."

"Thank you, Oma. For everything. I love you," Lila said, backing toward the door.

Oma remembered, "Lila, I need something to give Hazel to charm for the shadow spell."

"In my bag upstairs. There's a necklace. We'll be right back to go over a plan," Lila said as she grabbed her jacket.

"Lila, I love you too." Oma's face was proud, fearful and pained all at once.

Lila smiled assuredly and blew her a kiss before she skipped out the door.

Chapter 22

Stirling. I am coming for you. Lila spoke telepathically as she made her way to Cairo and his bike.

Lila, no. What are you thinking?

Gaelon is weak.

What do you mean?

Soon. I'll be with you soon and explain.

Cairo helped Lila onto his Harley and handed her his helmet. The black leather, tattoos, piercings, and brawn were no façade. It was all Cairo. She briefly thought that any woman who could domesticate him would be one lucky broad. He was playfully sexy and probably a god in the sack, but she was so glad he hadn't given into her easily when she begged him for a bond.

"Do you have any clue where your brothers might be?" he asked.

"Somewhere close. I called to them. They didn't answer, but I can feel them now. We need to track them; I just don't know where to start. Where do the local Incubi hang out around here?" Her voice was muffled by the helmet swimming on her head. She ripped the thing off and tossed it back to Cairo.

"This thing will fly off if we wreck," she said, annoyed.

"Just trying to look out for you, sis." He shrugged. There's only one place in this Podunk town where an Incubus would be caught dead in."

"Well then. Let's go."

Cairo slipped on black gloves that were cut off at the knuckle. Then he revved his bike backed it up slowly and positioned it in front of Hale's Cadillac.

"Hold on, Lila," he warned.

She wrapped her arms around his expansive, muscular frame, then he peeled off, down the street.

The ride was windy and cold, and Lila was grateful that she had always worn a leather jacket. Wind and cold couldn't cut through leather the way it did through other materials. She also loved the smell of it and was beginning to think leather was a Lilin thing. Every Lilin she had met wore leather. Pushing her trite thoughts aside, butterflies fluttered in her stomach as her anticipation swelled. Her hair whipped around her face and licked her eyeballs a couple of times, so she pressed her cheek into Cairo's back.

Soon enough, Cairo and Hale pulled up to a dive-bar. Numerous bikes were parked in the lot, and neon lights advertising Budweiser and Jack Daniel's hung in the dim windows. The place was a hole in the wall, a shanty, but it looked like the type of place where bar brawls were frequent, and Lila was sure any Incubus would love to find trouble here.

Cairo helped her off his bike.

She felt their presence stronger now. Just like Stirling had said, it was like gravity pulling at her inner being toward her kin, like how the planets were drawn to the sun.

"This is it, girl. If they aren't here, I don't know where else to take you," Cairo said, running a hand through his dark hair.

"They're here," she said confidently.

Suddenly, she got the jitters. What were they going to be like?

Cairo strode up to the bar first and held the door open for Lila.

"Well, hello," a busty blonde rasped at him. She was puffing on a cigarette, leaning against the brick exterior of the building. Lila looked back, and Cairo was sniffing the woman's hair and whispering something in her ear.

Hale approached and slapped him on the shoulder. "C'mon man," he ordered.

Cairo palmed the erection filling his jeans, and again, Lila thanked God she hadn't bonded with him.

Unmoving clouds of smoke hung in in the dreary space and music was playing from somewhere, loudly enough to obstruct conversation.

Lila, Hale, and Cairo stood near the door, scoping out the place and then at the bar, five men turned to look at them simultaneously. All the men exuded a dangerous presence. Two of them took down a shot and then they all stood in tandem and walked toward Lila and her new brothers.

The first Incubus to approach looked like Lila's father. He was tall, solidly built and had the facial hair her father had dapperly donned at one point. A thick mustache ran fluidly into his bushy grey beard.

"Lila," he said simply, and cocked his head to the side.

The others stood in a semicircle around her and her in-laws.

"You are my brothers," she stated, in awe.

"I'm sorry we have stayed so secluded, but Pearl wanted us to keep our distance due to our disruptive behavior. My name is Gage. I am your eldest brother. It's a privilege to finally meet you."

Lila took him in. He appeared to be in his early forties. He was wearing a black shirt, a leather jacket, black jeans and boots. Hardened features made him look lethal. He was a big, muscled man, and could easily be a match for Stirling or Cairo. A tattoo ran up his neck and along the side of his face, meeting long grey hair, which was pulled back into a ponytail.

"This is Roderick." Gage pointed to another Incubus decked out in all black: long-sleeved shirt with a leather vest over it and black chaps over blue jeans. He was also large and muscular but unlike Gage's, his face was kind. His features were rounder than the ones set in his older brother's rocky face. He looked ten years younger than Gage. When he offered his hand to Lila, she took it into her own with a smile.

"This is Holt, Brick, and Maximus. Max for short," Roderick said, gesturing to the rest of her brothers.

They each looked different but somehow the same, even the same as Lila. Holt was taller than the rest, and leaner too. He was probably in his early thirties in human years. His face was clean-shaven and he sported a bald head. Brick and Max were obviously twins. They were younger and a bit shorter than the others but built like dams. Both had short, dark hair. A cowlick forced their locks to lie stylishly to the left. Their faces were mean,

Al Capone-ish. While smaller than the others, they were much more intimidating.

Lila stood there and looked each of the men in the eyes. She was in total disbelief.

"Why don't we take this outside," Gage suggested. "It's too loud in here."

He took Lila's hand and led her out the door.

The minute they stepped into the parking lot, Gage grabbed her and embraced her hard. He sniffed her and kissed her on the cheek. She wrapped her arms around him, surprised by her feelings. She was misty-eyed over the strangers.

"You came," she squeaked.

Gage released her but stayed close enough that she felt his warmth. "I'm sorry, sister. But Pearl begged us to stay away. She didn't want us influencing her only daughter. And she was right. We're not a healthy bunch," he said, half-laughing.

"We've been near to you. You know, in case you needed us," Roderick assured.

"Yeah. We were pretty curious about you when we felt you activate. You don't feel the same as my brothers," Max commented stupidly.

"That's cuz she's your *sister*, dumbass," Brick chided and elbowed his twin.

"Fuck off. You know what I'm saying," Max huffed and pushed his brother back.

Lila covered her mouth and laughed at them. *Incubi will be Incubi.*

"I'm sorry. My mother only told me of you six years ago, right before I left home. Where are the rest of you? I was told I had fifteen brothers."

"Six are bonded and refused to get involved with you. Four of us have been murdered," Gage's voice was laced with hatred as he spoke the last part.

"Oh," Lila breathed, thinking about her random visions of unknown men. "I've seen them, felt them. I didn't understand any of it until my lifemate filled me in on all this demon stuff. I'm still new to this, and had I known I could have found you before, I would have."

"You're bonded already?" Holt asked, rubbing his slick head in wonder.

Gage shot Lila a look of shock.

"He's my soulmate."

"Holy shit," Max exclaimed, slapping his twin on the shoulder.

"That's impossible," Gage argued, shaking his head.

Lila slid off her jacket and pulled down the left front of her shirt.

"Unbelievable." Gage reached out and touched the brand in awe.

"No, what's unbelievable is that I'm pregnant," Lila admitted, brushing a hand over her belly.

"Double holy shit!" Brick yelped. He bumped his forehead with his fist.

"It's a girl," Cairo interjected.

"Okay, okay, my world just caved in on me," Max said, waving his hands back and forth. "How in the shit can you be bonded after only six years, and I'm still fucking to survive?"

"Would you shut the hell up, you idiot?" Holt barked and grabbed Max by the jacket, shoving him to the side.

Brick stifled a smile with his forearm. "You're such a moron," he mumbled to his twin.

Gage lifted a hand and the brothers quieted. "Lila, what's going on?" he asked and held her arm in concern.

"Uh, well, I don't really know where to begin," she stammered.

"It's Gaelon ...," Cairo started, stepping forward.

"The Destroyer." Gage's eyes squinted slightly.

"Yes. He tracked Lila and sent his goons after her. Gaelon means to demolish our race because of some stupid vendetta. Nasty Gaelon-son-killing-ex Succubus-lover drama. Now he has Lila's best friend hostage. My brother, Lila's soulmate, is on his way to exchange himself for that friend and will most likely be murdered in the process. Lila means to stop him and kill Gaelon."

"Thank you, Cairo," Lila said. He'd summed it up perfectly. She turned back to Gage. "This is Cairo and that's Hale by the way," she offered, gesturing to the men briefly.

Gage barely acknowledged them and tightened his grip on Lila's arm. "Your soulmate is letting you walk into a deathtrap with a child in your womb? Against a Destroyer, no less!"

"No. He told her to break their bond and stay put. She's just really stubborn," Hale explained, still churning from their heated night together.

Lila tore away from Gage. She glowered at him and then at her brothers.

"I'm not a fucking child. I know what I'm challenging. I appreciate you coming for me, but none of you truly know the weight of my situation; Stirling is my soulmate. Jenny is my best friend and Gaelon stole her from me. They're both at his mercy. None of you understand what that means to me but understand that he's out to irradicate our entire species. If you won't stand behind me, don't stand near me at all."

"Well then, we need to go somewhere to work this through," Gage relented.

"Thank you," she said quietly.

"Follow me." Hale signaled to Cairo and sprinted to his Caddy.

Chapter 23

Two of Lila's brothers rode in the same car. The others travelled on obnoxiously loud, burly bikes. On the way back to Maggie's, Lila decided that tough attitudes, rebellion, black clothes, and leather were definitely... How did she think of it? *Linin-Style?* Sure, she didn't wear black all the time, and even if she had a cheery attitude, acted like a good girl and hated leather, she would still be a Succubus. She would still belong right where she was now.

Hale led the caravan into Maggie's drive. Cairo parked back under the porch, and the rest of Lila's brothers had to fit in where they could. Cairo went ahead inside while Lila waited for her brothers.

Gage walked to her and embraced her. "Do you have any idea about how we're going to destroy a Destroyer?"

"Yeah. I think I do."

"Well, your plan better be good. Gaelon is not easy to get to."

"Well, isn't this place conspicuous?" Max chuckled, looking at Maggie's house as he strode toward Lila and Gage.

"Actually, it isn't. There's a shadow spell on it. You can't get here unless you know the house's exact location," Lila explained.

"Well, take us inside," Holt said.

The men followed Lila through the door. Maggie and her summoning circle were standing in the living room, bound by hands, chanting. When Maggie saw the bunch enter her home, she dropped her hands to her sides.

"These are your brothers?" Maggie asked.

Gage stepped forward, extending his palm to her. Maggie shook it but didn't smile. Lila didn't understand why. Maggie was so kind to everyone.

"Gage, this is my Oma. My soulmate's grandmother. Oma, these are my brothers," Lila said.

The men waved their hands and nodded, acknowledging her with the most charm they could muster.

"Were you able to spell my necklace?" Lila asked Maggie.

"Here you are, child," Hazel said, approaching Lila, holding out the black crystal necklace to her. "Put it on. When you are ready, you must hold the pendant and say these words: 'shadow of night, cloak me from light.'"

"Shadow of night, cloak me from light," Lila repeated.

"Yes. The spell will only last up to a minute at most, so be sure to use the seconds wisely."

"Thank you, Hazel," Lila said, brushing the old woman's sunken-in cheek.

"Good luck, Lila," the witch replied sullenly, returning to her coven.

"Lila, come. I will put this necklace on for you." Maggie took Lila's hand.

She led Lila into the kitchen, and Lila handed her the necklace. Maggie stood behind her, clasping it around her neck.

"Lila, they may be your brothers, but they are wicked. Especially the eldest. They have done horrible things. I don't wish them to be in my home after this night," Maggie confessed quietly.

Lila turned around and hugged her Oma. "Whatever you wish. I know they may be your average demons, but they're my family. And they're trying to assist me in winning this war. Wicked or not, I need them."

Maggie stepped back to look into Lila's eyes. "Yes. I'm sorry for having an aversion to evil ways. It's not fair, considering our breed, but I have gone to great lengths to live a decent life and avoid unnecessary torment."

"I don't fault you for anything, Oma. My mother taught me to have a good heart despite my malevolent power. I am more than grateful to have found you and your grandsons because you all have goodness in you."

Maggie kissed her cheek. "Here. Take this. It will help, but there is only one tremendous shock in it. It can only be recharged with my magic, so use it wisely." Maggie held an opal ring out to her.

"Stirling told me about you shocking his ass once," Lila mused. "This is awesome." She turned the ring over in her hand.

"It works wonders. Alright, daughter. Go out there and find a way to bring my boys home. Again."

Lila nodded and went back into the living room. Hazel, Helga, and Lisa walked past her toward the kitchen, each touching her before they disappeared out to the back porch.

"So, what do we know about The Den?" Roderick asked, now that the crew was alone.

"It lies beneath an old storage building in Barnesville, Georgia. There is one entrance on the west side. Inside is a barrier gate, a Reader and four Assassin guards," Gage stated surprisingly.

"How do you know this?" Hale asked.

"About a hundred years ago, I was an errand boy for Gaelon. I have... acquaintances who still hang around there."

"Well, how did you squirm your way out of his little club?" Cairo asked curiously.

"I had to pay him. With blood. Lots of blood."

Lila swallowed hard.

"A barrier gate, a Reader and four Assassins. Can't nine of us break through them?" Brick asked.

Gage answered, "The barrier gate will hold us if the Reader senses we're a threat. Then the Assassins will spring into action. Even with two hundred and fifty years of ass-kicking under my jacket, I wouldn't feel confident about us tackling four ancient Assassins. If we could breach the gate somehow, maybe we could slip by them, but only one of us can pass through the gate at a time."

It seemed impossible.

Cairo plopped down on the couch, and Gage took the yellow chair, elbows on his knees. Max and Brick leaned against a wall, and Holt and Roderick stood by Lila in the center of the room.

"We need a way in. An insider," Holt commented, rubbing his head again. Maybe the habit helped him think.

Silas, Lila. Stirling's call rang through her. *Call Silas.*

"Silas."

"What?" Cairo asked.

"I know an insider. I'll be right back," Lila answered and shot up the stairs like a bullet.

She busted into Stirling's room and skidded to a halt in front of the broken dresser. She looked around the floor and found his phone. He had dropped it before making love to her and leaving. She scrolled through his call log and found Silas's name. Holding her breath, she pressed the green button to dial him.

"Stirling? Man, Shit's crazy here. Gaelon has some human girl chained to a wall..."

Lila choked when she heard his words, but she forced a swallow. "Silas?"

"Who is this?" he asked.

"It's Lila. I need your help."

"Lila? Shit. I don't know what to say. Help you? Help you do what? Save the Lilin? I have no status here, I'm a nobody. Nothing I do will change the inevitable."

"You have to do something. I need your help to save my friend: the human Gaelon has chained to a wall."

"Christ, Gaelon is barely able to keep the Defilers away from her," he uttered.

"Rapists?" Lila's stomach turned.

"Worse. Much worse."

Fear snapped at her esophagus. She had to gather herself and shove away the images of Jenny being tortured unmercifully.

"Listen, I have to breach The Den. I'll have nine others with me, including Stirling. All Incubi. We're aware of the safeguards and specifics. But we're having trouble with this barrier gate situation. If the gate holds us, the Assassins could slaughter us."

"The only one who can deactivate the gate is Gaelon's siren." Silas said. "Her magic created it and only her magic can destroy it."

"Then you have to get to her! You have to persuade her to bring it down!" she cried in desperation.

"Lila, that is impossible! I will be killed for treason!" Silas exclaimed.

"He may kill you, but he won't take your soul," she assured firmly.

Silas thought dying wouldn't be so bad after living as long as he had, the way that he had. If Stirling's ass was on the line, he surely wanted to go to bat. The guy was a brother to him. "How do you know he won't destroy my soul?" he asked.

"Short version. My parents' souls are in Limbo. We summoned them and they say Gaelon can't destroy a soul without ailing for days. He won't risk his strength to soul-suck if we can get through that gate."

"Lila, I care for Stirling, and I can sympathize. But I can't be a part of what you're asking. No way can I convince the siren to do what you ask."

"I am pregnant, Silas. With Stirling's daughter. Do you know what he is going through right now? What fate awaits him? You're a coward with nothing to lose. Stirling has everything to lose," Lila seethed.

Silas was silent. He didn't know Stirling bonded with her or that she was pregnant. After a few long moments, he asked, "What makes you think Gaelon's siren will help me help you?"

"Every woman, demon or not, strives to crawl out from beneath the oppression of her mate. I learned this when my mother told me of Lilith's plight."

"Is that how it will be with you and Stirling? Will you feel oppressed by him and break your bond someday?" he questioned, sounding contemptuous.

"Fuck you. If you don't convince the siren to tear down that gate, he's dead. He's gunning for Gaelon on my behalf. We are soulmates, Silas, something so far beyond your comprehension I can't begin to explain."

He was beside himself. *Soulmates.* "No. I cannot comprehend what your bond is like," he confirmed.

"Still, you won't help me." Defeat threaded through her voice. She was about to end the call when he spoke again.

"Considering all of this...*shit* and trusting what you say about Gaelon's frailty is true, I will speak to the siren. Stirling is my only true friend. You say I have nothing to lose, and the truth is I don't. Other than him. I'll do what I can to help him and his unborn child."

"Thank you, Silas." She could almost breathe again.

"Is there anything else?" he asked.

"Yes. One more thing."

Chapter 24

Silas scanned the shack that was the home he shared with Stirling. The broken blinds suppressed just enough light, hiding the fact that they lived in total squalor. He had once asked Stirling why he hadn't duped some hot bitch into letting him move in with her and he answered, saying that he would surely lose control and kill her one day. Bonding with a Succubus wasn't in his wheelhouse and residing with a human woman was an even more outlandish thought. Stirling's temper was quick to violence and often caused destruction of anything surrounding him. He had even created a space in the backyard for breaking things when he was angry.

Nostalgically, Silas walked through the old house. The faucets dripped. The toilet barely flushed. The wooden floors were cracked and black with age and grime. All that filled the space were two old-fashioned dressers and two lonely mattresses. If Silas survived this fiasco, he vowed never to return to this place. Kicking bottles and can across the floor, he opened a dresser drawer and donned a blue tee and jeans. After swigging milk from a carton, in the filthy fridge, he left the house in his pick-up, resolute about his role in Lila's plan. The Den was only twenty minutes away. So was his fate.

He pulled into the lot of the storage building situated atop the club. The place was deserted. *Strange.* Usually, the club was packed by demons and some unsuspecting humans.

Silas stepped out of his truck and walked to the side of the building. Before he attempted to face the Reader, he cleared his mind. He had to fill his thoughts with something the Reader

wouldn't see past. What would do it?

The steel door opened for him. The gate was a fiery ring hovering just inside the doorway. He entered beneath it. The door slammed shut behind him and Silas acknowledged the Assassins positioned in the shadows. The Reader floated before him. The entity took no real form. It was smoke-like and gyrated rhythmically.

"Silas. You are known to me, but today you are different," the foggy thing echoed.

Silas felt his cover breaking, but he steadily concentrated on his miserable life, barring his intentions from his mind. He thought about the cockroaches scurrying across his stained mattress, the mold flourishing up the walls of his ramshackle cottage. The must, the filth, the loneliness, the suffering...

"There is a great sadness within you. You are fragile."

That's right. I'm harmless.

The Read swirled and evaporated, allowing Silas through the gate.

With a sigh of relief, he passed the Assassins and opened the door to The Den to set out on his mission.

He took the stairs down to a large rectangular room where demons and the occasional humans partied. The concrete walls were dark grey with graffiti sprayed across them. Usually, music was playing at offensive decibels this time of night, but the day lights were on, repelling the Defilers and the human woman Lila aimed to save hung from shackles in the near distance. The bar was open as usual, though, and a few demons crowded around it. Gaelon was nowhere in sight.

"Silas, come have a drink!" one of the minions called.

"No, I have to speak to Gaelon. Where is he?"

"In his quarters. He's bedding his lady," the demon replied, yanking on his tiny blue penis.

"Thanks, Murphy," Silas said nodding.

He continued down the only corridor in the building, which branched out into numerous other compartments. Most rooms housed Gaelon's sycophants. The others were private sex chambers, vaults for weapons and artifacts or kennels for supernatural animals.

There were only two ways out of The Den: back through the entrance, or through Gaelon's personal quarters, stationed at the end of the labyrinth. Silas had claimed a room adjacent to Gaelon's years back after earning his trust. Now, he only resided there when necessary, and squatters utilized the space when he was gone.

Nearing his home away from home, he regarded the Incubus and Redguard standing watch at Gaelon's door. Then he slipped into his room, leaving the door ajar in hopes the siren would appear.

As the minutes passed, Silas juggled his phone from hand to hand. He stood and sat; paced and bit his nails. Numerous times, he nearly abandoned his task. There was a chance that if the siren emerged, so would Gaelon, and then he'd have to devise a way to get her alone.

A door slammed, startling Silas from sleep. He sprung from the cot he was sitting on and pressed himself against the wall beside the doorway. He peeked out and saw a trail of red hair flowing down the corridor. *The siren.*

Silas waited a few moments in case Gaelon showed, but the guards remained frozen at their posts, meaning Gaelon was still inside. He stepped out of the room he was stowed in and followed the siren, allowing a good ten-foot lead. Then, as he was about to lose sight of her around a corner, she stopped abruptly and turned.

"Siren," Silas said with his heart in his throat. He glanced behind him, ensuring that the guards weren't tailing him.

Then, she was right in front of him. "What is it you want, Consumer?" she asked in a sultry voice.

The siren was as mesmerizing as the sun. Her fiery hair hung the length of her body in wondrous waves. Her lips were crimson against alabaster skin. Her licentious eyes flamed. Silas had only seen her from afar; now that he was face to face with her, he found himself staring at her like a pre-teen looking at his first porno mag.

"I wish to speak with you privately, if that is all right," he braved.

"What is this concerning?" she wondered aloud, moving closer to him until her breasts were inches from his chest.

Silas was tall, and her blazing eyes met his perfectly. "I may lose my life by speaking to you."

"By whose hand?" she pressed.

"By yours. Or Gaelon's."

"Interesting, Consumer." She touched Silas's cheek and seductively ran her fingers through his strawberry blonde hair. "Gaelon is sleeping. We may speak in my quarters." She beckoned him with a delicate finger.

He followed the siren down the hallway, and they stopped along the left side of a stone wall. She backed him against the cold rock with her voluptuous body. He thought she was going to make a move on him, but instead, she pressed on a knob to the right of his ear and the wall shifted, revealing a flight of stairs he never knew existed. She side-stepped him and he followed her up the stairs, eventually entering a room bathed in innocence. Her bed was adorned in billowy white blankets and pillows. The walls were painted white. The plush furniture was white, and the carpet and rugs were white.

The siren sat on her bed. A strange little creature hopped onto her lap and dropped a brush from its mouth, into her hands.

"Good boy, Paragon," the siren said, grooming the animal between its large, pointed ears.

The thing kind of resembled an albino Fennec with protruding fangs, bulging blue eyes and a long squirrely tail. It was deceptively cute. But Silas knew for sure that it would eat his hand off if he dared to touch it.

"Sit," the siren said, pointing to an elegant white chair.

Silas sat, entranced by her beauty.

She continued brushing her Paragon, in silence, ignoring him, which caused fear and anticipation to creep up his neck.

Finally, she shooed the little beast away and met his amber eyes. "What strong nerve is in you to have come to me in secret?" she queried.

Silas accidentally eyed her breasts. They were protruding from the red corset she was wearing.

"I'm sorry, Mistress, your beauty has taken me aback. I find it hard to speak with you," he confessed.

"Call me Rose. You have made it this far. You deserve to speak to me freely. No man or demon has ventured close enough to me in decades for a chat. This meeting is a breath of fresh air. The peril is great, however. Gaelon will kill you if he finds us alone. And he keeps me on a very short leash."

"I don't mean to overstep my bounds, but it is a risk I must take. The human woman Gaelon has bound to the wall downstairs is an acquaintance of mine. Her best friend's soulmate has set out to save the human on his bonded's behalf."

"Well, call this savior soulmate and bid your farewells," Rose said, standing and sweeping her hair behind her.

"But I need you," Silas said resolutely.

The siren had never been told she was needed in any way shape or form. She moved toward him. "What is it you need from me, Consumer?" she asked, nearly pressing her lips against his.

"Uh, well, how deep do your loyalties to Gaelon run?" *Dear Satan, I just got myself killed.*

"That is not as difficult a question to answer as one might think. I am his lover, yet he owes me more respect than he's given. I plan on killing him one day, but I must find a way to do it first. On the floor, where I stand next to him sitting on his throne, I have often thought of taking his head. I am very powerful but found a witch who is more powerful than me.

"I have protected myself from harm, but even if I went through with killing him, I couldn't escape this place. There is a binding spell that surrounds the only two exit doors from The Den, and the spell applies solely to me. This witch he summoned, took my hair and blood to cast it. Old bitch," Rose ground out hatefully.

"I thought being with Gaelon would make me even more powerful, and he promised me many things. Some things he delivered, most he did not, and he never told me I would be one of his captives. Apparently, he has trust issues. Now, my only wish is to take my Paragon and flee far from here."

"This '*old bitch*'—is she still around? Will she be a threat?" Silas asked. He didn't need any more hoops to jump through.

"No. She works for no one in particular, just exchanges favors."

Rose moved closer to him, and he refused to lean back. Her red corset forced her breasts into his face. The slits in the sides of her silk skirt revealed perfect, long legs. And her stilettos... He imagined taking them off with his teeth.

"Rose, if I could promise you a way to escape Gaelon, would you help me? I can find someone to lift the spell that confines you and you could flee, or command Gaelon's minions the way you see fit. You could start your own empire. Once Gaelon is defeated, I'm sure many of his followers will gladly bow to you. How could they not?

"Gaelon is not as powerful as you think. If he steals a soul, he becomes weak. So, my friends should be able to throw enough opposition his way to dissuade him from using his power."

"Now that is useful information, Consumer. Of course, Gaelon wouldn't trust me with that fact," she mused, staring through Silas's eyes. "Tell me what you will have me do. If you fail me, I will cast you aside and laugh as I watch you die."

Her gaze intensified and terrified him to the core, but he had won.

"I need you to break the barrier gate at The Den's entrance."

"And so it shall be done, comrade."

Rose held out her silky hand, and he took it into his own, kissing it gently. She unleashed a sinister giggle, then picked up her pet and sat at her vanity.

Silas took his leave. Once he was out of the hallway, he left The Den, opened his phone and called Lila.

Chapter 25

As Lila descended the porch stairs, she intently studied her brothers. They all seemed to be getting along except Max and Brick, who were bickering again. *Twin thing,* she thought. She couldn't wait to hang out with them after killing Gaelon. They made her laugh—something she could get used to. That is if everything went according to plan.

"I may have an in. But I can't promise anything until ..." Lila started. Then her phone rang. "Silas." *That was fast.*

The group of Incubi surrounded her earnestly. Lila pressed a finger against her lips.

"Yes. I'm here."

"The gate will be opened. You were right. The siren caved. You women are pure evil. You will do anything to step on us men. If you ever hurt Stirling ..." he warned.

"Silas, don't anger me. Stirling will give you the flogging of your life despite what you are doing for us."

"Then I definitely don't understand soulmate bonds. I guess the 'bros before hoes' rule no longer applies, huh?"

She ignored his remark. "Tell me what to do next."

"I have to contact a Transporter. He will take you to Stirling after you send me your locations. Call Stirling and get back to me. From there, I guess the rest is left to Fate."

"Silas, when we get inside, what are we looking at?"

"At the very least, the four Assassins at the gate, twenty lowly minions, a few Lethes, a handful of Defilers and one Redguard. He is the worst."

"Worst how?" she asked nervously.

"He is like Satan himself. Redguards are large, red, leathery creatures with bull heads, and they can travel on all fours, making their attacks hard to dodge. And it's smart to dodge. Then run. They are able to fly, dealing devastating aerial attacks."

"Okay, noted. What about the Lethes?"

"I suggest you strike them from afar. Shoot them, throw knives. If they touch you, they will implant thoughts in your mind and turn you against your allies."

"Anything else other than what we discussed earlier?"

"Nothing, Lila. I've done all I can do so far. The siren will not show herself unless Gaelon is completely incapacitated. She can be of no aid during the attack."

"I understand. You have been a great help to us, Silas. I will repay you with whatever you desire if I live through this."

"Well, the siren will need a witch to lift the curse that holds her captive at The Den, and I just want a place to call home."

"Then a home you will have. The siren will also be set free."

"Lila. It's up to you to pull this off. If it doesn't work…"

"I know the consequences, Silas. Thank you again." She disconnected the call.

Silas broke down the gate for us. We're coming for you.

Lila, I thought you wanted your friend alive.

Gaelon can't steal souls without it making him weak for days. He can't have us all.

All he needs is one of us.

He won't attempt that during a war. It would make him too vulnerable. We're coming for you. End of story. I found my brothers, and they are here to help.

Lila, stay behind.

No. If you die, I'll die anyway. I'd rather be at your side, fighting.

You're such a pain in my ass.

I know. And I'm sorry. I just can't be without you.

When will you be here?

Shortly. A Transporter is on the way. Compliments of Silas. I need your address.

I'll text you. I can't wait to hold you again. I love you, meine Flamme.

And I you.

"Lila? Lila? What is happening?" Cairo asked, on the edge of his seat.

She opened her eyes after calling to Stirling. "Sorry, I had to let Stirling know we're coming."

"You guys can communicate that long? I thought you were catatonic for a minute, there," Cairo said.

She shrugged. "Soulmate perk. Listen, the gate has been opened by the siren. Apparently, my contact is very persuasive, and the siren is very power hungry. Once inside The Den, we must come against Assassins, pesky minions, Defilers, Lethes, and a Redguard. There will probably be others as well. There are no guarantees that you will make it out of this alive."

She turned to her blood brothers. "You don't know me, and you don't know my soulmate, so I don't expect you to stay and war; but I am going, with or without you," she said resolutely.

"I live for this shit," said Max.

"Me, too," Brick conferred.

"You are my only sister, and I will go to bat for you. There is life in you that will help sustain our race. I'm in," Holt agreed.

Gage stood and walked up to Lila, placing a hand on her shoulder. "My sister, I have lived a horrible life. I've done despicable things. There is nothing that can save me, but if I do this one thing … this one good thing for you, I will carry it always. It will be the only pure thing in my life. I stand beside you, no matter the consequence. I always wondered what my purpose was, and when you found me, it finally clicked. My purpose is to protect you."

Lila placed her hand over his. "Thank you, Gage. Thank you all for watching over me."

Cairo stood up from the couch. "You know we are in this, Lila," he said, looking to Hale. Hale nodded, meeting Lila's eyes. He smiled at her sentimentally, and she smiled back.

"Thank you," she whispered to Hale, and he bowed his head in response.

Lila called Silas back after receiving Stirling's text and relayed their locations to him.

"So. What next?" Holt asked.

"We wait for a Transporter," she answered.

After a short while, there was a knock on the door. Lila sprinted forward and opened it. There was a seemingly ordinary man standing in front of her. Then she looked more closely at him. He was extremely pale, with dark hair and black eyes. He held out a hand to her and she was compelled to take it. As soon as she did, an electric blue bubble surrounded them. She touched the bubble, and it shocked her hand. She jerked back quickly, and as she looked around, she saw flashes of light and darkness. They were traveling through space so fast that she didn't even register moment the Transporter dumped her to the ground in front of a towering hotel. She stood, swaying a bit, as her eyes refocused in real time and she waited for her brothers, who appeared one by one in the parking lot of the hotel.

"I hate that shit," Max said, holding his head.

"A rush every time!" Brick bellowed.

Cairo and Hale appeared shortly after, just as a woman got out of her car. She looked at the group with a perplexed expression, but kept walking, and Lila sighed in relief.

Holt was next, and Roderick plopped down next to him, smiling. Lila thought he looked adorable. He had chipmunk cheeks when he smiled.

Gage was last, and he was carrying a long, black bag.

"Shit, I'm glad you remembered," Max said.

"Yeah, me too."

"Weapons?" Lila asked.

"But of course, young sister. Shotguns, knives, swords, a few homemade items."

Lila rose on her tiptoes and kissed Gage's cheek.

He smiled at her, then she took off inside the hotel.

Eighth floor, room 814.

As Lila waited impatiently for the elevator, the woman behind the desk tried to stop the eight large, scary men from further entering the building. Gage leaned over the desk and spoke with her. She was playing coy now and giggling. Hypnosis worked wonders.

Her brothers jogged to the elevator just as it opened. Lila punched the "8" button, and the elevator stopped on the fifth floor. A man stood in front of the door as it opened. He was a small guy who obviously scared easily.

"I'll take the next one," he stuttered, and the door shut in his face.

"Ha-ha," Brick chuckled.

Once on the eighth floor, Lila scanned the walls for room-number arrows. She darted down the left hall, and Stirling was standing in front of the door to his room. She swooned when she saw him. It felt like they had been apart for centuries.

"Stirling!" she cried and jumped into his arms.

"*Meine Flamme,*" he whispered against her neck.

She kissed his neck and shoulders and cheeks and then lifted her head and met his lips. They kissed the way they had the first time they made love.

"All right, you two, break it up," Cairo said, stepping behind them and into the room. Hale followed, but Lila's brothers waited for an invite.

Lila slid down Stirling's body but still hugged him tight.

"You must be the brothers. Thank you for your help," Stirling said cordially. "Come inside."

Stirling took Lila by the hand, and the demonic bunch entered the room. Cairo and Hale were sitting on one of the beds, speaking to Beckett, who was sitting on the bed across from them.

Stirling held his hand out to Gage and introduced himself.

"I'm Stirling."

"The soulmate. I didn't believe Lila at first. She had to show me her mark. It's good to meet you," Gage said, shaking Stirling's hand firmly.

"Trust me, we didn't believe it, either."

Pointing to Beckett, Stirling introduced his brother. Beckett waved and then resumed his conversation with Cairo and Hale.

The rest of Lila's kin introduced themselves and she hugged Stirling again. He ran his hand down her hair and breathed her in.

"I know you two want to get cozy somewhere, but we need to get a few things handled," Gage urged.

"Yes, I know," Stirling responded. "Lila tells me the gate has been deactivated."

"Yes. We will take out the Assassins and enter the lion's den. From there, there's no telling what we will face."

"I need to go in first to negotiate. The original plan was to reveal my bond to Gaelon, proving that I secured Lila. It would've been perfect leverage for Lila's best friend's life, trading myself for Jenny after Lila broke our bond. Gaelon would've lost his mind when he realized Lila had severed our tie. But now that Lila has refused to break it..." Stirling hugged her into him and shook his head. "She'll be in horrible danger and so will her friend. They are to be protected at all costs. As you know, not only Lila, but our baby is also in danger."

Gage looked at Lila hard. "Are you sure you want to do all of this for a human?"

"Gage, I was raised as a human. Not a Succubus. I am still struggling to fit into the world as you know it. As you've known it for quite some time. Jenny is a part of me, the way all of you are. I'd do this for any one of you, and I am damn well going to rescue my only human counterpart."

Gage nodded resolutely.

"In the morning, we're going to need a couple of rental cars," Beckett said. "I'll arrange that first thing."

"You will hang out for Jenny once I get her out of there, Beck. Lila, I will call to you and let you know when to muscle your way in," Stirling finished.

"Okay." She nodded her head, still taking in his stare.

"Well, sounds simple enough. Get in, rescue the human, protect Lila and murder Gaelon. You got anything to drink around here?" Gage asked, clapping his big hands together.

"Sorry, man. My brother and I killed a couple of bottles a bit ago," Stirling responded.

"Well, shit."

"I'll drive you to the liquor store. There's one a few blocks down," Beckett obliged.

"Then let's go." Gage beckoned.

Stirling leaned down and whispered into Lila's ear, "Come outside with me."

Her stomach fluttered and she followed him to the balcony, pulled the curtain shut, and closed the slider. Immediately, Stirling grabbed her up and kissed her. She tangled her fingers in his hair, and he sat her in one of the chairs, kneeling on the ground in front of her. Reluctantly, he pulled away from her mouth, and she leaned forward, wanting to kiss him again, but he pushed her back into the chair forcefully, pulling her hips forward.

He slipped off her sneakers and shimmied down her skin-tight leathery leggings, thankful that he didn't have to spend time unbuttoning and unzipping. She wasn't wearing panties either. *God.* He threw her legs over each arm of the chair.

"Oh," he sighed, spreading Lila's beautiful pink lips open, then he buried his face in between her legs.

She moaned over and over again. "I missed you so much."

"You taste so good, love," he murmured against her.

He did amazing things with his tongue, and she couldn't hold out any longer.

"I'm coming, baby," she whispered, her legs quivering.

He sucked her clit into his mouth. She bucked her hips into his face, and he grabbed them hungrily, pulling her closer. Her legs slid off the chair arms and over his shoulders. He kissed her bud and licked her juices from his lips. She was still moving her hips up and down, continuing even after he stood up.

"Are you a horny little girl?" he asked as he leaned down to look deep into her eyes.

He slid his fingers into her, and she thrusted into them hoping for a release, but she wanted him. She wanted his delicious cock, not his fingers.

"Quit teasing me, Stirling," she warned, grinding her teeth.

"Well then, get up and bend over that railing."

She backed her hips up until his fingers slipped out of her. She grasped the balcony railing and propped a leg up on it.

"Hell, yeah," he said. "That's my girl."

He dropped his pants and tilted her hips up just a bit. She was sopping wet, ready, and when he slid inside her he thought he would come as soon as he felt her warm billowy center. The way they fit together had him on edge. Coming now wasn't an option, so he ignored the swelling urge to ejaculate and set out to send Lila into blissful oblivion. He gripped the rail under her leg and held her waist close with his other arm, thrusting into her slowly but deeply. Each time he gave her his full length, small whimpers escaped her lips.

"I want to feel you against me. Hold me closer," she moaned.

He ripped off his shirt, and she lifted her arms so he could strip her of hers. He pressed his chest against her back and slid his hand up the front of her body, firmly clasping her shoulder. She wanted him even closer. Though he was inside her, they were never close enough.

"I couldn't stand the thought of you with him," Stirling growled, pounding into her harder.

She reached back and grabbed a fistful of his hair. "I tried to imagine he was you."

"You're mine."

"I'm yours. I'm yours. I'm yours!" she cried as she orgasmed. She would have fallen off the balcony had he not been holding her.

"Say it again," he demanded, still pumping into her, now with full force. He was claiming her all over again.

"I'm yours. Only yours," she sobbed.

Her words toppled him. He thrust deep inside her again and unleashed like he never had before.

"Ahhh, shit yeah."

He continued grinding into her, and spanked her twice, getting off on her cries. "You want it again, don't you?"

"Yes, yes. I want more."

She felt him shifting forms and he wrapped his ebony plated arms more tightly around her, pulling her upright against him. He bit into her neck with razor sharp teeth and she screamed out with pleasure. Blood snaked down her neck and he licked it up, savoring her taste.

"Love. You taste like love," he whispered.

Then he encased her in his wings and began rotating his hips, moving slowly inside of her. Gently this time.

The sliding door opened, and Max laughed at his stupidity.

"Sorry, guys. I should have known. Nothing like seeing your sister getting pummeled."

"Max!" Brick yelled and yanked his twin by the back of his shirt.

The slider closed again.

"He must be the dumb one of the bunch," Stirling deduced.

"Clearly," Lila laughed.

Beckett woke up at eight and wandered down to the lobby desk. He was met by a cute little blonde girl. She asked him what she could do for him, and he told her that he needed three rental cars. The girl picked up the phone, almost drooling as she did, and made a call. She promised the cars would be in the parking lot by noon; he just had to come by the desk and pick up the keys when they arrived.

The girl asked for his number, but he was hesitant to continue the conversation. The petite blonde was relentless though. His dick hardened and he succumbed to his demonic ways.

"Where would we go, if I took you now?"

After a five-minute fuck in the clerk's closet, Beckett hypnotized her into forgetting him completely. He left the woman and jogged a few blocks to burn off some of the life force he'd absorbed. Then, with sweat pouring down his face, he returned to the room.

He didn't intend on falling asleep again, but when he woke, the clock on the nightstand in between the beds said it was two-thirty.

Stirling was sitting up against the headboard, Lila asleep against his shoulder.

Beckett was dying of thirst and had to watch his every step on the way to the bathroom. The twins were out cold on the floor, and along with them were scattered bottles of beer and other booze. He wished Lila's brothers had gotten their own rooms, but everyone had been too busy shooting the shit, and they eventually took to passing out wherever was comfortable at the time.

Beckett grabbed his bag off the floor and set it on the bathroom counter. He drank as much water as his stomach would hold out of the sink faucet, then he shut the door to take a shower. He came out of the bathroom, and everyone was still asleep. No wonder. They had all gotten plastered, except Stirling, Lila, and himself.

Stirling and Lila had been too busy to drink. They fucked on the balcony, in the shower, and then in the bed after most of the guys were asleep.

Beckett rubbed his head. Holt and Roderick were both sleeping in two chairs at the table in the room. Cairo was outside on one of the chairs, slumped over, just the same as Gage.

Beckett considered dousing them all with cold water, but he had never been much of a prankster. He walked out onto the balcony and kicked the chair Cairo was hanging out of.

"What the fuck?" Cairo growled.

"Get up. We kind of need to put our heads together, eat, you know, prepare for the worst," Beckett growled back.

"Gage, man, get up," Cairo said, punching him in the shoulder.

Gage stirred, looking around. After finding his bearings, he stood up and cracked his neck. "Hey, I got your back tonight, bro," Gage said, slapping Cairo on the back.

"I got yours, too. I'd love to get drunk again and tear some shit up with you."

"Aw, isn't that cute. A bromance formed overnight," Beckett sneered.

Cairo flipped him off.

Gage sauntered inside and kicked Max in the side. Brick was next. "Get up, you idiots. Time to get some grub."

Max and Brick rolled around a couple of times before they were able to stand. Max yawned and went to the bathroom, but before he could get inside, Brick shoved him out of the way and slammed the door in his face, laughing.

"You're such a shit face, you know that?" Max yelled, pounding on the door.

Roderick and Holt roused.

"Where we going to eat, man?" Roderick asked Gage.

"I don't know. It's the city. A pain in the ass to get anywhere and nowhere to park when you get there. I guess we'll just drive around the block until we find something. I need to find me a lady, also." He rubbed his stomach with both hands, pooching his pelvis out.

Gage looked at Lila and Stirling. "You two need to get ready."

"I think we're gonna order in," Lila said, and Stirling kissed the top of her head.

"Disgusting, the two of you," Gage said, pointing at them.

Lila was glad when the boys left. She wanted Stirling all to herself. She shifted, and he fucked her in her demon form against the wall. When she shifted back from exhaustion, he transformed and ravaged her again on the bed. Insane with lust, they stumbled into the bathroom and made love on the countertop. With her legs tight around his waist, they held each other's gaze, then kissed intensely.

Afterward, they held each other in the shower, cherishing their reunion.

Lila was drying off, and Stirling hugged her from behind. "You know, I left all my stuff at Oma's. I was in such a hurry to get to you," she said.

"Use my stuff, then." Stirling smiled.

By the time Lila and Stirling were prepared for battle, it was nearing five. Lila sat on the bed with her heart in her stomach. "When are we leaving?"

"In an hour. It takes almost two to get where we're going." Stirling put his arm around her. "Be strong, my love. We will make it through this."

"I wish I knew that to be true."

Lila looked down at her stomach. She was a demon and so was her child. Jenny was a good human. All that mattered was her safety. But Lila truly wanted this baby and a long life with Stirling. The only thing she could do was hope for the best for them all. And fight like she never had before.

Chapter 26

Hale, Stirling, and Gage all pulled into the dirt lot at the storage building above The Den. Gage popped the trunk of his rental car and pulled out his bag of weapons. The other guys crowded around him, picking through his things. Lila watched as Cairo grabbed a shotgun and aimed it at the building.

"This is it, honey. There is no turning back," Stirling said, placing his hand on Lila's leg.

She kissed him longingly and pulled away too soon, trying to hold back her tears, even though Stirling felt the anguish inside of her.

"I like this whole beard thing you have going on," she whispered, and a tear slipped from her eye anyway.

"Then I'll grow it until you tell me to shave it off," he said, smiling at her as sincerely as he could.

Beckett opened Stirling's door abruptly. "Time to go in."

Stirling was aggravated, but knew Beck was right.

"I know. You stay out here and wait for the girl. When she's with you, drive far away. Get to Oma's if you can."

Beckett nodded, then, once Stirling stepped out of the car, he hugged his brother tightly. Beckett had never hugged Stirling like that before. He had always been so distant and smug.

"Thanks, man. For everything," Stirling said.

"Anytime."

Lila hugged Beckett's neck as well and he kissed the top of her head. "You'll be fine," he assured, in a way that made Lila believe him.

"Boys, are we all ready?" Gage yelled enthusiastically, holding a katana in the air.

As the men hollered back, Lila studied Stirling. His face wasn't expressionless, but it wasn't alive, either. She tapped into him and listened.

I know I shunned you decades ago. I know I am depraved and don't deserve your blessings, but please. Please. Take care of my soulmate and child.

He was praying. To God. He was sure they wouldn't make it out alive. Lila had never even thought about an afterlife without Stirling, but because of the way he lived, there was a real chance he may not join her after death. A chance she'd go to Heaven and he's go to Hell.

She was going to sacrifice everything for Jenny's life, but now, she had to save Stirling's, too. He had centuries in front of him to change his ingrained habits, centuries to enter God's good graces, and she swore right then that they would walk out of The Den alive. There was nothing in that awful place that could come before her and walk away to tell about it.

"Lila, take this. It's great for ripping heads off," Brick said excitedly, handing her a razor wire with a handle on each end.

"A garrote. I'm assuming this is one of the homemade weapons Gage was talking about."

"Naw, this creation is mine." Brick's smile was infectious.

Lila stuck the handles into the waist of her pants and let the wire hang beside her leg.

"Let's go," Stirling said in Lila's ear, and she let her inner demon unfurl.

Gage led everyone to the doorway and stopped. Slowly, he opened the door. "The gate is still up," he said over his shoulder.

"It can't be," Lila said. "Maybe it's a ruse. The Assassins would know if the gate went down. It has to be a fake."

"Well, who wants to try it out first?" Gage asked just as the Reader appeared in the doorway.

"Enter so that I can read you," the entity demanded in a ghostly voice.

Brick and Max barged through the gate, and Lila almost lost her mind, but they were in. Gage quickly followed them, immediately stabbing one of the Assassins in the chest.

"It worked!" Max yelped, and Lila followed the rest of the Incubi into the room.

The Reader was repeating that they were not worthy to enter, that they meant harm, and Lila wished she could have killed the annoying bastard. Instead, she pulled out her razor wire and yanked off a hovering Assassin's head with it. She looked at Brick, and he winked at her. Stirling and Holt took out the other two demons with ease.

"Well, that was fast," Roderick said, surveying the blood and guts on his boots. He shook his leg, and some of the goop fell off.

"You cannot enter. Your intentions are not pure," the Reader went on.

"Shut the fuck up!" Brick screamed at it.

"I have to go now, Lila," Stirling said.

He held onto her tightly. *"Meine Flamme*, I love you."

"I love you, too. We'll come the second you call me."

"Good luck, man." Cairo patted Stirling on the back.

"Don't worry," Hale said. "We'll get you out of there. I promise."

Stirling nodded to his brothers, rubbed Lila's cheek, and then opened the door to the basement.

He walked with heavy feet down the stairs and entered the familiar dank room he had once felt so comfortable in. Gaelon sat on his throne, which was an ornate, tall black chair donning spears on either side. Its arched beveled top was adorned with human skulls. As usual, minions cluttered the bar, and several others scattered around the open space. He felt all their eyes on him as he stared Gaelon down. The Redguard stood next to Gaelon's side, along with an impressive Incubus. Markus was leaning against the wall behind Gaelon, smirking at Stirling.

"Stirling, where is the girl?" Gaelon asked, tapping yellowed fingernails against the arm of his seat.

Gaelon's voice was gravelly and sinister, and his body was skeletal. He was a vomitous color, a mix between green and yellow and shit brown. Stirling had always thought it looked like something had puked all over him. His head was a skull with a thin membrane covering it, and his teeth and eyes seemed to hover in the spaces they should have been attached to. Gaelon pointed a bony finger at him.

"Where is the girl?!" he roared.

"I have a proposition for you," Stirling said steely.

"You are in no position to bargain with me," Gaelon laughed, his head bobbing up and down.

"Release the human, and I will give you the Succubus. She is just outside the gate. Your Reader allowed me in. My intentions here are true."

"What is so special about this human? Are you in love with her Succubus friend?"

"Yes, I am," Stirling admitted. "Her... Succubus friend would like her human to be released. We offer ourselves in your hostage's place."

"Well, I'll tell you what. I will keep the girl, kill you, and send another to hunt your love down."

"You don't need to hunt her. She is just outside. Let the human go."

Gaelon seemed to ponder the situation but signaled to the Incubus bodyguard next to him.

The bodyguard came toward Stirling and shredded the shirt from his body. He reached out and touched Stirling's brand, then met Stirling's eyes. The bodyguard's expression was one of compassion. Stirling knew then that he could get through to the Incubus.

"Come now, bodyguard. Step away so that I can see," Gaelon ordered.

The Incubus turned slowly and resumed his place beside Gaelon.

Gaelon gazed at Stirling's brand. "Interesting. You actually tried to use your Succubus as leverage. You didn't think I would look for a bond mark? I admire your bravery, but I don't envy your stupidity."

Lila, he found my brand. He's not going for it. Come now.

Stirling shifted and spread his wings out wide.

"You can't fight me, Stirling." Galeon rolled his floating eyes and crossed his bony legs.

"You aren't taking me down without one."

"I'm bored. Kill him." Gaelon signaled the crouching devils that surrounded his prey.

"One thing first," Stirling said. "Does your Incubus guard know that you have been torturing and devouring the missing Succubi?"

The Incubus turned on Gaelon with his jaws wide open, like he had been waiting decades for an opportunity to get at his boss. Just as he was about to pounce, the Redguard lifted him up into the air by his throat and hurled him across the room. The demons attacked Stirling just as Lila and her brothers invaded.

"What is this?" Gaelon hollered. "I will have your soul, Stirling!"

Lila used her weapon to slice through a few of the lower life-forms coming at her. A Scavenger popped up behind her, and she strangled it with her tail until its eyes popped out. Gage was busy fighting another Assassin. Brick and Max put their backs together, dealing deadly blows to little brown Scamps.

Lila quickly surveyed the space and saw Jenny hanging from the far-right wall. Disgusting creatures were clawing at her legs, but she was too weak to fight or scream. Blood dripped from her body and her clothes were torn to shreds. Lila couldn't see her face because her head was down; her limp golden locks were caked in sweat, dirt and grime.

She fought her way over to Jenny and was caught around the throat by one of the Defilers. The thing had razor claws and rows of sharp teeth. It stuck its barbed tongue out for her face just as Cairo shot it in the chest, spraying its guts all over her body.

"Get the girl!" he yelled.

Lila scampered forward and flew into the air, reaching Jenny's wrists. Cairo kept popping off shots below her.

"Jenny. Jenny, wake up, honey."

Lila lifted Jenny's head to hers. Jenny slowly opened her eyes and looked at her.

"Lila?" she whispered pathetically.

Her lips were dry and cracked. She'd lost a significant amount of weight and her skin looked thin and scaly from dehydration.

"That's it. I'm going to take you to the doorway. Once you get up the stairs, there will be a man waiting for you. He will take you somewhere safe."

She looked down at Jenny's legs, noticing they'd been infected. Damned Scavengers. There was no way Jenny could keep her baby. Not after this.

Rage filled Lila's heart, soul and eyes. She could only see red. She yanked the chains out of the stone wall, not bothering with the manacles that were still attached to Jenny's wrists and ankles. She cradled Jenny's limp body and flew across the room with her. Cairo followed below, blowing a few more demons' heads off.

"I'm out, Lila!" he called before he smashed a slimy creature in the face with his elbow. Lila landed on the ground just in front of the doorway leading to safety.

"Jenny, hurry to the top."

But Jenny couldn't go anywhere. She couldn't stand up. Cairo bolted forward and scooped her up, just as Lila got hit by a Lethe, which looked surprisingly human except for

its freakishly long appendages. It took her to the ground, but before it could take over any of her thoughts, it shot off her body onto the floor, convulsing. Stirling wasn't joking about Maggie's ring. It packed a mean punch. Lila looked behind her, and Cairo was running up the stairs with Jenny, and Lila sighed in relief.

Where is Silas?

She looked through the bodies lying on the floor. Human heads were scattered around, eyes still open, spines exposed. She stalked toward Brick, who had his leg caught in a spider-like demon's web. The thing cackled as he fell to the floor. It opened its mandibles and started dragging him toward its mouth. Roderick sliced the web with a blade and stabbed the demon in its side. It shifted into a pretty young woman before collapsing.

"Max! Max!" Brick cried.

Lila ran to Brick's side and helped him to his feet. Brick turned to see the Incubus bodyguard coming for him. The Lethes had gotten to the Incubus, turning him against his own kind. Without hesitation, Brick stormed for the infected bodyguard, Ignoring his size. Lila couldn't make out who was who for a moment while they grappled and clawed and bit. They were a black swirling tornado.

The Incubi separated and regrouped, expelling air from their lungs in louds huffs. Then they flew into the air, meeting head-on, horns against horns. Neither budged. Brick dove quickly, and Holt flew into the Incubus's face. The bodyguard looked for a way out, but Brick came up behind him and slashed off his wings with two clean swipes of his claws. The Incubus crashed into the ground and shifted. Roderick stood over his human form and regretfully drove his blade into the cursed dying man's heart.

Lila found a human-looking Max squirming in a pile of bodies. She knelt by him and held his hand.

"I'm so sorry, Max," she cried. Guilt shrapnel stuck into her heart, surely to leave deep scars.

"It's nothing, sis. I've been looking for some decent action for decades. Bar fights just don't cut it anymore," he laughed weakly, spitting up blood.

"Max!" Brick screamed and sank onto the ground next to him.

Lila released Max's hand, and stood up slowly, backing away from them. She couldn't hear what last words they shared. She didn't deserve to. She had only known them a day and had asked them to die for her. She closed her eyes briefly, and the sight of her dead brother invaded her mind. She felt him slip away.

"Another wave," Hale said, sprinting to Lila's side. "Are you okay?"

"Neither I nor Stirling have taken a hit we couldn't handle. Are you okay?" she asked, trying to sound grounded after just losing another brother.

"I'm fine, but there's another wave coming from there," Hale pointed into the only other hallway in the place.

"The Succubi. They're alive. We need to release them," Lila said urgently, grabbing Hale's shoulders.

"I'll go."

"Thank you, Hale. For everything."

He kissed her on the forehead and headed toward the hall.

Lila quickly whirled around to survey the situation. Almost every demon was down. Gage, Holt, and Roderick were headed her way. Cairo was back inside and kicked a Scamp across its face, sending it flying across the room. Stirling snapped the last Assassin's neck and took a step toward Gaelon and the Redguard. They were still in serious danger.

Lila had almost given up hope when she saw Silas sprinting out of the hallway with numerous other abominable beasts.

Stirling, wait. Bide your time.

Stirling backed away from Gaelon and flew to her. When he did, Gaelon laughed wildly. "Weaklings, all of you!"

"Hale is going to release the Succubi," Lila said to Stirling.

She looked Hale's way and saw him hovering over the hall entrance, waiting for the demons to finish flooding out.

"Stop him!" Gaelon roared, pointing at Hale.

Stirling, Cairo, and Gage tore through the streamline of little bastards, and Hale dipped into the hall.

Silas bounded toward Lila, turning into a yellow lizard of sorts. Just as he leapt out at her, she turned and kicked up her leg, planting her foot into his chest.

"Silas," she breathed.

"Release the dogs!" Gaelon ordered.

"The werewolves. Lila, you can't stay here. You need to get out. You have your friend! Go!" he yelled, punching her lightly in the ribs.

"I can't. My brothers are in the dungeon. They are releasing the captured Lilin," she explained and backhanded Silas across the face.

"I will do as you asked, but I think you're making a horrible decision." He ducked another one of Lila's punches.

"This ends tonight." She flew off toward her brothers.

Lila felt her shoulder tear open. She looked at it, but it was fine. *Stirling.* She scanned the mass of demons below her and saw a huge wolf perched on Stirling's chest. It had bitten into his shoulder, and another wolf was closing in on him. She dove down and shredded the wolf's back wide apart. The beast whined and rolled off Stirling, just in time for him to get to his feet and headbutt the other one in the side.

Gage sent the smaller demons flying, splattering them into walls. He ripped off their limbs and chomped at them as they came forward. Blood rained from him, creating a river as he stalked around until a third werewolf slammed into him from behind. It bit into his neck and tore out most of his throat. Before he fell to the ground, Gage stabbed the abomination in the stomach with his sword, driving the blade all the way through its body and out its back. Lila saw flashes of her brother dying but didn't have time to process the scenes. Sadness invaded, but instantly turned into rage.

She watched Stirling as another wolf circled him. Whistling and taunting the canine, she confused it a bit. The wolf eyed Lila with yellow eyes. The thick grey hair on its back bristled.

This one's mine, Lila.

As if it had heard their telepathy, the wolf turned, and Stirling sprung at the same time. They both hit the ground hard, and Lila ran to Stirling. She didn't feel his pain, if he was in any.

"Is that all you've got, Gaelon?" he roared.

Lila held her hand out to him, helping him to his feet. His eyes were glowing and dangerous. Pieces of fur and flesh were caught in his teeth, and he howled, flexing his biceps and puffing out his chest. She thought he had gone mad. This was definitely his primal, animalistic side. His "depraved" side, as he called it.

"I have saved my Redguard for you. Too bad I won't be able to stay for the battle. It was entertaining, but I've seen enough. Now I'll be going," Gaelon chuckled.

What a fucking coward, Lila thought, fists clenched.

"No, you won't," a woman's voice rang out.

Stirling and Lila turned to see a coven of Succubi blocking Gaelon's exit. Hale lowered himself to the ground, and Cairo had his burly arm around the waist of one of the Succubi. She was decked out in bond marks. Of course, she would have piqued his interest. She was obviously a wild card.

There was still one werewolf scouting the grounds, but it hesitated to act. The other demons had scattered and cowered in small groups against the walls.

"Worthless! All of you!" Gaelon screamed.

He balled his bony hands into fists, and his eyes went black as he glared at the intruders. "The first one of you to touch me shall die and lose their soul!"

The twelve-foot Redguard went down on all fours and rushed Stirling. It crushed him against wall, and Lila felt his ribs break. Her knees buckled, and she dropped to the ground. Hale

rushed to her side.

The Succubi, and a few captured Incubi, flew in around the red demon and backed it against the wall Stirling was lying in front of. He tried to stand up, but the Redguard rammed his horns into the unprotected flesh of Stirling's armpit. It lifted Stirling off the ground and thrashed its head back and forth wildly. It reared back and started to gallop toward Gaelon with Stirling still pinned to its horns. With a quick head-toss, Stirling rocketed off the Redguard's spikes, landing just short of Gaelon's throne.

The Redguard took off into the air, and the rescued Lilin descended on the huge demon. It smashed its enormous hoofs into some of them, and they corkscrewed from the air, screeching like dark falling angels.

Cairo and Roderick rushed to Stirling's aid, pulling him as far from Gaelon as they could. Brick and Hale stayed with Lila, and

Holt tore after the wailing red beast, stabbing into him, while the Succubi tore apart his wings and then settled for eating his eyes out.

"Lila?" Hale said. "Lila, you have to get up."

Lila was in so much pain, but she tried to tell herself it wasn't real. Her ribs weren't broken, Stirling's were. Her lung had not been penetrated by Redguard horns; Stirling's had.

She still felt him breathing, and she turned her head to the side to look for him.

Stirling. Not like this. We won't die like this.

She spotted Gaelon running toward the hallway, which was now unguarded. She gathered her strength and rose from the ground slowly. Hale and Brick helped her steady herself.

"Lila, are you alright?" Brick asked.

She pointed to Gaelon. Brick immediately flew across the room and grabbed the skeleton by his shoulder. Gaelon spun around and stabbed Brick in the heart with a dagger he had apparently pulled from the back of one of his underlings.

"No," Lila whispered, extending her arms toward her brother as if to touch him.

Gaelon turned for the exit again as Silas and the siren appeared in the hallway.

"What is happening?" Hale asked Lila in fear.

"Don't worry, brother. Gaelon is about to die," she answered venomously.

She rubbed her pendant. "Shadow of night, cloak me from light," she said and disappeared before Hale's eyes. Carefully, she made her way over to Gaelon. She crept up behind him as he looked at Silas and the siren.

"Help me, Silas. My Rose," Gaelon begged.

"Your thorn, Gaelon," Rose corrected.

"What are you saying?" Gaelon's hideous face scrunched in confusion.

"I'm saying that I am no longer your slave," the beautiful siren answered evenly.

"This is treachery!" Gaelon squawked.

Lila brought her razor wire from around her neck. While it was painful, she outstretched her arms, holding the wire taut.

"Gaelon. You are going to die," Silas told him.

"I will end you all," Gaelon threatened and turned, thinking he could sprint to the doorway that led out of The Den.

He didn't have time to see the wire stretched out in the air. He walked right into it. Lila wrapped the razor wire around his neck. It cut into his thin flesh, and he oozed a green phlegm-like substance. Appearing in front of Gaelon, Lila hissed. Her incisors gleamed, and she tightened her hold on him.

Gaelon's black eyes sagged, and his jaws hung open. He raised his frail arms to Lila's and grabbed her for his life.

"You really chose all the wrong women, Gaelon. First, it was your Succubus, then it was Rose, and lastly, it was me. Silas is going to consume your power, and after I kill you, he will destroy your soul," she said numbly.

"Please," he pleaded pathetically.

"Surely." Lila nodded to Silas, who took off his gloves. He placed both hands on Gaelon's feeble shoulders.

Lila pulled both handles at the end of the wire as hard as she could, and Gaelon's head slid off his body onto the cold concrete floor. She watched as a grey misty energy left his body. It turned, revealing its rotting expression: an even more twisted version of Gaelon's face, saturated in sheer horror.

Silas grasped the mist and pulled it toward him as it struggled to get away. He closed his fist, and Gaelon's soul dissipated into thin air. Lila closed her eyes and fell back. Hale caught her before she hit the ground.

Chapter 27

"Stirling?" Lila whispered.

Stirling opened his eyes and was immediately annoyed by the light blinding him. He draped his arm over his face.

"Hale, get the light," Lila said. Back to Stirling, she asked, "Honey, are you awake?"

Lila knew he was doing better. She was able to walk around now without much pain. It would have been a much faster healing process if Stirling could have made love to her. Without exchanging life forces, they were struggling.

"Where am I?" Stirling asked. "Uh, I need water."

"I'm on it, bro," Cairo said and left the room.

"You're at home. In your bed," Lila said.

"Lila? We're at home? Where's the light?"

"We turned it off, honey. You spent a week with a demon doctor. I didn't even know they existed, but he took care of you, and now you're home."

He moved his arm off his face and looked at her. "We're at home?"

He sat up in the bed, and she quickly threw two pillows behind his back. He winced as he rested against them.

"Yes. We made it out. Jenny was at the doctor's with you, and he healed all of her serious wounds. He said that because Jenny is human, she was easier to fix. Her baby is fine!" Lila said excitedly, grabbing Stirling's hand.

"I thought the light was coming for me," he whispered and looked at her again, making sure she was really there.

"Look around, Stirling. We're here."

He looked around the room and saw Hale and Beckett. Hale had bond marks, at least two that were visible.

"Where's Cairo?" Stirling asked urgently, trying to get out of the bed.

"Dude, calm down. I'm fine. It's good to know you don't really hate me. Here's your water," Cairo laughed as he came through the door.

Stirling noticed he had new blue tattoos as well, on his arms. *What the hell?*

Maggie was on Cairo's heels. "*P'tit boug*! You're awake! Poor Lila has been hobbling around, tears dripping down her pretty face."

Maggie placed a wrinkled hand on Stirling's.

"Poor Lila, huh?" Stirling chuckled weakly, then grabbed his ribs.

"Now that you're awake, you should really let Lila take care of you," Cairo said, winking at him. "I'm starving, Oma. What's for lunch?" He put his arm around her small shoulders.

"You know, one day you will have to move to Manhattan so Beckett can cook for you," Maggie said, shaking her finger in his face. "Stirling, you let me know if you get hungry let me know. I'll have one of your brothers bring it up for you."

"Well, you should have seen it, Stirling. Lila tore Gaelon's head clean off. She planned a scheme with that Consumer friend of yours before we even left to meet you at the hotel," Hale said.

"What?" Stirling asked, looking to her, cocking an eyebrow.

"After I located my brothers, I found your phone upstairs. I called Silas and asked if he could consume Gaelon's power. When he said yes, I asked him to help. He was able to turn Gaelon's siren against him, and Hazel charmed my pendant with a shadow spell. I went invisible, crept up on that bastard and he turned right into my razor wire. His head came off quite easily." She shrugged as she smirked.

"You crazy, smart, wonderful woman. Come here." Stirling held his arm out to her, and she gently laid her head against his chest. "I'm so lucky to have you. You saved us, you know that?"

Lila's feeling of triumph was short-lived.

"I lost three more of my brothers," she said quietly. "The Cleaners cremated them, and Holt and Roderick are taking the ashes with them to wherever they decide to go. I also found my parents' bodies in the torture chamber. I had them cremated as well.

"My brothers stayed long enough to cross over my parents with me. The whole thing was terribly sentimental and pathetic. We cried like babies after our parents crossed and again when we said goodbye. I have closure with my mom and dad, but open wounds for my brothers. They said they will keep in touch, but I had to promise to stay out of trouble. They say good luck and to take good care of me."

"Lila ..." Stirling started.

She lifted her head up from his chest and pressed a finger against his lips. "Don't."

"Well, if you need anything, let me know," Hale offered and patted Lila on the shoulder. He left the room before Stirling could ask about the bond marks covering him and Cairo.

"Little brother, I have to get back home," Beckett said, tucking a strand of his silky blonde hair behind his ear. "My wife won't quit calling."

I'll explain later, Lila.

You'd better.

Beckett held his arms out to Lila, and she wrapped herself in his embrace.

"I love you," he said.

"I love you too, Beckett. We'll come see you in Manhattan. I can't wait to visit your restaurant."

He let Lila go and smiled. She saw tears welling in his blue-lensed eyes.

"Stirling, I promise not to be a stranger anymore. Don't get me wrong, I still can't stand being around you grunts for too long, but I want to see the baby, hear the stories."

"And I want to meet your wife. Any human who puts up with our kind deserves a big diamond ring. It'd better be huge, Beckett." Stirling grinned.

Beckett leaned down and hugged his brother. "Behave from now on, okay?" he said.

"Sure thing, Beck." Stirling waved to him, and Beckett shut the door on his way out.

Lila sat back down on the bed next to Stirling, tears falling from her eyes.

"Honey, don't be sad. I know you'll miss them, but we have plenty of decades to see them. Before long, we'll be avoiding them," Stirling chuckled before she started full-out bawling.

"Hale's leaving this week, but I won't have to miss Cairo. His big ass is moving to an ugly green house a few blocks away."

"Why won't you miss him?" He looked at her suspiciously.

She batted her eyes innocently. "I thought we could sell my parents' house and stay here with Oma and Opa. We can fix the place up and raise Deva here on the lake."

"If we stay, Cairo has to move to a different state," Stirling groaned.

"Honey, c'mon. You know you love the guy."

He grunted, and she started laughing, wiping her tear-stained face.

"Oh, yeah, Silas wanted you to call him the minute you got up. He's shacking up with that spiteful bitch, Rose. I think you need to talk him out of it before she kills him," Lila suggested and sniffled.

"Then Silas will be thinking I'm asleep for a while. I can't deal with that shit for at least another week or so." Stirling rubbed his forehead. "You said Jenny's baby is all right?"

"Yes! The doc was amazing. She got checked out by her regular doctors once she didn't look like she'd been hanging from a dungeon wall, being attacked by demons. They did a sonogram. The baby is fine, and her boyfriend proposed! I promised to check in on her every few months." Lila beamed briefly, then began to sob.

She tried to arrest more tears, but she continued blubbering anyway. "It's best this way. We have our own lives now, and we don't fit in each other's worlds comfortably anymore. We just have to give each other space."

Stirling touched Lila's face and wiped her tears away.

"Come here," he said, hugging her into him.

After a few moments, she stopped crying and closed her eyes, inhaling his scent.

"So, when is someone going to tell me how Hale and Cairo bonded so many times in the week I was out?" he asked, vexed.

"Oh, yeah. That. Their bonds are broken. Most of the trapped Succubi were burning and close to death. Cairo and Hale claimed a couple of them, then passed them off to the few Incubi who were also locked in the cells. Cairo ensured that his bonds were broken immediately. Hale, I think, wanted a bond, but he just didn't find a close enough match. He passed the last few Succubi off to another Incubus."

"Jesus. I bet Cairo had the time of his life fucking without burning."

"Yeah. He was ranting about how great it was, but how it wasn't good enough to make him settle. He didn't sound so sure though. I think secretly, he wants it too, now that he got a taste of it. We'll see."

"Yeah, we'll see. My bet is that he dies single."

Lila ran a hand along Stirling's bandaged chest.

"You know I dreamt of you several times while I was out," he said.

"I believe it. You popped a few erections at the doctor's place," she snickered.

"Really?" He laughed, and they both grabbed their ribcages and grimaced.

She looked at him and sighed. She had mourned all week, and now she could finally relax a bit and enjoy her time with him. It was a wonderful and free feeling she hadn't felt since they had met. Nothing was obscuring their joy now. She touched her lips to his.

"Did the doc have to shoot us up to stave off our needs?" he asked sexily against her mouth.

"Yes. Adrenaline. He said it replaces the need for life forces temporarily," she whispered as she carefully climbed onto his bandaged body.

Licking his bottom lip, she ground her pelvis into his.

"Yeah. It keeps the body going for a while, but your mind eventually leaves. And I'll lose my mind if you don't take off your clothes. Now, *meine Flamme,*" he commanded, lustfully.

Lila was all too eager to oblige. She transformed into her true form while shaking her tattered clothing to the floor and proceeded to ravage the sexiest beast she'd ever known.

About the Author

Scarlet Clearwater lives in Colorado with her wonderful husband, three grown beautiful boys, and four beloved dogs. She's also mother to a gecko, several fish and a gorgeous daughter who models. Writing came easily to Scarlet at a young age, beginning with short stories and poetry. Winning several awards in school, a fire lit up her passion for penning to paper. When She's not writing, Scarlet dabbles in digital art, painting, woodworking and dog training.

www.ingramcontent.com/pod-product-compliance
Lightning Source LLC
LaVergne TN
LVHW040136080526
838202LV00042B/2927
* 9 7 8 1 9 5 6 0 7 4 9 9 4 *